JUSTICE MATTERS

Ron Vergona

Published by:

S_{hepherd}
H_{all}

Coeur d'Alene, Idaho

To my wife Addie, and children Jessica and Michael, for their love and support.

"If the citizens neglect their duty and place unprincipled men in office, the government will soon be corrupted . . . . If a republican government fails to secure public prosperity and happiness, it must be because the citizens neglect the Divine commands, and elect bad men to make and administer the laws."

∞ Noah Webster ∞

JUSTICE MATTERS

CHAPTER 1

His eyes blinked, trying to keep the stampeding images from blocking his concentration.

But what bothered him most was the feeling that no matter how hard he focused on the pictures inside his head, essential pieces remained fractured. Dark, distorted slivers that never took form.

The doctors at the VA hospital had a name for it.

As he'd grown accustomed, he forced his mind to shut out the broken streams of data and return to the here and now.

After today's decision, none of the rest mattered. A split-second act—no doubt his last—would seal his legacy. The final details hit him when he woke up this morning. He had swallowed the usual regimen of meds and then devised a lie to tell Corey.

It touched him again, as a long breath rolled over his dry lips.

A twitch? No, maybe a tremor.

Ethan Galloway yanked his finger from the trigger guard as if fearing a bite from a deadly serpent. The barrel remained resting in its cradle. He squinted at his hand, expecting some indication of betrayal.

Dry. Steady. Not the slightest bit of shaking.

A brief smile flitted across his face; then turned into a frown. It'd been more than a year since his last drink. He knew the exact day and time. He could still see the bottle crashing into the fireplace and imagined the comforting aroma drifting from the wet stones edging the hearth.

Would've been his first drink of the night—then second—then third; until he lost count again.

He fought with the lingering sensation of the evaporating liquid entering his whiskey-soaked pores from that mid-June evening of last year. But he couldn't shake the look on Corey's face when he'd given him the news.

No fifteen-year-old should ever hear those words.

Keeping his eyes closed, Ethan Galloway's other senses absorbed the surroundings and steered him back. The distant background sounds and the occasional slight rocking motion anchored him to the present. But it didn't bring much comfort, just a stark reminder of where he was and what he intended to do.

Corey's stricken face faded into the dark recesses of the broken remnants of Ethan's tormented mind. Right now, the last thing he needed was to think about Corey. But another voice popped into his head.

If you were a real father—Corey is precisely who you'd be considering.

Ethan took in slow, deep breaths and his heart rate steadied, dropping into a familiar, comfortable state, readying to get back to the task at hand. He opened his eyes and thanked God he saw no traces of Corey.

And not the slightest image of Kinsley—*don't you even go there tonight.*

When he looked down on the scene, nothing had changed. From this vantage point, a few intervening structures hampered his visual, not allowing him to see the bigger picture.

But that was okay.

His only concern—a clear shot at the target.

At this point there was little else to worry about. Besides, he couldn't afford to stay in the Captain's Suite on the deck above him, which included a more panoramic view of the theater.

Corey could use that money to live on if....

He checked his watch. Little time remained. He tried not to think about the finality of those words. Or maybe that's precisely what this was all about. He grimaced and almost shouted out loud.

Somewhere in the distance, Ethan heard a dog bark. In a reflex action, he glanced to his side and reached down. He whispered a name. One that still haunted him.

Chopper.

Keep it together, Ethan. Just a couple more minutes.

Out the window, down the street; the scene shifted. As Ethan's eyes drank it in, everything played out in slow motion. The tunnel vision angle from the corner room gave him an odd perspective. He'd experienced this before, only in Afghanistan, not so close to home.

Home? Yeah, right. How long has it been since this felt like home?

His mind flashed images again with no details, like someone had erased a portion of his world, leaving shadows; hollow remnants of an encrypted file scrubbed from a hard drive.

The front doors to the Eagle Theater slammed open. It sent shockwaves through the mob waiting outside the historic building on Front Street in Old Town Sacramento.

Ethan noted that the number of tourists had been larger than normal. It was Halloween night and hordes of costumed partygoers bustled along the streets. But many more had shown up for a glimpse at the governor of California who was attending this evening's opening performance at the theater.

Governor Nicholas Blackwell: democrat candidate for president. With the election only days away, the entire nation had gotten caught up in the growing fervor, and this occasion presented a rare opportunity to see the man who might be the next president of the United States.

That's why Ethan Galloway was here. Although he intended to cast his vote early.

As the noise of the doors crashing into the theater's old wooden siding reached his ears, Ethan watched someone stumble through the opening and leap off the planked walkway.

The sounds of gunfire echoed up and down the narrow streets.

In Ethan's head a familiar ember sparked to life, throwing him back in time. A blurry reflection—muzzle flashes—a spine-chilling howl—a whimper—then silence.

He tamped down the past, using every ounce of resolve and pulled himself back to the present.

Down on the street, the running figure faltered and slapped a hand against a shoulder. An instant later the form rounded the corner and disappeared from Ethan's line of sight.

But not before he saw a red splotch spreading from underneath the hand.

She—at least that's what Ethan's mind translated from the fleeing image—headed toward the river.

The next blast cried from inside his head as disjointed memories jolted him again into the void. The madness returned; obliterating any meager gains he'd made since returning from Afghanistan. Maybe this was the reality he'd face for the rest of his life. He wished he could transfer this nightmare to the sonsofbitches who ran the country. Give them a dose of their own medicine.

Ethan rose and glanced at his hands, pushing his troubled past back. The tremors he now suffered were real, overshadowing the rhythmic river currents that had earlier shaken his concentration and still slapped gently against the hull of the docked riverboat.

He wondered what memories the flowing water triggered in the ancient boards of this old vessel. Permanently docked and converted into a luxury hotel and restaurant, the Delta King, frozen in time, now served the tourist clientele of Old Town Sacramento.

From the upper deck room on the docked riverboat, he walked to the front window. It offered a more expansive vista over the ship's bow. His body reacted to a gut-wrenching punch as he saw the same person reappear below.

He chanced a quick turn over his shoulder and glanced toward the side window. His rifle sat nestled in its cradle, still pointing accusingly toward the theater. What he saw through the glass reassured him that her pursuers hadn't picked up on her location. Things changed quickly as frightened onlookers steered them in the right direction. He refocused on the front window.

A head turned up as if staring straight into Ethan's eyes. Although the face remained shrouded—only the eyes visible—Ethan accepted he was looking down at a young female wearing traditional Muslim garb. He recalled it was Halloween but dismissed any notions of a costume. The moment lasted for a fraction of a second before the girl's posture reflected the approaching danger.

The windows vibrated as another sound interrupted Ethan's concentration. As the rumbling grew louder, he watched a train plodding along a siding that paralleled the river. Ethan saw the girl's head crane back and forth. He could feel her hopelessness at the sight of the monstrous machine blocking her freedom. She cast a final glance behind her, undoubtedly sensing her fate.

"Oh my God," Ethan heard himself mutter as the girl's body sprang forward; at the same time, dropping, rolling, and vanishing beneath the spinning wheels. The endless stream of freight cars rattled, screeching behind the powerful locomotive.

He placed both hands to his head.

Two men emerged from the corner and stopped. Guns drawn in outstretched arms, sliding left; then right. Their shoulders slumped and the weapons lowered. Ethan watched their silent shouts. And the classic motions—relaying messages, communicating positions and observations.

"They didn't see her go onto the tracks." Ethan shrugged. "Small consolation. Wait till they gawk at the mangled, bloodied—"

Ethan's eyes bulged and blinked in disbelief. He caught sight of the far side of the moving train and gasped as the girl burst free from the steel wheels spinning on the rails. Her body lurched headlong, arms and legs flailing for purchase on the graveled slope, struggling to right herself.

The train now provided an effective barrier from her pursuers; a more welcome transition from what Ethan first identified as a surefire deathtrap. He couldn't keep his eyes off her, and his mind formed the obvious question—*what the hell happened inside the theater?*

While he considered the preceding events that triggered her dilemma, the girl moved toward the river with new purpose.

Ethan had no trouble recognizing the demeanor, the actions, and the dress of the two men attempting to stop the girl. Security team or bodyguards—but not secret service agents.

He looked back at the girl. It was clear what would happen next. Ethan nodded as she reached the end of the pier, and after a brief glance over her shoulder—jumped into the river.

He smiled to himself and mouthed the words, "Good luck, darlin'. I don't know what you were up to, but—"

As Ethan looked on, the girl thrashed, her head bobbing like a cork in the flowing water and then disappearing. Each time her head broke the surface, she spent less time gasping for air before dropping further into the depths.

Not realizing his actions, Ethan reached the outside door to his room and pulled it open. He gave a final nod to the sniper rifle, cursing as he removed his gloves and stuffed them into a pocket. In a half dozen quick strides, he crossed the promenade deck and leaned over the side.

No one else had seen her make it this far.

The lighting along this portion of the river was sparse and gloomy. A near full moon hanging above the unfolding drama struggled to shrink the shadows and frame the image of the drowning girl.

Forgetting everything that had brought him to this place—at this time—for one purpose, Ethan Galloway grabbed the deck railing. He climbed over and dove into the river.

Chapter 2

Ethan's body hit the cold water and the shock took his breath away. The world turned black as he plummeted below the muddy waters. In the back of his mind, he sensed this was real, not the murky threads of his past. Fighting his way back to the surface, he wiped his eyes clear and spun around trying to locate the girl. He smelled the rancid remains of dead and putrefying organisms spreading from the delta wetlands and hugging the night air like a moldy blanket.

In the dim light, he saw arms stretching up and the momentary sight of the girl's head right before it disappeared. By instinct, he swam toward the spot. His lungs sucked in a generous gulp of air and he plunged into the depths, arms stroking and legs kicking. Without seeing her sinking form, his hands grasped onto a patch of material. Clenching it tight, he reversed his body and pumped his legs in an all-out effort to drag the girl from the river.

As his head broke the surface, the weight he was pulling lightened dramatically, leaving him with a fist full of wet and torn fabric. While watching the remnants of the garment drift away, he reached down and his hands connected with a more tangible object. He looped an arm around the girl's chest and pulled her head out of the water.

The girl coughed and spit and coughed again more violently. Ethan spotted her left shoulder bleeding. He didn't see any spurting but couldn't determine the extent of the injury—his mind darted back to the charging men and the gunfire.

He worked to keep her head high enough for her to breathe and not swallow any more water. What she wore beneath her now lost outfit looked like a type of tactical vest. It was bulky and acted as an added weight to pull her back underwater. And the girl fought any attempts for him to keep her head above the water.

From experience he understood the usual panic and involuntary resistance to his efforts, but this girl's movements appeared directed—deliberately trying to free herself from his grasp. Amazed, Ethan heard the girl speak; not scream or cry out, but articulate clear, precise words.

Her face was inches from his ear. "Let me go. I must die. There's no other way."

"That's not gonna happen." He found the zipper on her vest and yanked it down. She tried to stop him, punching at his arms and chest. This had no effect on Ethan's goal, and soon he had ripped off the vest. He watched it bob several times in the current before sinking out of sight. The girl was much lighter now, and Ethan had little trouble handling her, even as she struggled harder.

"No! Nooo! You don't understand. Now you'll die too. You should've left me alone. I am meant to die. I've dishonored my family. I must die."

The girl's speech sounded clear and forceful in spite of their predicament. Her next move caught him off guard.

She slapped him in the face, saying, "You need to get out of the river."

"No kidding. That's why I'm here. So let's get with the program. I suggest we head to the opposite shore. Those guys from the theater may be waiting to finish the job."

"May Allah save you. My vest—you've triggered it—we've less than a minute before it detonates. Go! Quickly!"

"If you holler *Allahu Akbar* I'm gonna knock you out cold," Ethan shouted and grabbed a tighter hold on the girl. He swam toward the opposite shore. Over his shoulder he saw the lights of the Delta King riverboat flickering in the misting fog that rolled across the water. High above, the moon's once guiding beacon waned.

Ethan didn't need to estimate the time remaining on the detonator to know they'd never reach the opposite bank. Before those thoughts registered, a muffled blast shook the night air. A shockwave followed and slammed a wall of water into Ethan and the girl.

The gushing tidal surge pummeled their bodies. The spreading vortex catapulted them away from the underwater blast and deposited them onto a marshy finger of land that jutted out into the river. With waves ripping in all directions as they impacted against the banks, Ethan and the girl became wedged and tangled in a collage of debris scattered along the tiny peninsula.

The receding waters left their inert bodies exposed.

CHAPTER 3

Wailing sirens intensified and filled the void after echoes from the blast died out. People scurried in all directions, not knowing the source of the explosion. Those near the river were drenched as sheets of water sprayed in a concentric pattern.

On the docked riverboat, the underwater detonation shook glasses, china, and silverware off tables. Upturned chairs left patrons thrashing in heaps of dangerous shards. Those seated at the bar witnessed the instantaneous destruction of one of the more distinctive collections of fine libations in the entire city. Delta King hotel guests got the ride of their lives; tossed from their beds and onto the plush, padded carpets in their staterooms.

In a corner room on the starboard side of the upper deck, one floor below the Captain's Suite, a twenty-inch barreled SR25, fitted with a maximum-range tactical scope and a custom wood stock, sat abandoned on the floor adjacent to the partly opened side window.

As the sirens grew louder, they penetrated the spidery depths of Ethan Galloway's ears. Still motionless, his mind compiled a torrent of afferent pain signals from all his peripheral body parts. That told him this was real, not another imaginary voyage to a previous hell.

Ignoring his body's cries to remain still, Ethan pushed himself to his knees and scanned the area. About ten feet closer to the river and dangerously near the shifting currents, he saw the body of the girl, the lower half of her torso submerged in the river. The erratic waves worked to draw the slight frame back into the waters and finish the job.

He crawled closer, and in the wavering rays of dying moonlight, got a brief look at her.

My God. She's a child. About Corey's age.

This had escaped him while fighting to save her from a sure death at the hands of the river, the suicide vest, or the approaching guns of her pursuers.

The sirens reached a nerve-shattering crescendo and Ethan acted. He struggled to his feet and lifted the unconscious but still breathing young girl in his arms. After a quick survey of the scene and the converging onslaught of first responders to the waterfront, he turned away from the river, headed up the grassy banks, and trotted west along the narrow pathway in the meandering riverside park. He disappeared under the Tower Bridge and listened to the last of the approaching emergency vehicles roar by overhead. Moving as fast as he could, he'd gotten about fifty yards past the bridge when he chanced a look over his shoulder.

He noted a number of stationary flashing lights cutting through the developing fog which encroached the center of the bridge. Several rigs had stopped on the span, but for now all eyes appeared focused to the east, trying to pinpoint the location of the blast. Ethan knew they'd soon widen the perimeters.

He pushed himself forward.

Ahead and to the north, he saw the floodlights bathing the inside of Raley Field. He listened to the booming PA system instructing the spectators to vacate the stadium in a safe and orderly fashion. Ethan picked up the pace and ran toward the outer parking lot. If he hurried, he'd be at the spearhead of the first wave of vehicles spilling from the lot and avoid getting trapped in the monumental traffic jam that would come next. Later, he'd congratulate himself on having the foresight not to park his truck in one of the closer parking structures in Old Town.

The first wave of patrons began flooding from the stadium as Ethan yanked open the rear door of his black Ford pick-up truck. He absently chided himself on forgetting to lock it. He placed the girl across the crew seats and checked her left shoulder. The cold water had stemmed most of the bleeding. The bullet had only grazed the flesh. He kept a first aid kit in the center console, but fighting against time, Ethan chose to cover the wound with a clean rag he pulled from the seatback pocket, wrapping it several times around her upper arm and snugging the end underneath the makeshift bandage. A more thorough inspection could wait until he got her—

What the hell am I doing?

There weren't a whole lot of choices as to where he'd be heading.

Still got time to flag down one of the first responders and let the authorities handle this.

Ethan's brain hiccupped again. The image of the sniper rifle brought him back—with all it represented—the rest of his past stayed jumbled in his head. No way could he return to the riverboat now. He'd been careful about leaving prints in the room, but after witnessing the girl drowning in the river, his mind couldn't recall the details about what happened next.

He looked back at the girl and brushed damp strands of hair away from her cheeks. The interior dome lighting underscored the dark features: oval-shaped face with a slightly jutted jawline. Deep brown eyes framed by long lashes and hooded by prominent arched brows. Her straight nose was punctuated by full lips. Ethan imagined the remaining elements of baby fat sculpting a vacant smile. Her long, matted black hair stuck to thin shoulders on a slender, still developing frame.

The girl's eyes blinked open, and Ethan's body jerked against the back of the driver's seat. Her lips parted. Ethan, recovering from the momentary shock, leaned forward.

"Wh—who are you?" Her words all but drowned out by the escalating sounds of the approaching crowd from the stadium as they pushed through the turnstiles and spread onto the tarmac.

"Ethan. Ethan Galloway. Pleasure to meet you," he responded mechanically, ignoring the inanity of the conversation.

"I'm Patas Ta'anari...." The girl's words became swallowed up in the shouts and the revving engines coughing to life. Her eyes slid closed again and her head canted to the side.

Ethan decided that if he wanted to stay ahead of the stampede, he had only seconds to hit the road. He grabbed a blanket off the floorboards and placed it over Patas. After slamming the rear door shut, he jumped into the driver's seat. For a moment, he feared the keys were lost somewhere in the Sacramento River. Even that was a far better scenario than the thought of them forgotten in the room on the riverboat.

Surprisingly, when he stuck a hand into the wet pocket of his jeans, he found the key fob and extricated the prize. He'd worry about the drenched electronics later. Right now he was thankful for small favors. He jammed the key into the slot and twisted the ignition switch.

The pleasant tune of the powerful engine made him smile, and he dropped the gearshift into drive, threading his truck into the line of cars maneuvering toward the exit. Most of the patrons had yet to reach their vehicles, and Ethan found himself rolling through the exit gate before a major gridlock developed. Traffic was directed left, and then left again at the Tower Bridge Gateway. In the opposite direction, crews slapped barricades across the roadway a block from the blinking emergency lights of the rigs straddling the two sets of bridge spires that were now barely visible in the crushing fog.

Ethan allowed himself a deep, cleansing breath as he guided the Ford onto the entrance ramp to the 80 freeway and headed west.

CHAPTER 4

For the umpteenth time following his awkward introduction to Patas Ta'anari, Ethan Galloway considered his reckless actions since diving into the murky Sacramento River. He excluded any thoughts of the upper deck corner room on the Delta King, the left-behind sniper rifle, and how close he came to finishing things tonight.

Ethan glanced in the Ford's rearview mirror, trying to catch a glimpse of Patas. He then stared at the dash clock.

"And the night's not even over yet," he mumbled. From the rear seat he heard a stifled murmur, but the girl's eyes remained shut.

About thirty minutes later Ethan passed the Yolo County Airport and turned onto an unpaved roadway, the truck's headlights reflecting off the irrigation ditches bracketing the narrow lane. The tires crunched against the sparse gravel, making more noise than Ethan wanted. He stopped the truck in front of his house. A faint flickering glow from a TV screen peeked out from the edges of the drawn drapes in the living room.

Before he shut off the engine, a corner of the drape pulled back, and a moment later the outside floodlights came on. The front door opened, and Corey stood staring at his father. The glare from the harsh lights prevented Ethan from catching the expression on Corey's face, but Ethan knew the time had come for him to sprinkle a little bit of truth on all the lies.

You think that's going to erase everything that happened leading up to the day Kinsley died?

Ethan opened the door and stepped down from the truck. Before closing it, he glanced into the back seat. The blanket had slipped below Patas's shoulder and exposed the makeshift bandage. The white cloth was soaked in blood. So far none had dripped beyond the borders of the wrapped material. Patas appeared to be asleep or unconscious.

He let out a long, slow breath and took a step toward Corey. He now got a better look at the twisted features on Corey's face, while hearing bits and pieces of a TV newscast coming from the living room. As expected, the events in Sacramento dominated the latest news cycle.

Corey's young body was rapidly changing, becoming lean and tall like his father. Any remaining pudginess had long since melted away. But the similarities ended there. Ethan's complexion was olive-toned—his black hair, straight and well-behaved. His large brown eyes erased most of the surrounding white.

Corey's sandy light brown hair reminded Ethan of Kinsley's. Corey also had his mom's fair skin, with a sprinkle of freckles under his eyes. And right now, his bright blue eyes burned into his father.

It suddenly occurred to Ethan that Corey was no longer a child, and there was a strong likelihood his son knew a lot more about what was going on than Ethan imagined. Instead of bolstering his resolve, those thoughts made Ethan feel even worse about his actions. Before he could confront Corey with some version of the truth, he needed to address a more pressing issue.

Ethan watched as Corey approached the truck. He could see Corey straining to look into the back seat. Ethan reached an arm out, but Corey ducked away and yanked open the rear door. Patas let out a short squeal and attempted to sit up. She wound up flipping her body off the seat and onto the floorboards. She cried out one more time as her hand clutched at the bloody bandage, and she once again passed out.

"Corey, we must get her inside the house. She needs help."

Corey spun around, ignoring the tears and spitting out a response. "I thought," he started and stopped. "No, no, no. What I prayed for… was that you weren't gonna go through with one of your insane plans. And you really did just meet up with some old Navy buddies. That was the story. Wasn't it?"

Ethan watched Corey's shoulders heave, but he didn't dare take another step forward.

It's been more than a year since my last drink, just let me get through one more night.

"Just a wild guess—but is this the suicide bomber every cop in California is looking for? She kinda fits the description on the news."

When Ethan stammered, Corey shoved on. "So, you're working with a Muslim terrorist? What the hell is going on? Thank God Saba isn't alive to see this."

"Corey—this has nothing to do with your great grandfather." But Ethan thought of the stories Saba must've told Corey about the violence Kinsley's family endured before coming to America.

"And to think I wanted to be a Navy SEAL. Be like my dad and kill those damn Muslim terrorists all over the world. What happened to you?" Corey swallowed hard. "Y—you were gonna blow yourself up and...."

This time Ethan grabbed Corey by the shoulders and stared into his eyes. "Corey. We'll talk. I promise. But right now, this girl needs help. She's been shot, and she's bleeding. Now—go inside and put some sheets on the bed in the guest room."

CHAPTER 5

Corey stood in the corner of the bedroom with his arms folded. Every now and then his father barked orders. Corey responded and then resumed his robot-like stance. For the past hour, Ethan had worked on Patas's shoulder. After giving her a powerful painkiller, he cleaned the wound, stitched it closed, and applied a sterile bandage. He finished injecting her with an antibiotic and administered a sedative to keep her calm. Gathering up his instruments, Ethan turned to Corey.

"Corey, I want you to keep an eye on her—till the drugs take effect. Give me a minute to clean up." He hesitated and added, "Then we'll talk."

He glared at his father and remained mute. After Ethan left the room, Corey took several deep breaths and began pacing, trying to look at anything but this intrusion his dad had brought into their lives.

A short time ago, he'd been watching the news. Live footage of the chaotic scene in Sacramento. Descriptions of the mysterious figure fleeing the theater.

Shots fired.

Another Islamic extremist at work.

Then the bomb blast in the river.

He shuddered from the troubled vibes of his father being involved with—but prayed it was only his overactive imagination.

After months of listening to the agonizing groans from his father's almost constant tortured nightmares and attempting to understand his bizarre actions, he had suspected that earlier today his father had reached an important decision.

Corey had worked hard to dismiss the meaning of what his father was up to tonight. Then the lights of the Ford bounced off the living room window. So when he'd spotted the girl in the pick-up, his own nightmare became a reality.

He stopped in front of his mom's old desk. Over a year, but it was as if she'd just stepped out for a breath of fresh air, taking a short break from her work. When his dad had attempted to box up the books, the laptop, and the rest of her personal items, Corey lashed out and told him to leave everything alone.

Lost in thought, Corey picked up a familiar picture from the desk. He stared at the proud image of his great grandfather dressed in the olive-green uniform of the Israeli military.

A dreamlike slurry of words drifted across the room.

"Wh—who are you?"

Corey placed the picture back on his mother's desk and turned, locking eyes with Patas. "So, your accomplice never mentioned he had a son?" His whole body remained rigid.

Patas's face scrunched up. Her arm moved to the bandaged shoulder and touched the fresh dressing while snugging the edge of the blanket to her neck. She started coughing and her throat retched. Corey grabbed the small metal bowl from the bedside table and thrust it under Patas's chin as she dry-heaved and spit up small amounts of saliva. As she settled back onto the pillow, her eyes drooped momentarily but then opened wide, trying to focus on Corey.

More slurred words came from her lips. "You... saw me... naked. I... now you must marry me."

Corey's face turned bright red. He stood back and the metal bowl fell to the floor, clattering across the scarred hardwood. "I—I just saw a small part of your shoulder—the wound...."

By the time Corey uttered his puzzled response, Patas's eyes had wavered and shut. He could hear faint snoring sounds emanating from the young girl. As he picked up the bowl and placed it back on the table, he kept his own eyes diverted from the rise and fall of Patas's chest. He glanced at the picture of his great grandfather and said, "Sorry, Saba. I don't like this anymore than you. What the hell is a Muslim terrorist doing in our house?"

When Corey walked into the living room, his father was sitting in the leather recliner, holding a photo. His eyes were closed. Corey didn't have to strain to catch the deep snores. After returning his mother's picture to the end table, he picked up the embroidered blanket bunched up on the sofa and draped it over his father. Out of habit, he drew close and checked his father's breath. Thankful he didn't detect any signs of alcohol. Although his father's rollercoaster emotional changes still unnerved him.

"Good talk, Dad," Corey mumbled and headed toward his bedroom.

CHAPTER 6

The governor worked at handling the situation in his customary manner.

Staff, aides, and security personnel buzzed about the governor's mansion, trying to look busy and avoid any unnecessary contact with either the governor or his wife.

Anita Blackwell shook her head and said, "Jesus Christ, Nick. Do you have no limits as to how low you're willing to go?"

For the moment, Governor Nicholas Blackwell and his wife sat alone in his office in the historic residence on H Street. From the start, Anita had disapproved of moving into the newly redecorated landmark in Sacramento. She was content to ride out her husband's term at their coastal estate in Malibu. The short commuter flight by private jet could be tolerated a lot better than squeezing into this *'quaint old relic'*, as she called it, stuck in the middle of this God-forsaken city.

"Trolling for eager-to-please Pepperdine coeds was starting to bore you?"

The governor flashed his best—photo op—campaign ready—smile. "She was a senior in high school—we've played with younger ones—"

"I'm not talking about her age, Nick. She's a Muslim. Or hadn't you checked out her unusual style of dress?"

"So what. And don't tell me you never wondered if they wore anything under those sheets."

Anita ignored her husband's comment. "You told me Petricello took care of everything. And there was no way the tramp could blow the whistle on your little indiscretion."

Before the governor could answer, he heard a commotion coming from the outer office, followed by a rapid-fire knocking on the door.

"Come in," he said, relieved for the potential opportunity to lash out at one of his minions instead of being hassled by his wife.

Blackwell's chief of staff pushed the reluctant head of the governor's private security team through the door. As someone slammed it shut, the governor's wife began the expected tirade before either of the two newcomers had a chance to utter a single syllable.

CHAPTER 7

Ethan Galloway stood at the kitchen range cooking breakfast and biding his time. The phone rang—causing him to drop the wooden spoon into the scrambled eggs bubbling in the cast iron skillet. Corey stepped into the room and grabbed the handset before his father could retrieve the spoon. Seeing Corey had taken the call, Ethan worked on rescuing the sausages from a smoldering frypan and saving the toast from a fiery death.

He caught the tail-end of the phone conversation as Corey said, "Ahhh… thank you, Ms. Torrence, two o'clock should be fine."

Ethan glanced at Corey who had grabbed a carton of orange juice from the refrigerator. Knowing Corey deserved an explanation, he attempted an abbreviated version of last night's chain of events that ended with him diving into the river and dragging Patas back to shore. He denied knowing anything about her wearing a suicide vest until pulling it free from her body and neglected to mention anything regarding the sniper rifle left by the window in the upper deck room on the Delta King.

For now, he'd let those details remain buried. Maybe that phone call could get him off the hook. The name Corey spoke before hanging up sounded vaguely familiar, but Ethan had no clue as to the nature of the conversation. "That call sounded important. Who was it?"

Corey stared hard at his father before turning away and reaching for a glass in one of the upper cabinets. "The lady who works at Mayacamas Shepherds in Sonoma—Catori Torrence."

"Oh, yeah… right." Ethan picked up his coffee mug and took a slug of the tepid brew. He racked his brain. This was something important, but he still couldn't put the pieces together. "So how is *Connie* doing?"

Corey let out a deep breath and opened his mouth to speak, when the sound of a door closing caused them both to turn toward the living room.

Patas Ta'anari stood in the archway to the kitchen, her entire body wrapped in a bedsheet which dragged behind her as she walked into the room. Her head and most of her face were also covered in what looked like a pillowcase.

Patas's eyes shifted between Ethan and Corey. She pointed at Ethan. "I remember you from the river." She turned with a blank expression to Corey. "Who are you?"

Corey downed the remaining juice in his glass and said, "I guess the wedding's off."

Ethan glanced at Corey, narrowing his eyes, but then spoke softly to Patas. "You shouldn't be walking around.

Let's get you back to bed. I'll bring you something to eat." He took several steps toward the young girl.

Patas stayed still and, for a second, her eyes lowered. When she looked back at Ethan, her head shook and her words shot back at him. "You have no idea what you've done. Why didn't you let me die?" She paused and her voice cracked. "It was my duty to end my life inside the theater along with the one I—I... seduced. When I failed to restore my family's honor, I had no choice but to die in those waters. You are a complete stranger, why did you get involved?"

The glass in Corey's hand slipped through his grasp and shattered in the sink. "Dad? You two *really* don't know each other?"

Ethan stared at Corey. He couldn't blame Corey for harboring any doubts as to the veracity of his story. Especially when he'd left out the critical parts.

Patas responded to Corey. "So, he's your father." She nodded. "I didn't know who he was—only that he shouldn't have interfered."

"Then you aren't working together?" He turned to his father.

Ethan remained silent and shook his head. He watched as the features on Corey's face transitioned from confusion to relief; finally settling on anger.

"You rescued this... this... suicide bomber? This... this... Islamic terrorist? I thought your job was to wipe these jihadists off the face of the earth. But you helped this one?" Corey's jaw contorted as the words escaped his lips. "And brought her home?"

He turned, pointing a finger in Patas's face. "They said you tried to kill the governor inside the theater. You were wearing a suicide vest and planned on blowing up the whole place. You would've killed hundreds of other people inside too."

"I don't think your father knew what I'd been up to. And he had no idea that pulling off my vest would trigger the explosion." She looked at Ethan. "I tried to warn you to leave me alone. If you had, I would've dropped to the bottom of the river and ended this."

"And you had nothing to do with her plot to kill the governor?" Corey asked his father while pointing a finger at Patas.

Ethan's mind flashed back to the room on the Delta King and the sniper rifle aimed out the window.

That was another story.

He knew the time was drawing near when he would have to confront Corey with that narrative.

His head gave a quick shake, and he raised his arms toward Corey. He could see the confusion grow on Corey's face and absorbed the pleading look in his eyes as his son grasped at anything to dismiss his father's potential role in the attempted assassination of the governor of California.

"So… you *were* with your old Navy buddies tonight, Dad?"

Ethan gazed at Patas and then back to Corey. "No more lies," he said, but knew he wasn't even close to revealing the whole truth. "Corey. I never met up with the guys. I needed to do something." He hesitated and walked over to Corey, placing his arm around his shoulder and pulling him tight. Before he spoke, he saw Patas turn away and march out of the kitchen.

"Corey, I promise I won't let you down." As he said these words, he wondered if this wasn't a greater lie.

Ethan heard the latch on the front door open and the sound of footsteps pounding down the porch stairs. Patas had already spanned the short distance across the gravel driveway and had opened the door to Ethan's truck by the time Ethan and Corey reached the porch. Finding no keys in the ignition, she stumbled back out and ran toward the open pasture.

Ethan bounded down the steps and easily closed the gap as Patas's feet caught in the loose bedsheet that draped her body. She crashed to the ground.

"Let her go, Dad! Please. Let me call the cops. They can come and get her. If Saba were alive, he'd take care of this terrorist." Corey continued shouting, as he watched his father scoop up the struggling girl in his arms and carry her back to the house.

Patas flailed her arms at Ethan. Several blows landed squarely on his jaw, drawing blood. Finally, her efforts subsided, and Ethan walked up the front steps and into the living room. He placed Patas on the sofa.

Corey stood behind his father as Patas's hands flew to her face and she sobbed.

Ethan reached back and grasped Corey's shoulder. In a slow, determined voice, he said to Patas, "Tell us what happened."

CHAPTER 8

As usual, Anita Blackwell's words sounded venomous and echoed across the governor's office. The governor felt grateful that, for the moment, she aimed her fury at his chief of staff and the head of their private security company.

"Tom," said Anita, pointing a manicured finger in the face of the governor's chief of staff. "What the hell good are you if you can't keep our damn security personnel in line?"

She pivoted so fast that Victor Petricello, head of security, almost fell back on his ass. The expression on his face assured the governor that he was close to pulling out his pistol and placing a bullet between Anita Blackwell's eyes. For a split second, or perhaps a little longer, Governor Blackwell willed Petricello to do exactly that.

Anita switched gears and aimed her wrath at Petricello. "And what did you not understand about getting rid of the little Muslim bitch?"

Victor Petricello opened his mouth to answer, but before any words formed, the governor's wife spit out, "And then what? The little whore gets a theater ticket to attend last night's performance. Not to mention she's wearing a suicide vest under her clothes."

Thomas Steadman, the governor's chief of staff, took a breath and attempted to intervene. "Now, Anita, you know with the election right around the corner we're faced with the presence of secret service personnel. While they lend an air of presidential atmosphere to our operations, they make it difficult to carry on with business as usual. That's why we tried keeping them away from the theater."

The governor chimed in. "Glad they're not on our payroll too, Tom." He chuckled in a lame attempt to lighten the atmosphere and quell Anita's anger.

In response, Anita stared briefly at her husband, but then faced off with Steadman and Petricello. "Speaking of business, gentlemen, can you at least confirm that our meddling secret service agent no longer presents a threat?"

Petricello answered. "Yes, ma'am. You no longer need to concern yourself about Agent Anson Kostelecky snooping around. The local police have been keeping me up to date on the investigation into his unfortunate death. They don't appear to have any leads in the case."

Anita Blackwell held his gaze before taking a deep breath and walking over to the window. With her back turned, she said, "Well I'm glad you can congratulate yourselves on taking care of a secret service agent. But tell me again." She spun around to face the men. "How in the hell did you let a high school girl disappear from my husband's office and get out of this dreary old mansion? I don't understand how that could happen."

Petricello coughed. "As you know, the installation of the security system has not been completed. The original schedule didn't have the governor moving into the house until—"

Anita interrupted. "My plan was not to move into this place at all. And if everybody remains on task and we win the election, we'll be moving into a much more significant historical mansion. I'm tired of listening to these pathetic excuses for not doing your job."

The governor decided to step in. "At least we know she'll no longer be a threat. After that explosion in the river, I doubt there'll be much left to identify the girl's body," he said, shrugging.

It was time to move on. "I take it, Tom, you barged in here with something a little more substantial than what we've been discussing?"

With a relieved look, Steadman nodded at the governor and said to Petricello, "Victor, could you run back to the security office and get Agent Davenport?"

Although the governor had no clue as to what this newly assigned agent could add to the mix, he had the feeling it would not go over well with his wife.

CHAPTER 9

Patas Ta'anari's sobbing grew louder while Ethan and Corey stood towering over her prone and shaking form. Ethan nudged Corey, and they both sat down across from the stricken girl.

Patas sat up on the sofa as her eyes gazed at the surroundings in the home of these two strangers. Her breathing slowed, the tears subsided, and she found her voice. "I dishonored my family and seduced a married man. I had no choice but to follow the demands of my father and my brother. My brother drove me to the theater last night and ordered me inside. He said our family was ruined unless I carried out his demands."

She swallowed hard and added, "But I couldn't push the button to detonate the vest my brother strapped to my body. I didn't want anyone to die. And now I've failed in my duty."

Her next words came out as a whisper as she imagined the rebukes from her father and brother. "I am still alive, and so is the governor."

Patas closed her eyes and described the events of two weeks ago.

* * * * * *

It was late on a Friday afternoon. Patas arrived at the governor's mansion at her scheduled time following her last class for the week. A senior in high school, she was part of the new intern work program where gifted students from local schools got the opportunity to participate in the final restoration processes at the recently reopened historic site. During the construction phases, documents and artifacts had been stored in several maintenance structures located on the grounds. Now that the work had been completed and a sitting governor once again took up residence in the mansion, the warehoused articles would be sorted out and returned to the proper locations. On occasion, the students also got the chance to interact with the governor's staff and play minor roles in the escalating prep work for the presidential campaign.

With election day on the horizon, the campaign momentum had reached a feverish pitch. This presented a firsthand experience for the interns to witness the inner workings of the political practices of our government.

Patas Ta'anari had worked hard to become a part of the intern program. The rigorous selection process required not only high academic achievements, but also the demonstration of strong community values and commitment. The students who vied for these positions were required to compete in civics debates in front of the student bodies of their respective high schools, as well as compose a term paper on the importance of maintaining the state's historical archives as a way to preserve political history.

Those aspects of earning one of these coveted positions did not present any major obstacles for Patas. She excelled in her schoolwork and tackled the additional prerequisites with enthusiasm, easily outshining most competitors for the job. The biggest challenge Patas faced involved convincing her family—in reality, her father and older brother—to allow her to participate.

The Ta'anari family had fled to the United States from Yemen before Patas was born. Although her family followed strict Islamic traditions and disciplines, to her father's displeasure, Patas immersed herself in the culture of her family's new homeland. Not that she dared show any disrespect for her father's wishes or the teachings of her religion. In fact, Patas cherished Islam and the beauty of a God that brought her love and comfort. She isolated herself from what she considered cultural aberrations orchestrated over the millennia by misguided and evil individuals who wove their dogma into the souls of the masses.

Patas's father and brother did not share her views. When she attempted to question her mother, she received either silence or hushed reprimands in response.

Patas represented one of the scarce Muslim students in the intern program. She was the lone female. While attending classes at her high school, Patas's father allowed her to wear just the hijab, or traditional headscarf. As a concession to allow Patas to participate in the after-school intern program, he insisted that she be covered in the niqab, which revealed only the eyes. Patas still considered herself the victor in this epic battle with her father over the timeless repression of the female body. She embraced the love and support of Allah and willed her soul to forgive the failings of her faith's human components.

Patas understood that at this point in history she was still a frightening minority in her beliefs. Perhaps the world would change, and in her lifetime, others too might experience the joy of Islam without the rhetoric and hate that espoused and dampened the love for Allah. With all her heart, she could not fathom her God instigating the hatred and intolerances preached by the Prophet since the fiery birth and transitions of Islam through centuries of warfare.

In the quiet moments at night before falling asleep, she often fantasized about leading a reform movement to modernize her religious beliefs to conform with the world and bring peace and hope, rather than war and hate.

She, of course, kept those thoughts hidden deep within her heart. To question Mohammad would kindle her father's resolve to keep her shrouded in his own and accepted cultural manifestations of Islam.

"Patas," Thomas Steadman called out as she passed by his office, "could you please step in here for a moment?"

Patas stopped and looked through the open door to the governor's chief of staff's office.

"Come in," he added.

She lowered her head and walked into the office. In her hands she held a cardboard container filled with files she was bringing to the mansion's library.

"Just place the box on the credenza." Steadman pointed a finger to the far corner of the office.

She did as she was told and turned back to Steadman, keeping her head lowered.

"Patas, I've been told you are one of our best interns. Working harder and staying later than the other students. I want to commend you for your dedicated efforts."

"Thank you, Mr. Steadman. I am honored to work here." Her eyes darted up quickly and lowered again. She allowed a small smile to crease her cheeks, hidden beneath her garb.

Steadman cleared his throat. "Patas, I have a different job for you to do now."

She glanced at the container on the credenza. "Should I take care of those files first?"

"No, no. I'll have one of the other interns do that." He reached for a thick manila folder on his desk and handed it to Patas. "The governor has asked for you to work directly with him for the next several shifts. The remarkable job you've been doing has been brought to his attention, and he has an important task for you to tackle."

Patas stared from the folder to the governor's chief of staff.

"Go on now. Please take this folder to the governor. He's waiting for it." He tapped a closed fist on the desk. "You do know where the governor's office is, don't you?"

Patas nodded, but did not move, reluctant to leave the container behind and not finish her assigned duties.

Steadman tapped his fist harder on the desk. "Get going. You shouldn't keep the governor waiting."

CHAPTER 10

Ethan and Corey had remained still while Patas spoke in a hypnotizing cadence, but when her voice began to crack, Ethan rose to get her a glass of water from the kitchen. As he returned, he heard Corey questioning Patas.

"I get it," Corey scoffed. "You must've been hiding explosives in that container, waiting to slip the vest under your clothes. That's why you didn't want to put it down."

Ethan placed a hand on Corey's shoulder and passed the glass to Patas.

"You should've let her go, Dad. If she worked on the governor's staff, they already know she's the suicide bomber. And now you're linked to this whole mess."

"Corey, let Patas finish her story."

Sounding angry and worried, Corey said, "Dad, what exactly were *you* doing near the theater last night? Is there any way they could find out you pulled her from the river?"

Ethan didn't answer Corey, but the questions forced his mind to replay the events leading up to him jumping in the river. He was pretty sure he'd left no traces in the room on the Delta King, and rifles like the one he'd abandoned could be bought at any gun show. He'd had the SR25 fitted with a custom-engraved wood stock but still didn't think it could point the authorities specifically at him. His mind flickered wildly at that carved image, and then last night's horrors faded away.

Corey relented to his father's tight grasp and shrugged. "Okay, Patas, let's hear the rest of your—*story*."

She took a huge gulp of the offered water, placed the glass on the coffee table, and continued.

* * * * * *

Patas left Steadman without saying a word and headed off in the direction of the governor's office. As she walked, she thought about the conversation with the chief of staff.

Work directly with the governor?

She'd obviously gotten that part wrong. Why would he pick an intern when he surrounded himself with a professional staff? By the time she reached the outer door to the governor's office suite, she had convinced herself that her only task would be to deliver the folder and be on her way.

No big deal.

I'm nothing special. Stop reading anything more into what Mr. Steadman said.

Patas knocked lightly on the open door. The governor's secretary waved her in while finishing up a phone call.

"Yes, Tom. I understand." She pulled the handset away from her ear and spoke to Patas. "You must be Patas Ta'anari?"

Patas nodded.

"She's here now. Yes, I will. I was just on my way out anyway. Okay, I'll see you in the morning. And Tom? Remember, the staff meeting has been pushed back to 9:30."

The secretary ended the call and punched another button as she motioned for Patas to take a seat. After a brief conversation, she placed the phone in the cradle and stood up. "Ms. Ta'anari, the governor will see you now."

With those words, Patas's whole body froze. Although the governor's secretary couldn't have known because of her head covering, Patas's mouth opened wide, and her jaw fell.

"Let's go, young lady, the governor is a busy man. It won't do you any good to keep him waiting."

She ushered Patas into Governor Blackwell's inner sanctum. "Goodnight, sir. Would you like me to lock up before I leave?"

The governor, sitting behind a monstrous desk, with his back to the door, gave a quick nod and a wave. Patas jumped and almost dropped the folder when the door slammed shut behind the departing secretary. She looked around the spacious office and confirmed that no one but the governor was present.

And, of course, her.

Besides her father and brother, Patas had never been alone with a man. An unbidden image of her brother reared its ugly head.

Calm yourself, silly. Calm yourself.

This is the governor of California. Governor Nicholas Blackwell.

I think Dad voted for him too.

You're here to do a job.

Maybe I can toss the folder on the desk and run out before he sees me.

Patas had taken two steps forward when she heard the governor's chair squeak as he turned to face her.

She stopped in mid-stride, feeling like an unbalanced store mannequin in a display window. As she tried to right herself, the folder fell from her hands, and its contents spilled onto the grayish-green carpet.

Patas dropped to her knees and rushed to pick up the papers. Before she realized, the governor had stepped around his desk and stood behind her. A sharp electric jolt coursed through her body when Governor Blackwell reached down and placed his hands below her armpits and eased her back up to her feet. For a moment Patas imagined slender, groping fingers extend and stroke the rising contours of her breasts.

The papers fluttered back to the floor and her entire body spasmed.

He's merely trying to help me, she told herself and repeated that thought several more times.

Patas could not will her body to move.

In her ear, the governor whispered, "Leave the papers."

From somewhere in the distance, she heard herself say, "It won't take a minute. I'll clean up this mess and leave so you can get back to work, sir."

The governor's voice turned from a whisper to a breathy wheeze. "What's your hurry?"

Those same fingers slivered down her spine. When his hand stopped and cupped her buttocks, she gasped. Her body burned from embarrassment and shame. Dark thoughts of her brother erupted in her head again, but she willed them away.

She heard the rebukes from her father.

"Only whores allow themselves to be alone with a man. Any female who does this is inviting the man to ravish her and take what she is offering. There is just one reason for a female to meet with a man under those conditions. She is evil and has the desire to seduce the unwitting man. It is the ultimate dishonor to her family."

As her father's words etched into her soul, Governor Blackwell spun Patas around to face him. The look on his face scared her almost as much as his next words. "Patas Ta'anari. I think it's time we get to know each other."

Blackwell's hands ran lightly over the fabric covering her face. His fingers outlined the edges of her underlying tremoring lips. As he grabbed the end of her headscarf, he hesitated and let it drop back in place. His smile widened, and she watched the tip of his tongue slide across the upper row of his teeth. "For now—your clothes stay on. Even your headscarf. We'll skip the usual foreplay, and I'll use my imagination."

He let out a brusque laugh that made Patas close her eyes, forcing several tears to squeeze out and streak beneath her shroud. Blackwell's hands shot forward and roughly fondled her breasts. Before she could twist away from his grasp, he snatched her up and threw her onto the large sofa in the back corner of the office.

Patas experienced what came next as if watching the unimaginable horror happening to someone else. She saw the flowing garb forcefully yanked up to the girl's shoulders, white cotton panties torn off and flung across the room. What transpired over the following minutes spun her consciousness to a place she never knew existed.

All the time she prayed to Allah for forgiveness.

When it was over, Patas's mind melded once again with the girl on the sofa, staying motionless and unfeeling. She sensed movement and heard several dishes fall from a serving cart parked beside the sofa. One eye blinked open briefly; in time to watch the governor grab a linen napkin off the cart. A moment later he tossed it on the sofa and cursed. He pulled up his pants and let out a huge sigh.

Patas remained rigid. The beating of her heart felt distant and shallow. The governor's finger pressed against the side of her neck and then his hand slapped her cheek. She forced herself not to move or breathe.

She heard a final oath from the governor—followed by footsteps—then the whole office shook from the slamming door.

Patas stayed silent and stiff on the sofa. As her senses returned, she absorbed the smell and the stickiness of blood and other fluids oozing between her legs. She reached down and her hand brushed against the linen napkin. Grasping it, she thrust the material between her legs to staunch the flow.

But nothing could stop the tears.

From the outer office, the governor's voice shouted into the phone. She heard another door open. Then footsteps fading down the hall. And then silence.

CHAPTER 11

Ethan sat forward in his chair, hands steepled and covering the lower portion of his face. Corey got up and stared out the living room window, trying to focus on anything but the horror coming from Patas's lips.

"Not sure why I did what I did next," Patas continued. "Everything happened so fast. I must've acted without thinking."

She tried to explain what took place after being brutally raped by the governor of California, but the words sounded desperate and incomprehensible. When she finished, her voice softened and she spoke with clarity. "But none of it matters. I dishonored my family by putting myself in an unthinkable situation. According to my father, I am no longer his daughter. And my brother demanded I restore the family's honor. He told me what needed to be done. There was no other way."

She paused, shaking her head and tightening her lips. "But I couldn't go through with it. And by fleeing the theater without detonating the explosives, I diminished myself even more in the eyes of my family. I had no choice but to put an end to my shame and die in the river."

The tears now flowed freely down Patas's cheeks, and she turned to face Ethan. "But you came along and ruined everything. My life had already ended. Don't you understand? It's the one thing I have left to give to my family." She lowered her head in her hands and sobbed.

Corey walked away from the window and stood behind his father's chair. Confused, he looked at him and said, "Dad?" His gaze turned to Patas.

Ethan stood. He gave Corey's shoulder a quick pat and walked to Patas, kneeling in front of her. He gently peeled her hands from her face and attempted to adjust the pillowcase that had long since tumbled from her head. Patas sat up a little straighter and swallowed hard, fighting off the next round of tears.

"You're wrong, Patas," Ethan said, his voice barely above a whisper.

She blinked back the last remaining tear and nodded. "Yes, that's the reason I must complete my brother's demands."

His head bursting with conflicting emotions, Corey edged forward and said, "What happened wasn't your fault. You didn't dishonor anybody. But you can't go around trying to seek revenge. Or whatever your twisted religion tells you to do. You need to go to the cops and explain what the governor did. Right, Dad? Tell her."

Ethan didn't respond. Instead, his knees buckled and he grabbed onto the coffee table for support. He yanked himself to his feet and stumbled off to the bathroom.

Patas watched him leave and jumped at the sound of the banging door. "What's wrong? Is he okay?"

Corey shook his head. He was about to answer when his face turned a bright red and he backed away from Patas as she pulled the sheet higher and tucked the pillowcase snugly over her head. He realized they were once again alone. Placing his hands in his pockets, he stared at the closed bathroom door.

The last thing he expected to hear was the stifled giggle coming from the girl who had just poured out her heart and fiercely lamented the fact she was still alive.

Corey turned to Patas, eyebrows raised and mouth wide open.

"Sorry, but after all that's happened…." She waved her hands and covered her mouth. Turning serious, she pointed to the bathroom. "I'm worried about your father. What's wrong?"

Corey attempted a small smile and said, "Well, I guess you don't care about being alone with *me*. You don't consider…." His face got hotter, but this time he didn't turn away from Patas.

"I did suggest you marry me, didn't I?"

"What? I thought you didn't remember any of that."

Patas smiled, shyly. "Some of it's coming back." She looked again to the bathroom door. "You should check on your dad."

Corey walked closer to Patas and lowered his voice. "He does this once in a while. He's been getting better, but recently it's started up again. When he experiences any kind of stress, he needs to take higher doses of his medications. That's what he's doing in there now."

Patas, still looking anxious, nodded. "Corey, do you have any idea what your father was doing near the theater? Why he was there in the first place?"

Startled, they both looked up as the bathroom door opened, and Ethan strode back into the room.

CHAPTER 12

For the next several seconds, the governor's office remained silent. Governor Blackwell stared at the closed door after the head of his private security team stormed off to find the new secret service agent assigned to his protection detail.

The governor's chief of staff, Thomas Steadman, turned to Blackwell. "Nick, the secret service has hinted at new developments from last night's assassination attempt. But we need to be careful about what we say in front of this new agent, Olivia Davenport. Victor's still trying to figure out what the hell she's doing here. That's why we told her to wait in the security office until I had the chance to warn you."

"So, what have they got?"

Steadman shrugged. "Victor said this new agent's been guarded about telling him anything."

"Great. For now, I'm pissed enough that one of my fucking interns tried to blow me the hell up. Not to mention the incompetence of my security staff to let a damn teenaged girl get away—*for the second time*. Hell, even with the added support of the secret service covering my ass, I still came damn close to getting killed last night."

The governor's wife had been sipping a martini when she all but choked at her husband's words. "Yeah, darling. Who would have thought? Another *fucking* intern. Next time you choose to dabble in an underaged tramp, you should avoid the one wearing the suicide vest."

The governor chuckled and walked over to Anita. He kissed the top of her head and said, "She wasn't wearing the vest when I had the pleasure to work with her. You're jealous you weren't there to see for yourself."

Anita smiled back. "For starters, if I *had* been on call a few weeks ago, the poor helpless slut wouldn't have disappeared from this office right in front of our top-notch security force. And now I hear that a particular item which could implicate you in all this nasty business is still missing."

This reminded the governor that he hadn't finished the tirade against his staff. Since only his chief of staff was present, he continued with him.

A knock on the door interrupted the governor. With a relieved sigh, Steadman hustled across the room and opened it.

CHAPTER 13

When Steadman opened the door, Victor Petricello walked in. Several steps behind, Agent Olivia Davenport followed. Governor Blackwell's annoyed expression transformed into a leer.

The governor's tastes tended to gravitate toward much younger flesh, but something in him stirred as his narrow blue eyes washed over the body of Olivia Davenport. He brushed fingers through his wavy, light brown hair and chanced a quick look at Anita. Although she remained silent, he thought he detected a slight shake of her head as she placed the glass to her lips and took a sip.

The governor spoke to Petricello but kept his focus on Davenport and appraised the agent's features. Ordinarily, Blackwell dismissed any female with the strong, no-nonsense athletic build that Davenport possessed. It tended to make him self-conscious about his tall, but softening frame. There was something about this woman, pushing the wrong side of forty, that had him envisioning her body writhing in a fast-paced bout of undercover sports.

Olivia Davenport pressed a hand against the tight bun of her dark brown hair. Her large green eyes riveted on the governor as she replaced the slight harshness on her face with a sudden smile. "Governor Blackwell, it's a great honor to meet you, sir." Olivia stepped forward and extended her right hand. "I'm Agent Davenport. The D.C. office has reassigned me to your protection detail."

She tilted her head and added, "And if all the polls are correct—I'll soon be calling you *Mr. President.*" Her eyes appeared to grow larger as they pierced into Nicholas Blackwell.

The governor shook hands with Davenport, the brief contact sending sharp jolts through his system. He held her hand longer than necessary and savored the building heat coursing through his body.

Davenport eased her hand from the governor's grasp as her face clouded over. "I'm the replacement for Agent Anson Kostelecky. I'm sure you're all still feeling his loss. Such a senseless act of violence."

"Yes, of course, Agent Davenport." Blackwell glanced at the head of his security team. "Although we only had a brief opportunity to work with Agent Kostelecky, we all mourn his untimely death."

"They told me the local authorities have no leads in the case," Olivia said.

Blackwell nodded and turned to Petricello. The head of security cleared his throat. "That's correct, Agent Davenport. It appears he was another victim of our city's crime epidemic. A random encounter on a popular jogging path."

"From what I understand, Kostelecky was a careful person and could handle himself in almost any situation. It's hard to imagine him reckless enough to allow a stranger to get so close. Shot at point-blank range, no less."

Petricello responded to Olivia's remarks. "The path was dark and isolated, especially at that late hour. Sometimes the best of us can let down our guard. So far, neither his wallet nor gun has been recovered."

"It surprised me to learn he was on the path by himself."

"I'm not following, Davenport," Petricello said.

"Well, it's difficult to comprehend why Kobe wasn't with him."

The governor stared at Petricello. He then turned to Olivia. "Who the hell is Kobe?"

"Kostelecky's trained K9 partner."

Petricello shrugged. "Right. We all thought it a little unusual when Kostelecky reported for duty with a dog. And let me tell you—it gave the local authorities a tense moment when they went to his apartment after the incident and confronted the beast."

"So I heard. To gain access they had to call in the breeder who trained the dog," said Olivia.

"Did you know Agent Kostelecky—personally?" Anita Blackwell asked. She placed her empty martini glass on the bar counter and walked up to her husband, lightly touching his shoulder.

Olivia shifted her attention to the governor's wife.

She had seen numerous photos of Anita Blackwell and instantly recognized the woman. Although she appeared short in comparison to the governor, with her high cheekbones and prominent jaw, she presented a formidable image. Anita's shoulder length dark blond hair obscured the rounded contours of her face, making it seem more callous. And right now, her hazel eyes looked up at the taller female agent.

While Anita's words sounded innocent enough, Olivia sensed an underlying danger in this woman. Before answering, she glanced back at the governor. All she saw there was an animalistic desire to jump her bones. Olivia smiled inwardly. The governor's wife would be her biggest threat, and she needed to keep that in mind.

"No, Mrs. Blackwell. I only knew Agent Kostelecky by his reputation." She delivered this lie without any hint of fabrication, and added, "Those who did know Kostelecky described him as one of the most competent agents in the service. They say he had an uncanny investigative eye, with a knack for sifting through layers of subterfuge to find the truth."

"The truth?" the governor stammered.

The governor's wife tightened her grip on his shoulder but responded with a cool, penetrating voice, her eyes never straying from Olivia. "Well, it's a pity a man of his talents was assigned to such a trivial detail at the California governor's mansion." She shook her head. "And then to die so needlessly at the hands of some petty criminal looking for money to buy drugs."

The governor's chief of staff broke in. "Agent Davenport. While we're all sorry for what happened, I'm sure the appropriate authorities are doing their best to find the perpetrator. But for now, we should focus on last night's attempted assassination of the governor. We're preparing to leave on the governor's final road tour before next week's election. Victor tells me you've uncovered some additional information." He looked at Petricello. "Something our own private security people missed?"

"That's what they've been saying, Thomas," Petricello responded. "Agent Davenport, let's get to the point, so the governor can get back to the task of solidifying his base and winning this election."

Anita Blackwell said, "The assassination attempt failed, and the suicide bomber is dead. We should all move on. Let's concentrate on kicking that hot-headed fool Tyler Griffin out of the White House and sending him back to New Jersey. The Oval Office is within Nicholas's reach, and we wouldn't want anything to change our momentum in the race."

She paused and added, "So, Agent Davenport, what is it that's so important?"

Olivia's skin crawled as she listened to Anita Blackwell's words.

CHAPTER 14

Ethan Galloway's legs grew shaky, and his body swayed as he entered the living room. He tried to smile at Corey and Patas, but knew the attempt was lame. At least his breathing seemed more normal, and his heart had stopped trying to break free from his chest.

Looking at the expectant demeanor fixed on their faces convinced him to switch gears for the moment. He cleared his throat. "Ahh... Corey? Two o'clock? What happens at two o'clock?"

Corey's mouth opened wide. "W—what?"

"The earlier phone call. You were talking to the girl from Mayacamas Shepherds in Sonoma. Catori Torrence. Did she call to tell you they might have a puppy ready? I thought the next breeding wasn't scheduled until after Christmas."

Ethan watched the medley of changes cross Corey's face as he listened to his father's words. Ethan had surprised himself while walking back to the living room. All of a sudden, he remembered the discussions with Corey about getting a puppy. For months, Corey had worked on him. He had done hours of research and at every opportunity found a way to bring up the subject.

Somewhere along the line, Ethan agreed and Corey had gone ahead and submitted an application form to a kennel in Sonoma that bred and trained German Shepherd Dogs. At the time, Ethan had paid no attention to the questions and background information requested by Steve Casella, the owner of Mayacamas Shepherds. He left it all up to Corey to fill in the answers. He simply signed the application where Corey indicated and wrote out the deposit check.

Although Corey pleaded the case of wanting a puppy as a companion for the long hours spent alone while Ethan worked his security shift at the university, he realized that, in fact, Corey thought having a dog in the family might help his father's fragile mental state. Ethan wasn't positive that bringing a dog into his life at this point was something he could handle, but maybe Corey had the right idea.

Ethan's face froze as his mind fixed on an image of Chopper. The horrendous howling. All the blood. And his companion—motionless on the dirty floor. Ethan had reacted swiftly and cut down the charging terrorist before anyone else would die. But it was too late for Chopper. His K9 partner did his job, so Ethan could live.

That thought haunted him every day. For some reason his mind replayed that terrible moment with a harsh clarity. But what happened next as he stood staring down at his fallen companion eluded him. As did the details of so many events during his last tour in

Afghanistan. When least expected, some of those memories rushed back into his head, but almost as quickly they disappeared as if a door had slammed closed before he could recognize the importance of what his head tried to tell him.

On his last visit to the VA Center in Sacramento, he found out his case had been turned over to another team of physicians. They'd started him on a different treatment regimen. The new drugs supposedly worked to decrease the incidences of his bizarre episodes of twisted memories, but on occasion, when the images broke through, the terror he felt intensified to the point where he imagined losing his remaining sanity.

So, when he had run to the bathroom to take extra doses of this latest series of drugs, he instead spit out the pills before swallowing them. Without thinking, he flushed the remaining pills down the toilet and tossed the empty bottles in the trash.

The doctors had warned him about serious consequences if he abruptly stopped his medications. They outlined a frightening litany of complications to such an action.

As he had watched the last of the pills swirling out of sight, he thought, *Well screw them all. My gut is telling me those sonsofbitches are full of it. I don't trust them. Hell, I don't think I'll ever trust anyone from the government as long as I'm still breathing.*

And right now, Ethan didn't think he had a whole lot of time left anyway.

He looked at Corey and repeated his last question.

Corey nodded. "Catori—she told me it was okay to call her that—well, you're right, Dad. They don't have any new litters. But she asked if we might be interested in an older dog. She wanted us to look at a particular one. It belonged to someone else, and recently—Mr. Casella, the owner—brought the dog back home."

"Did Catori say what prompted that action?"

"No, she said there's no pressure to take the dog, or anything like that, but she didn't want us to miss out on the opportunity to see it."

"I guess it can't hurt to take a look. At least we'll get to see the facility firsthand."

Ethan stopped talking and looked at Patas, who had risen and wandered over to the window. He considered the consequences of leaving her alone and the likelihood of her running off again. He didn't want that to happen, although he still had no idea how to handle the situation.

Looking at his watch, he said to Corey, "You still got the stack of old clothes that don't fit anymore? The ones we planned on dropping off at Goodwill?"

Corey scrunched his face and nodded.

"Go get them and put them in the guest bedroom." He turned to Patas. "Patas, please follow me." He headed into the kitchen.

Corey and Patas stared at each other. He shrugged and left to find the box of clothing. Patas followed Ethan into the kitchen, pulling the bed sheet tighter.

After dumping the box in the bedroom, Corey walked into the kitchen in time to witness the first clumps of Patas's long, luxurious black locks raining down on the tiled floor as his father's hands pulled, parted, clipped, and thinned her hair, using the set of barber shears he'd brought home from the Navy.

Corey gawked at Patas, and she turned her head to meet his gaze.

"Careful," Ethan said. "Don't move, or you'll lose an ear."

Corey laughed. "He tells me the same thing every time he cuts my hair. But see," he said flicking the edges of his ears, "they're both still there."

"That's reassuring. Mr. Galloway? How many times have you cut a *girl's* hair?"

"I'm about finished with my first victim."

"Ahh… Dad? Why are you doing this?"

Patas answered, "Your father is trying to change my looks, so I won't be recognized. He doesn't trust me to stay here alone. He's afraid I'll run off again."

"Would you?" Corey asked.

Patas lowered her head. "I—I'm not sure I can answer that."

Ethan stepped back and looked at his handiwork. "I think Patas should stay close to us until, well… until we determine the best course of action. She's is going to accompany us to Mayacamas Shepherds. And if this young lady hurries, she still has time to wash up and try on some new clothes before we leave."

Patas got up and Ethan added, "Don't get the bandage wet. Give me a holler when you're ready and I'll come in and check it again. And I have something else for you to try." When he finished speaking, he watched Patas glance at Corey as she slipped through the door. Both their faces glowed with a brilliant red hue, but he also caught slight smirks before they turned away.

About thirty minutes later, Ethan and Corey looked up in response to the guest bedroom's door opening. With her uncovered head lowered, Patas took a cautious step into the living room. She finally looked up and faced the two men staring at her.

Ethan smiled and Corey gasped. "Oh my God!"

Ethan had given Patas several containers of Kinsley's make-up items and left Patas's feminine instincts to work their magic.

Patas cringed and covered her face with both hands. "I'm hideous. And just like my father accused me, I look like a whore. But I'm dressed like a man."

Ethan turned to Corey, raising his eyebrows.

Corey stammered, "No—no. Patas, you're beautiful. I hardly recognized you. You look so different than—" He shook his head, making his face turn redder, the tips of his ears on fire. "Wait, I mean you were pretty before, but with your new hairstyle, and even in my old clothes, you—you—"

Ethan stepped in and saved Corey from any further embarrassment. "I think what Corey is trying to say, Patas, is we're confident you're ready to go out in public and not be recognized." With a final glance at his watch, he added, "Let's see what the rest of the day has in store."

CHAPTER 15

Olivia Davenport took a breath and filed away any further thoughts of Anita Blackwell. She understood it would be prudent to redact certain parts of what was uncovered during her initial investigation of the attempted assassination.

She turned to the governor. "As you know, sir, the FBI has taken the lead on this investigation. I'm speaking to you with their permission and as a courtesy to you and your security staff." Finished, she added a fake smile.

Thomas Steadman leaned forward. "What do you mean coming in here and—"

Victor Petricello placed a hand on the chief of staff's shoulder. "Relax, Tom. Agent Davenport is just doing her job. We've already discussed those details in my office." He looked at Olivia. "We all have procedures and guidelines to follow, but we're all on the same team. Isn't that right, Agent Davenport?"

Olivia raised both hands out in front.

"Please proceed, Agent Davenport," the governor said.

She nodded. "Let me start at the beginning and fill you in on what we know." Planning to take this step by step, Olivia wanted to gage every reaction to what she said. Doing this solo complicated things. She usually had a partner to stand back and observe. At one time Anson Kostelecky played that role. More recently the president had teamed her up with another agent. They had worked a series of cases involving national security issu es.

Damn it, Mike. Whether you like it or not, you're getting involved in this whole mess. I don't give a crap if you're retired from the agency. What the hell were you thinking?

"Okay, gentlemen." Olivia observed Anita stiffen before heading off to mix herself another martini. "First, let's set the record straight. A Halloween costume? Who the hell tried to push that story on the media?"

From behind the bar, Anita said, "Well, it *was* Halloween night. With plenty of parties going on in the area. It seemed logical to presume the obvious, wouldn't you agree?"

"Remind me never to go trick-or-treating at the governor's mansion. I'm not so sure I'd want to be greeted by a team of armed security men chasing me down the street, firing semi-automatic weapons. What the hell kind of candy did she ask for?" Olivia riveted her eyes on the governor's wife, who looked away and proceeded to stir her martini.

Petricello responded, "Let's not get carried away, Davenport. We're in the final stages of a heated campaign. No one likes to jump the gun and shout out the words *Islamic terrorist* at this juncture without proof. The governor's wife thought it best to downplay the event until all the facts were in."

"The governor's wife is still here, Victor, and is capable of addressing *Ms. Davenport's* concerns. If she finds it necessary to do so." Instead of looking at Olivia, Anita Blackwell diverted her eyes and took a large gulp of her drink.

Olivia pulled out a notebook and read through several pages before continuing. "Here's what I'm looking for," she mumbled and cleared her throat. "Several theatergoers, *not* in costumes, distinctly recall the girl wearing—for lack of a more precise term—what we Americans refer to as traditional Muslim garb. They heard her shouting out a litany of familiar words. The same words used by many Islamic jihadists prior to blowing themselves up."

She looked up and studied their faces. "I have the exact phrases written in my notebook if anyone's interested." Nobody took the bait, so Olivia continued, "And there's additional evidence now being recovered from the Sacramento River and the adjacent shorelines. It seems like this girl brought a bomb to a gunfight. Hard to understand how you all survived this event."

Although Olivia was well aware of the potential devastation and loss of life that could have occurred if the suicide bomber had detonated her vest in the theater, she needed to keep the governor's staff off guard and wait for them to make mistakes. She was convinced a lot more was going on than anyone present dared to admit.

The president himself had sent Olivia Davenport here. He was in a difficult position with Nicholas Blackwell being his opposition in a crucial presidential election. Disturbing data had been leaking for months from various intelligence departments in the administration. Most of the intel came from on-the-ground sources within the agencies, not from the senior officials. This troubled President Tyler Griffin, as it indicated that certain elements in both political parties appeared determined to cover up any potential illegal activities of the Blackwells and the far-reaching tentacles of their behemoth organization.

If word got out that Tyler Griffin was secretly investigating Governor Nicholas Blackwell, the democrat candidate for president, he would face an insurmountable outcry from both congress and the voters. It would look like Griffin was underhandedly trying to discredit his opponent. This would ensure Griffin's defeat in the upcoming election.

Olivia again turned her thoughts to Agent Mike Finley.

Now that I'm thinking more clearly, this operation has your fingerprints all over it, Mike. Retired—my ass.

Referring to her notes again, Olivia said, "Pieces of material that may be from the girl's outfit have been recovered. There were blood stains on several sections."

She held up a finger. "More on that in a minute." She browsed through her notebook again. "We have a tentative identification of the perpetrator. The girl walked into the theater with a ticket. The ticket had her name printed on it. And at least four members of your staff claimed they knew her despite wearing clothing that hid most of her features. She was an intern, a high school student taking part in your after-school program." Pausing to look up and assess their response, Olivia said, "Patas Ta'anari. She is sixteen years old. And by coincidence, she appears to be a Muslim. Do any of you recognize this name?"

Anita Blackwell murmured a few incomprehensible words and turned to refill her glass. The governor looked at his shoes. Steadman and Petricello exchanged glances, and Steadman answered first. "We have also been made aware of this fact. When it was brought to my attention, I checked our employment records and confirmed this person had worked for several months in our intern program. I do remember seeing someone dressed in similar garb on several occasions, but personally, I don't recall having any direct contact with her."

Olivia looked at the governor. "Based on the odds, sir, it's logical—you were the primary target of last night's assassination attempt. Do you have any idea why Patas Ta'anari would want to kill you?"

The governor paled and shook his head. His mouth opened, but no words escaped.

"We still need to talk to the rest of your staff. Perhaps someone saw something suspicious about the girl or observed an incident that could have precipitated such an extreme response."

"It's possible this girl is part of a larger terrorist cell with aims to wreak havoc on our election process. We've received warnings from Homeland Security regarding potential threats planned as we get closer to election day," said Petricello. Both the governor and Steadman nodded in agreement.

"The FBI is looking into those activities. You sure you're willing to give up blaming this on a Halloween prank gone bad?"

Nobody commented and Olivia continued, "Now here comes the interesting part. You do have time to hear this, don't you?"

Steadman let out a long breath. "For God's sake, Davenport—"

The governor interrupted. "Take all the time you need, Agent Davenport."

CHAPTER 16

Ethan's earlier attempt at making breakfast had wound up in the trash, but before they left for Mayacamas Shepherds he rustled up a quick bite to eat. As they walked out the front door, Ethan tossed the keys to the Ford at Corey and said, "Your turn to drive."

Four months ago, Corey passed his driving test and held a provisional California driver's license. They headed out to Ethan's pick-up. Corey jumped behind the wheel and adjusted the seat and mirrors. Ethan opened the rear door for Patas before climbing into the front passenger seat. Corey started the engine, shifted into drive, and the truck jolted forward.

Ethan turned over his shoulder and winked at Patas. "Letting Corey drive reminds me of that suicide vest you had on last night."

"Da—aad," Corey moaned.

Ethan's stomach clenched when he saw the painful look on Patas's face. "Sorry, Patas," he mumbled. "Poor choice of words."

She shrugged and tweaked out a thin smile.

As they reached the 80 freeway and headed west toward Mayacamas Shepherds in Sonoma, Corey periodically glanced in the rearview mirror at Patas, but his overall driving remained focused and steady. Ethan resisted the urge to make any additional comments, although his foot pushed down on a phantom brake pedal from time-to-time.

The Ford's GPS navigation system did an accurate job of getting them to the kennel's isolated location on the narrow and winding country lane high in the eastern hills above the town of Sonoma. A simple but professional-looking sign stood at the opening to a parking lot in front of a large teal green metal building. Corey pulled up next to the lone car parked near the front entrance. A sign above the door read *Training Center.* Attached to this building, on the east side of the parking area, was a long, low structure with a small placard on the vertical siding stating it housed the kennels and boarding facilities.

Ethan and Corey stepped out of the truck and gazed at the panoramic vista spreading as a backdrop to a large A-frame dwelling directly across the gravel road from the training center. Patas remained inside the truck, hunkered down in the rear seat. Ethan rapped lightly on the window before pulling open the door and coaxing her out.

For several moments, they stood in silence and looked at the breathtaking view. Corey shielded his eyes with one hand and pointed. "Look. That's the town we just drove through—Sonoma." His voice grew more animated, and he waved his arm. "There's San Pablo Bay. And I can make out some of the taller buildings in San Francisco. If it weren't for those pockets of fog, I bet you could see the Golden Gate Bridge."

Ethan watched Patas's face light up at Corey's enthusiasm, part of her anxieties pushed into the darker recesses for the time being.

They flinched at the sound of the soft, but confident voice at their backs. "No one can resist the beauty of this place. Every morning when I arrive, and in the evening when I leave, I take the time to appreciate such a wonder."

Turning, they saw a young woman bracketed by the open doorway to the training center. Ethan stole a quick look at Corey and understood that the sight of this alluring female speaking to them had eclipsed the majestic views he'd been admiring.

She took a step forward into the sunlight. Her waist-length dark brown hair shimmered about her shoulders and framed a slender body that on tippy toes stood under five feet.

"I'm Catori," she said and smiled, making her olive-toned complexion appear even more captivating.

Ethan found himself mesmerized by Catori Torrence as the sunlight glittered from her slanted, almond-shaped eyes.

To Ethan's surprise, Corey responded first. "Hi Catori, I'm Corey Galloway, and this is my father." He hesitated and added, "And this is our friend... Patty." The name they'd agreed on to call Patas while they had driven from Davis to Sonoma. Patas stood half-hidden in

Ethan's shadow. He stepped aside and Patas managed a slight smile.

Catori shook each of their hands. Ethan thought he detected a subtle shift in Catori's eyes when she greeted Patas. When she extended her arm to him and their hands touched, he sensed a peculiar sensation. Not unpleasant, but none-the-less disturbing and reassuring at the same time. He exchanged a brief glance with Patas. Looking at Corey, he noticed the wide grin plastered on his face.

Catori moved on as if all this was nothing unusual for her. "It's a pleasure to meet you all. And thanks for coming out on such short notice."

"Corey tells me we've been placed on your approved wait list for the next available litter, but you wanted to show us an adult dog someone brought back. We can take a look, but I'm not sure we want—"

Catori raised a hand. "I understand, Mr. Galloway. Rest assured; you are under no obligation to consider adopting this particular dog. Your name will remain on the list for our next planned breeding." She paused, as several loud barks escaped from the open door.

"This is a unique situation for us, Mr. Galloway. I'd like you all to follow me inside." She turned and entered the building. Ethan shrugged and motioned for Corey and Patas to go through the door. He followed close behind.

Once inside, Catori pointed to several chairs and a small table in a partitioned area in the front corner of the building. They moved silently and seated themselves as directed, facing the large open arena. At the far side of the building, they saw a man working with a jet black German Shepherd.

The man, dark-haired, tall, and in excellent physical shape, signaled the dog to sit at his side and then threw something across the room. The dog remained still, eyes riveted on the object as it bounced and rolled over the pale blue rubberized matting. They could see the dog's limbs and flank humming in anticipation. The handler next did a quick hand movement, and the magnificent creature exploded from the man's side and pounced on the object; then spun around and galloped to a sitting position in front of the man.

"Give," the man said as he reached out.

The dog released it.

"Good boy."

The dog barked as the man roughed up his fur. He next shook the object, which could now be seen as a tube-like canvass form with a looped handle at one end, and held it out for the dog.

"Take it, Kobe."

Kobe lunged and its powerful jaws latched onto the pull toy as the man held tight to the handle. The two wrestled and rolled around the floor. The dog never let go but seemed to gear its tugging to exactly counter the man's efforts to pull it away.

"Give." The dog instantly released the object again, and the man signaled Kobe to down. When the dog responded, the man glanced over at the spectators. After commanding Kobe to stay, he strode purposefully toward them.

Steve Casella introduced himself and took a seat across from Ethan. "I've read over your application, Mr. Galloway. Given your background and experience, I can see why Catori brought it to my attention."

Ethan glanced to his left at Corey, who appeared busy studying one of the Mayacamas Shepherds training brochures. He looked back at Steve and smiled.

What the hell did Corey put on that application? Guess I should have read it before signing on the dotted line.

Steve held Ethan's gaze before continuing. "Well... we have a difficult situation regarding Kobe. To be frank, Mr. Galloway, I've never run into this before. At least not with a dog having Kobe's particular training. I'm not sure how much Catori has discussed—"

Catori touched Steve's arm. "They know nothing at all about Kobe. Only that you had reason to bring him back to the kennel."

"Before we go too far," Ethan said, looking at Catori. "Let me repeat. The original plan was to get a puppy for my son. I'm not sure an older dog is something that suits our needs at this point."

He hesitated and turned to Steve. "But I must say, you've tweaked my curiosity about this dog."

"I understand what you're saying, and let me assure you—"

The side door to the training facility burst open, interrupting Steve's response. This door opened directly into the training area and everyone at the table turned to see a very young girl charge across the floor toward Kobe.

Alarmed, Ethan looked at Steve. He saw a slight tensing in his jaw muscles, but otherwise the man remained calm.

"Kobe! Kobe! You're back home again." the little girl shouted. She slowed while approaching the dog, stopping about ten feet short of Kobe. Steve smiled, keeping an eye on the dog. Kobe didn't move, his head staying stretched out on his front paws.

"Sorry, Daddy. I almost forgot. Is it okay to pet Kobe?" She turned her tiny body sideways to the dog.

"Just a second, Rosa." Steve maintained his attention on the prone animal. "*Bitte aus*, Kobe."

As soon as Steve finished the command to release him, Kobe padded over to Rosa. When Kobe got close, he sat down. Rosa extended a closed fist and allowed him to sniff. She then turned and broke into a big smile. Kobe licked her face, and she wrapped her arms around him.

"Good job, Rosa." The voice came from the open doorway. A woman wheeling a baby stroller stepped inside and turned to pull the door shut. She waved at Steve. "My fault, Steve. Rosa got the jump on me again. I know we shouldn't use this entrance."

Before the door completely closed, a large white German Shepherd stuck its head in and plunged through. She took a quick look at Rosa and Kobe, barked twice, and headed for the table near the front of the building.

Ethan's mind had been processing the prior events when the sight of the white dog caused him to stand up so abruptly his chair screeched back, crashing into a metal file cabinet. As the boom echoed throughout the cavernous space, the dog skidded to a halt several feet from the wooden ring gates closest to the table.

For a moment, Ethan stood still, his body frozen in time.

With his eyes glued to the white dog, he muttered, "Excuse me."

He turned and fled the building.

Corey, although startled, attempted to explain his dad's abrupt behavior.

Edie Pauling, Steve Casella's wife, retrieved Rosa from the training ring. With one hand pushing the baby stroller and the other holding Rosa, she introduced herself and apologized for the interruption.

"I'm sorry. I forgot Rosa let Amber outside. I thought she was sleeping on the back deck."

Rosa looked up at Edie, her eyes welling with tears. "Did Amber frighten that man, Mommy?"

Looking at Rosa, Corey stuttered, "Don't worry, it's nobody's fault. My dad once had a dog and… I think Amber reminded him of it."

"Chopper," Catori whispered.

"Right," Corey nodded, scrunching up his face. "How did you know that?"

Catori shrugged. "Oh, I must've read it on your application." She walked over to Steve, who was busy fastening a leash on Kobe. After a brief conversation in hushed tones, she took the lead from Steve's hand and watched as he strode back to the table.

"Why don't we all sit down so Corey can finish telling us about Chopper," Steve said.

"But my dad. I should go check on him."

Steve reached out and touched Corey's arm. "Give him a little time, Corey. Trust me."

"Daddy?" Rosa broke in. "Where's Catori going with Kobe?" Her eyes filled with tears again.

Steve smiled at Rosa. "Don't worry, sweetie, you'll get a chance to say goodbye to Kobe before he leaves with these nice people."

Corey and Patas stared at each other.

Steve pointed to the Galloway's application sitting on the table and prodded Corey to talk.

CHAPTER 17

(two weeks ago)

Puget Sound Creamery, a small but prosperous dairy farm situated to the south and east of Parkwood, Washington, utilized the Washington State ferry system to transport raw milk to a bottling and processing facility in Seattle.

Starting two months ago, for a period of three weeks, a private investigator studied the scheduling routines and documented the transportation equipment owned by the creamery. Next, he shipped this information along with detailed photographs to a private mail pick-up location in San Francisco. He made no copies of the data. Once those papers were retrieved, a courier transported them to an automotive body shop in an industrial section of Tacoma, Washington.

Yesterday, the owner of the body shop placed a *'closed'* sign on the rotting overhead garage doors and set off to start a premature retirement as the result of the substantial windfall earned from his last job. As it turned out, his retirement ended before the lights had been switched off.

The bodies of the private investigator, the courier, and the owner of the body shop were deposited somewhere in the vast wastelands beyond the dazzling city lights of Las Vegas.

Under several brown tarps inside the body shop was a 2006 Dodge Ram diesel pick-up truck outfitted with a double-insulated 700-gallon stainless steel dairy tank. As per specific details outlined in a separate set of instructions, other important changes were planned for the vehicle. From the exterior, the modified Dodge Ram appeared identical to the Puget Sound Creamery dairy transporters.

Chapter 18

The silence in the governor's office was deafening. Olivia Davenport could hear the ice tinkling from the glass held in Anita Blackwell's hand. She nodded at the governor's invitation to discuss the evidence, and then looked at his chief of staff and the head of his private security team to make sure she had their attention.

"We have no conclusive proof that Patas Ta'anari died in the blast."

She turned to the sound of glass shattering on the marble bar counter as the martini slipped out of Anita's grasp.

"Of all things. Damn. What a mess," she uttered, stepping back and pulling the gin-soaked blouse away from her skin.

Olivia stared hard at the woman before continuing. She wondered what mess the governor's wife was referring to: her wet clothes, the lost drink, or the fact the Ta'anari girl may still be alive.

The governor interrupted her thoughts. "H—how can that be possible—if the vest exploded and you found pieces of her dress covered with blood?"

"Well, first," Olivia said, her eyes still glued on the governor's wife, "witnesses reported the girl may have been shot. And while the FBI and the local authorities have done an extensive search of the river, other than lots of dead fish, no human remains have been found in any of the debris."

The chief of staff commented, "It's a big river with swift currents. The body could be snagged below or carried away by now."

Olivia shrugged. "Sorry, Mr. Steadman, while that's possible, if she were wearing the vest, we'd be looking for body *parts*. More likely the blast would've—well—I— something should've turned up. Of course, the authorities will continue searching."

She flipped over a page in her notebook. "Ahhh… the Delta King. You all know what that is, right?" Without waiting for a response, Olivia continued, "Several witnesses reported seeing a man jump from the upper deck into the river."

Steadman raised both arms. "Jumped? The shockwave from the blast probably knocked him overboard."

Olivia looked up, shaking her head. "No. Every witness was positive they saw him jump into the river *before* the explosion. In fact, all accounts about the timing were consistent. The gunshots had occurred first. People were panicking and looking in every direction, trying to pinpoint where the shots came from. When they saw someone jump from the Delta King, many speculated he could've been the shooter."

"You know damn well it was my men firing at the assailant fleeing the theater," Petricello huffed.

The governor said, "This doesn't make any sense. If someone jumped into the river before the blast, you should've found two bodies."

"Like I said, so far no bodies have been recovered, but there's another piece to this puzzle that makes even less sense."

The governor's wife finished blotting off her blouse and threw the towel in the bar sink. "Chrissakes, Davenport. Why don't you just spit it all out?"

Maybe I should pour you another drink, Olivia thought, but nodded instead. "After being informed of the eyewitness reports, I accompanied the FBI when they checked out the Delta King. We found a sniper rifle in the starboard-side corner stateroom on the upper deck. The room had an exit door to the same deck where witnesses saw the man jump over the railing. In addition, Governor Blackwell, one of the room's windows had an excellent view of the theater." She turned to Petricello. "Is it safe to say you hadn't placed one of your men in that room as a precautionary measure to surveil the area?"

The governor and his chief of staff stared at Petricello. He slowly shook his head. "So… you're saying this Ta'anari girl had an accomplice?"

Olivia Davenport hiked her shoulders and remained silent.

Either that or a guardian angel, she thought.

Deciding she'd shared enough information about this part of the investigation and planted seeds of her own, Olivia said, "I've asked the FBI to update me immediately if anything else turns up. And by the way, it looks like with my new assignment, I'll be accompanying you on your final campaign tour. And this time, Governor Blackwell, you may want to allow us a little better access."

Olivia smiled and turned to leave, waving with her notebook. She had at least one phone call to make regarding the evidence found on the Delta King. In her summary to the governor, she hadn't mentioned the fingerprints lifted from the deck railing, nor did she provide a description of the custom stock on the sniper rifle found on the riverboat.

Recalling the unique details of the carved image on the gunstock, her last thought was that if the owner of this rifle was, in fact, a Navy SEAL, her list of suspects just got a whole lot shorter.

CHAPTER 19

The black Ford pick-up cruised through Sonoma and headed toward the Galloway home outside Davis. Sitting behind the wheel, Ethan kept glancing to his right.

"Da—aad," Corey said in a mock accusatory tone from the rear seat. "Don't drive distracted. Keep your eyes on the road."

Ethan grunted and mumbled a response, while Kobe, sitting on his haunches in the front passenger seat, chuffed and swiped a paw on the dash. Ethan swore the damn dog smiled at him. Before leaving Mayacamas Shepherds, Kobe had jumped into the truck and selected the front passenger seat. Nobody seemed interested in challenging him.

Once again Ethan's head swam with discordant images, but this time the details he tried to sort out came from a more recent episode. After fleeing the training center and staggering toward his truck, he was startled by the appearance of Catori Torrence and her disturbing words—and the sensation of Kobe's wet muzzle sniffing his hand.

Corey's voice brought him back to the present.

"It's not safe to let him ride up front—especially without a seatbelt."

Ethan didn't need to see Corey's reflection in the rearview mirror to conclude his grin was bigger than Kobe's.

"Not like we had much choice," Ethan said. He tried to hide his own smile but knew he more than likely failed. He heard snickering from the back seat and caught a glimpse of Patas slapping a hand over her mouth after adding words of agreement.

"Well, well. *Patty* can speak. You haven't uttered more than two words since we got out of the truck at Mayacamas Shepherds," Ethan said, laughing. He reached for the radio and turned up the volume to Willie Nelson's *'On the Road Again'*. He focused his attention on driving and whistled along with Willie.

In the back seat, Corey and Patas spoke in hushed tones for the remainder of the trip home. All signs of levity evaporated well before the truck turned onto the gravel drive leading to the house.

Ethan cut the ignition, but no one exited the truck. He listened to the fading ticks of the heated engine. Corey broke the silence by saying, "Dad, I'm going to take Kobe for a walk. A long walk. Patas needs to talk to you."

"Corey!" Patas protested; eyes narrowing. "I'm not sure it's—" She stopped in mid-sentence at the look on Corey's face as he opened the door. Corey's hand lightly touched Patas's shoulder before he grabbed Kobe's leash, jumped out, and pulled open the front passenger door.

"Let's go, Kobe. Time to check out the perimeter before seeing the inside of your new home."

The sun was already settling below the far western ridges as Corey led Kobe away from the house. For several seconds, Ethan watched them in the fading light and then said to Patas, "Guess we should go inside. How about I heat up some water and make a pot of tea?"

He opened the door for Patas, and they headed inside. After catching the dark look on her face, Ethan cursed himself for never replenishing the whiskey bottles he'd destroyed last year.

For some reason, I'm not sure a cup of tea is going to cut it tonight.

Patas sat at the kitchen table while Ethan prepared the tea. Willie Nelson's lyrics had long since disintegrated from his head. Ethan remained quiet as he placed the steaming mugs on the table and sat across from Patas.

Patas took several sips of her tea while Ethan waited. He could see a deep flush rising up from the collar of Corey's old plaid flannel shirt which hung loosely on her slim shoulders. He was about to coax her to speak when she stood up and turned her back to him.

Her words sounded so soft, he barely heard them. "Corey said I should've told you—"

Patas shifted her weight, and Ethan thought she might keel over. Instead, she twisted around and grasped the edge of the table. Her forehead looked damp, and her color had transformed to a deathly shade of white. Ethan didn't know what to do. Kinsley had always been the nurturer in the family. So he sat back and waited.

Patas wiped non-existent tears from her eyes and shook her head. "I didn't tell Corey everything. I couldn't get myself to say it. But when I told him there was... *evidence*... he insisted I had to tell you. That you'd know what to do."

Ethan motioned for Patas to sit, and this time he reached across the table. He placed his hand over hers. Cold tremors shot up his arm, and he felt her hand relax.

A faint smile formed, and a slight coloring returned to her face. "Corey guessed I was holding back and was too embarrassed to come right out and say it to him. That's why he insisted on taking Kobe for a walk."

Ethan nodded and raised his eyebrows. He patted her hand once and sat back, folding his hands on the table.

Patas met his eyes briefly and focused on the mug as she twirled it around in front of her.

"You remember the linen napkin? When I told you the story of what the governor did with it, I glossed over the more delicate parts. But after I pressed it against my... between my legs... to try and stop the bleeding, I realized he had used it to wipe *himself* before he pulled up his pants."

She looked up expectantly. "That's important, isn't it? It can prove he...."

Ethan narrowed his eyes and said, "*If* you had the napkin and could get it analyzed. But I'm sure the governor would've destroyed it by now, don't you think?"

"What if he couldn't find it?"

A small smile etched Ethan's face. "Any idea where it might be?"

Patas nodded. "Corey said you'd know what to do. Should we call the police and explain what happened? They could go in and get it back. I should've done that right away, but I was too scared and embarrassed. My family blamed me, and… well, I guess you know the rest of the story."

She took a deep breath. "Is it too late?"

Ethan's mind whirled with images almost too much to fathom. He looked at Patas. Her vulnerability smacked him in the gut. The thought of Blackwell—this predator—becoming the next president of the United States made him sick. He could feel himself receding back into the past, wishing he hadn't flushed his medications down the toilet. Not to mention there wasn't an ounce of liquor in the house.

His mind scrambled to keep it together, when almost as an afterthought, Patas said, "While I worked at the governor's mansion, I saw and heard things. I tried to ignore them, but…."

As Patas talked, Ethan pulled himself back to the present. Slowly, her words resonated.

He hadn't seen Corey return, but as Patas finished talking, Ethan turned around to his voice. "Dad? So we can go to the cops, right? Let Patas tell her story. They'll take care of this, won't they?"

Ethan didn't answer right away. His mind was still spinning, but he now thought of the future and the consequences of his past.

Kobe padded to his side and sat back on his haunches. Ethan absently scratched the dog's neck and looked at Corey and Patas.

He shook his head. "This is what we're going to do."

CHAPTER 20

Olivia Davenport sighed one more time and tucked her head into the welcoming curve of Mike Finley's shoulder. From the smile on her face, it appeared any lingering anger from her confrontation with the governor two days ago had been forgotten.

But this interlude wasn't all about pleasure. When she'd returned to her temporary quarters across from the governor's mansion in downtown Sacramento, retired agent, Mike Finley, had been waiting inside the tiny, no-frills efficiency apartment. She hadn't questioned how he'd gained entry, but immediately grilled him on what he'd turned up from the information she'd sent him the day after the assassination attempt on the governor.

Then they'd jumped into the sack for a comforting reunion.

Finley whispered, "Makes me wonder how you'd react if I brought better news."

She smiled. "I learned a long time ago—don't shoot the delivery boy."

He pulled her tighter. "I don't know. At my age, these kinds of bedroom gymnastics can be fatal too."

"Gee. Yesterday the FedEx guy said the same thing."

Olivia twisted out of the bed before Finley could react.

Finley turned on his side and propped up his head using an elbow stuffed into the fold of a pillow. As he gazed at Olivia's naked body, he saw the muscles in her neck tense while she cocked her head.

She lifted a finger and took two steps toward the only window in the apartment. Easing back the heavy drapes, the harsh rays of a streetlight intruded on Finley's enjoyment of the soft glowing reflections radiating from Olivia's body.

He watched her lean closer to the parted drapes and turn her head to the left. She reached back with her right arm and pointed to a large canvass bag heaped on the floor next to the bed. "Mike, I got binoculars in the bag. Grab them."

Finley shrugged and twisted his legs to the floor. Sticking his hand in the bag and fumbling around inside, he said, "Don't think I need them. My eyesight's still pretty good for an old man, and you're close enough for me to pinch your lovely backside."

Finley didn't expect a response. He heard the same sounds that had drawn Olivia's attention to the outside, but didn't register anything unusual about the screeching brakes, the barking dog, or the shouting and irate voices. After living in Washington, D.C., for most of his adult life, this was all minor league compared to the nightly bombardment of more menacing noises. He usually fell asleep to the repeated retorts of gunfire and the waxing and waning of the inevitable sirens emanating from emergency response vehicles crisscrossing the city streets until the dawning hours helped quell the nightly neighborhood activities.

He walked over and handed Olivia the binoculars, as well as a cotton bathrobe he found slung over the back of a desk chair. "Here… why don't you cover-up so you don't distract whoever you're staring at from whatever bad thing he—or—she is up to."

Olivia let Finley place the robe over her shoulders. With one hand, she drew it across her breasts. In the other hand, she raised the binoculars and focused on the scene playing out near the Sixteenth Street entrance to the governor's mansion.

She kept her body still, and the binoculars glued to her face. After what seemed like an interminable amount of time, she dropped the binoculars to her side and let out a long breath. "Hey, Mike. You got Steve Casella's phone number handy?"

Finley peered around Olivia, pulling back the drapes a bit further. Even without the binoculars, he could make out an old man shouting and waving his arms at what appeared to be a teenage boy—and a large, angry black dog with its leash caught on a fence picket. The dog struggled to free itself while growling and lunging at the old man.

He thought, *I'm sure this is something Steve would want to get involved with.*

Then he corrected himself. *No, this is more like something Edie could sink her teeth into.*

For a fleeting instant, a vision of Catori Torrence flashed through his head. That's when his nervousness ratcheted to a higher level.

He turned, looked around the room, spotted his pants, walked over, bent down, reached into a pocket, pulled out his phone, and hit speed dial number *three*.

Olivia Davenport was number *one*, President Tyler Griffin was number *two*. But he'd keep that to himself.

After a dozen rings the voicemail message kicked in and Finley left an abbreviated message for Steve Casella. It had to be brief because he had no idea why he was making the call.

CHAPTER 21

Thirty minutes before Olivia Davenport heard the barking dog, a black Ford pick-up truck pulled into a closed public parking lot east of the governor's mansion in downtown Sacramento. From this location, the historic residence's main gate and the narrow service alley could be observed.

Ethan Galloway brought the binoculars to his face and scanned the grounds. Flipping through a tiny notepad, he scribbled in some changes. He'd spent the last two days making solo trips to Sacramento, trying to scope out the governor's mansion and the surrounding locale.

He also utilized online resources to research the recently reopened home for the California governor, familiarizing himself with the renovated building and the changes made to the secondary structures on the historic grounds. Although this data proved helpful, he preferred hands-on reconnaissance to Wikipedia and Google.

Ethan and Patas were sitting in the rear seat of the pick-up, dressed from head-to-foot in black clothing. When Ethan returned home from his last trip to Sacramento, he'd tossed Patas a bundle containing the new wardrobe and told her and Corey to get ready to go.

Corey now sat in the driver's seat with Kobe next to him. When the truck had gotten near the governor's mansion, Kobe's demeanor changed. The dog kept a sharp eye on the building and the surrounding neighborhood. He strained against his harness, making frequent whining sounds, interspersed with low growls.

"Dad! For the last time, I should be going inside with you. Patas can stay in the truck with Kobe."

Ever since Patas confided in Ethan about how she grabbed the linen napkin with the damaging evidence against the governor and hid it while making her escape, he'd fretted over how to handle this.

Corey vehemently argued a case for going to the authorities and letting them take care of the whole mess. Ethan could see his son was desperate to ignore his father's culpability and any potential consequences should his presence on the Delta King be discovered. Ethan had been vague about his own intentions that night. Corey rationalized that Patas would not be held responsible for the thwarted attempt on the governor's life once the facts were exposed and the governor's behavior made public.

Ethan did not trust the authorities to handle these matters in a way that assured justice would prevail. At least not before the governor had time to destroy any evidence and twist the truth. Besides, this was personal for Ethan. He owed it to Kinsley to set the record straight and salvage what little left existed of his own dignity.

Ethan always fostered a healthy skepticism when it came to the motives of individuals in positions of government power. Those feelings had intensified in an explosive manner during his last tour in Afghanistan and his untimely discharge from the Navy. Hidden amidst the terrifying images tormenting his sanity, he tried to hang on to his principles regarding matters of justice. Although some days it got jumbled up in the weeds of self-pity and revenge.

With the election looming on the horizon, he needed to act before the unthinkable could happen. Although feeling guilty about asking Patas to join him, she'd been ambiguous about the exact location of the hidden evidence and had persuaded Ethan to take her in with him. She described the lack of a functioning alarm system, having listened to the governor's private security team's constant bickering over why the governor insisted on moving into the house before it had been rendered more secure.

Besides, Ethan told himself, since the governor had left for his final campaign blitz and would not return until after the election, this was an opportune time to sneak inside. He found out from his earlier surveillance trips that the mansion was all but deserted, with only one or two caretakers remaining on site. If Patas's reports of no electronic security system in place were true, this should be a piece of cake.

"One more time," Ethan said. "Let's go over the plan."

After reassuring himself that Corey understood what to do, Ethan smiled at Patas and gave her a thumbs-up.

As he opened the door, Kobe pulled harder and his barking escalated.

When Ethan hesitated, Corey said, "Don't worry, Dad, I can handle him. Right, Kobe?" He scruffed the dog's neck.

Ethan nodded and stepped out of the truck. He reached for Patas's hand and helped her down. He closed the door and strode off with Patas by his side. Kobe's barks faded as they crossed the main thoroughfare and walked north, past the mansion. They circled the grounds and approached the service alley from the opposite end.

Crouching in the shadows of a rusted blue dumpster, Ethan checked his watch. He leaned against the exterior side wall of the old carriage house that formed the southeast corner of the grounds. This section of the one-acre site was secured by a five-foot high wood batten-board fence. A lower and more easily scaled wrought-iron picket-type fence surrounded the front and opposite sides of the property but was more exposed to the bright lights and traffic of the main roads bordering the mansion. This narrow, dark alleyway gave them better cover for gaining access to the grounds. On an earlier visit to check things out, Ethan had disabled the two closest streetlamps to the carriage house. They waited in the thickened shadows for Corey to carry out his part of the plan.

"We've got a few minutes before Corey gets in position. Don't know if we'll hear anything from this far away, so I'm counting on him to keep to the exact schedule."

Patas nodded. She pointed to the carriage house and whispered, "This is the building they utilized to store papers and artifacts while the main residence was being renovated. We spent a lot of time sorting through boxes and carrying stuff back to the house. Eventually it'll be turned into the caretaker's cottage. For now, like you read on the internet, the caretaker is living in a temporary structure nearer to the main house."

Ethan could tell by her babbling that she was nervous. He glanced at his watch again and placed a hand on Patas's shoulder. "Patas? You don't have to do this. Tell me where to look, and I can go in alone."

"No way, Ethan." After multiple assertions, he had convinced Patas to drop the *'Mr. Galloway'* when addressing him. "With all that's happened, I need to see this through to the end."

Ethan recalled that a short time ago Patas had decided on a more final ending to her ordeal. About to protest one last time, Ethan's words were cut off by a cacophony of barks, snarls, growls—followed by horns blaring, brakes screeching, and shouts—then more barks, snarls, growls. A floodlight near the caretaker's quarters snapped on.

No longer seeing any need to reference the time, Ethan touched Patas's arm. "I'd say it's showtime."

"Ya think?" Patas said. As Ethan yanked her toward the old wooden fence, she added, "The barking sounds a lot louder than I thought."

* * * * * *

After Ethan and Patas disappeared from Corey's sight, Kobe continued to act up. Corey's confidence melted away, and he wondered what would happen once he took the dog out of the truck as planned. He tried to soothe Kobe with reassuring sounds, pleads, and the occasional treat. None of that worked and, in frustration, he yelled out, "Knock it off, Kobe!"

Kobe instantly quieted down and sat still, eyes focused on Corey.

"Humph." Corey folded his arms. "This dog training stuff isn't so complicated after all."

Kobe chuffed and continued to stare at Corey. Corey reciprocated, maintaining the stand-off until he realized it was time to go.

He attached the lead to Kobe's collar and removed the seat harness from the dog.

Once he opened the door, Kobe reestablished the alpha role and yanked Corey straight across the parking lot and onto Sixteenth Street. Fortunately, with the light traffic at this late hour, the two made it to the other side with only one or two horns blaring and brakes screeching. Although the subtle smell of burning rubber clung to the cooling night breezes.

Corey was supposed to bring Kobe around to H Street and approach the main gate near the front entrance to the mansion. He planned to toss food or a toy over the fence and have Kobe get the caretaker's attention from inside his temporary housing unit by barking and lunging at the fence. This would allow his dad and Patas time to gain access to the opposite side of the grounds and enter the building while the guard was distracted by the commotion near the front lawn.

Patas had explained that the security office inside the mansion would be vacant, since the governor's entire entourage was traveling with him on his final campaign tour. She also reminded him that the alarm sensors were not yet functional. Since the caretaker's temporary unit had no direct access to the mansion, once they gained entry, there should be little chance of discovery.

Kobe had a different idea.

Struggling at the end of Kobe's leash, Corey held on tight with both hands and stumbled behind the charging black German Shepherd until his left sneaker smacked against the curb and sent him sprawling onto the narrow strip of gravel bordering the sidewalk near the side gate. One of Corey's hands slipped off the leash. He reached out and grabbed onto a parking meter.

This was all the help Kobe needed.

The leash ripped through Corey's other hand and Kobe bounded across the sidewalk and perimeter landscaping. With a final surge he launched himself up and over the wrought-iron fence, landing in a thick hump of mulch surrounding a beautiful grouping of Camellia. The exotic flowering shrubs didn't stop Kobe, but at least cushioned his landing.

The looped handle at the free end of the leash snagged around one of the wrought-iron pickets, stopping Kobe in his tracks.

After a slight break in cadence, Kobe's barks and lunges started up again. This assured Corey that the damn dog had not been injured. Corey leaned back against a nearby Chinese Elm and caught his breath.

"I guess we're going with plan B."

* * * * * *

Hidden in the shadows of the carriage house, Ethan boosted Patas over the fence. By the time his feet dropped inside the perimeter she had already spanned the distance to the south-facing porch. After kneeling down next to a huge potted plant, she looked over her shoulder as Ethan slipped in by her side.

Ethan pulled Patas close and whispered in her ear, "You're positive this is the best way in?"

"Don't know for sure, but it'll get us where we need to go."

Ethan glanced around, listening to the growing commotion near the Sixteenth Street gate. He couldn't see what was going on and wondered why Corey hadn't stuck with the plan to make his approach on the far side of the mansion. Kobe's barking showed no signs of letting up, and the caretaker appeared entrenched in a heated argument with Corey. Not much he could do to change things now, so he motioned for Patas to lead the way. The southeast corner of the building still shielded them from the activity near the street.

Patas proceeded toward the right side of the porch and unlatched the metal gate to the narrow catwalk. Ethan stayed close, and they climbed the first set of iron rungs on one of the mansion's multiple fire escapes.

The aged wood-framed structure had been deemed a firetrap years ago. That was one of the main reasons for Governor Reagan and his family's short tenure in the mansion during his term in office. He was the last sitting governor to reside here until Governor Blackwell's hasty decision to leave his Malibu estate and move into the recently renovated house.

Ethan and Patas stepped onto a wider platform after climbing the second flight of exterior metal steps. Ethan stood facing a large window, his hand grasping one of the thick steel bars bolted to the frame and secured with a heavy-duty lock. He turned to Patas with a resigned look and raised eyebrows.

She shook her head and pointed to a small circular window—with no bars—about ten feet beyond the platform's right-side railing.

"I watched some of the other interns use that window to sneak out to the fire escape when they wanted to disappear for a while. Prob'ly for a quick smoke or…."

Even in the dim light cast from a distant streetlamp, Ethan could see Patas's face redden.

She placed a hand over her lips and said, "Or I think maybe to fool around."

"Guess you missed out on the fun. With your required wardrobe, you couldn't've climbed through the window."

Patas opened her eyes and mouth wide. "I never would've—" She stopped when she saw the smile forming on Ethan's lips.

"After you," Ethan whispered, the grin still fixed in place.

Patas stood up and climbed over the railing. While facing the platform, she held on to the railing with both hands and stretched out her left foot until it touched the arched roof centered below the small window. She next twisted her body around, leaning toward the lower portion of the window frame and grabbing an iron handhold. With her opposite hand, she grasped the ornamental wood finial attached to the eave to steady herself while straddling the center of the arched roof. In one quick motion, Patas pushed inward on the lower part of the window and disappeared inside.

Ethan looked down and shrugged. If he fell and failed to grab hold of the narrow catwalk one story down, the stacked cooling units below wouldn't provide much of a soft landing. Following the same sequence he'd seen Patas use, he soon found himself sitting on the floor next to her.

Patas poked him in the stomach and giggled. "Little tight getting through the window?"

"I'm not fat, but I could stand to lose a few pounds. By the way, you're the first Muslim I've come across with a sense of humor."

"That's because nobody's pointing a sniper rifle at my forehead."

"Good point. Where to now?"

Patas headed across the room. The faint glow from the streetlamps seeping through the window provided sufficient light for them to reach an interior door, but after entering a large central hall, they were encased in darkness. Ethan chanced flicking on a small flashlight and handed it to Patas. She pointed the light in several directions before focusing on a u-shaped staircase to the left.

They walked slowly, making almost no noise on the tiled floor. Patas headed down the steps leading to a landing with glass-paned double doors in the center. She pushed open one of the doors and crossed the threshold. She extinguished the flashlight as sufficient outside light filtered through one of the open doorways across from where they stood.

For several long moments, Patas stared down another set of stairs at the far end of the corridor, her body stiff. When Ethan moved in next to her and pressed his hand against her shoulder, she jumped and let out a small cry.

"Sorry, Patas," he whispered. "What's wrong?"

She took a deep breath and said softly, her voice cracking, "Down there... it's the governor's office... that's where he... he...."

Ethan put his arm around her and pulled her close. "Don't worry, if that son of a bitch ever tries to touch you again...." He closed his eyes and imagined himself looking through a rifle scope with Governor Blackwell's head centered in the crosshairs.

Patas sniffed and nodded. She turned back to the opposite wall and took several steps toward two sets of bi-fold door panels. She thought for a moment and pulled the left one open. The look on her face had Ethan half expecting a monster would leap out and gobble them both up.

She shook her head and repeated the same routine with the second set of doors. This time she looked up at the top shelf, all the way to the right side of the closet. She swallowed hard. "It's behind the yellow shoebox. If it's still there." As she reached up for the box, Ethan pulled her back.

"No, Patas. I'll get it."

When Patas turned, she saw Ethan had put on a pair of vinyl gloves and was holding a clear plastic bag. He removed the shoebox from the shelf and handed it to Patas. At first, he didn't see anything in the space behind it. She turned the flashlight back on and Ethan found the linen napkin scrunched into a slight space between the shelf and the wall. He picked up the material near the edge and dropped it into the open bag, running his thumb and forefinger along the top locking tabs to seal it shut.

As he stuffed the evidence bag into an inside pocket of his jacket, he heard Patas reciting a prayer in Arabic.

He looked away trying to elude Patas's anguish. After placing the shoebox in its original location, his eyes stopped on a stacked paper tray on a lower shelf. There was a brochure sitting on top. He picked it up and turned it toward the light, gazing inside at the timetable and hand-written markings in the margins. He shrugged.

Placing it back in the tray and closing the closet doors, he mumbled, "We should go. We got what we needed. You don't have to stay in this house any longer. Whatever it is—"

"If what I think is true, there's no way I'm leaving without it."

"Patas, you never told me what else you were looking for."

She stared at him, and her lips trembled. "If I'm right… probably better evidence then what you've got in your pocket."

"I don't understand."

"Come on, Ethan. Follow me."

Before he could say anything else, she had climbed back up the stairs to the central hall and was halfway to another door on the south side, next to the room from where they had climbed through the window.

Ethan identified this room as the master bedroom. He didn't get much of an opportunity to look around because Patas had already strode across the space, opened a mirrored door, and stepped into an adjoining room. She motioned for him to follow. Once he was inside, she closed the door and shut off the flashlight. When he looked toward the door, he could see the outlines of the furniture from the bedroom in the light reflecting from the outside.

He heard Patas's hand sliding against the wall, when a sudden sharp click sounded. The room was bathed in a dim light coming from a small overhead fixture. He was about to shut off the light switch when he looked around. All the windows were covered with lowered shades and heavy draperies.

Patas said, "No one can see the light from the outside. Or—from the master bedroom."

Ethan stared at the closed door. "A two-way mirror," he said almost to himself as he glanced around the space. At one end of the large closet, he saw a plush love seat. His eyes followed Patas's stare to the large-screen video monitor mounted on the opposite wall.

Although Patas spoke in hushed tones, Ethan was still startled by her words.

She led him to a massive antique armoire with ornately carved double doors reaching to the arched top of the eight-foot-high piece of furniture. Ethan was surprised when Patas pulled open both doors. He expected them to be locked. Several shelves lined the inside of the cabinet. One of the shelves was stacked with electronic equipment. From the other shelf, she pushed aside a pile of sweaters and picked up a black lacquered jewelry box. After retrieving a key from inside, she placed the box on the floor.

Her hand shook as she kneeled down in front of the armoire and pointed to the lower of the two drawers spanning the unit below the doors.

She inserted the key into the lock and hesitated, speaking in a soft voice. "One day… before the governor… *raped me*…."

She paused, swallowing and giving her head a quick nod.

"I overheard him and his wife arguing in his office. She stormed up the stairs and bumped into me as I was carrying a large container across the center hall. I was heading into the sitting room—the room we entered from the fire escape. She barreled into me, knocking the box to the floor. Everything spilled out."

Patas twisted the key and slid open the drawer. "The… the… woman—"

"You mean bitch, I suppose."

She looked up with a knowing grin. "The governor's *wife* never looked back or apologized. Don't think she ever noticed me. She had a small object clutched in her hand. While I crawled around the floor and put the stuff back in the box, I kept an eye on what she was doing. That's how I knew where to find the key. At the time, I could only guess at what the object was in her hand. I saw her unlock this same drawer and stick it inside. I'd heard rumors of the kind of things they were involved with, but couldn't imagine our governor was capable of—"

Patas turned her attention back to the drawer and ran her fingers along the edges of the stored cases inside. "After what happened two weeks ago in the governor's office, I finally realized what's in here. The alarm system isn't functional, but the governor and his wife made sure their toys are in place."

As Ethan listened to Patas tell her story, he grew more nervous by the second. His attention shifted to the sounds coming from outside the mansion. He pulled open a small slit between the drapes and pushed aside an edge of the shade, trying to get a look at the grounds.

He could still hear Kobe's barking; accompanied by shouting, presumably between Corey and the caretaker. If anything, Kobe's barking had escalated, but he didn't know how long they had before the caretaker decided to check out the rest of the grounds. He had to convince Patas to get the hell out. They already got what they were looking for.

When he turned back to convince Patas to hurry up, he realized she had left the room. He glanced into the open drawer and froze at the sight of the rows of DVD cases lining the entire space.

His blood turned to ice—Patas had discovered another monstrous manifestation of the sick and depraved actions of the governor.

After endless hours of wading in the murky depths of his tortured brain, he suddenly saw everything in crystal clear technicolor. And it scared him more than the thought of losing his mind. For an instant his hand hovered over the cases, his eyes speed-reading the information on the labelled spines.

Without thinking, he plucked a DVD from the drawer and stood up straight. He locked the drawer and placed the key back in the jewelry box, returning it to the shelf and covering it with the sweaters.

Staring at the date and the name written on the spine, he felt his body separate from the reality of what he was seeing.

A pungent smell brought him back to the present. He saw Patas kneeling in front of the fireplace in the master bedroom. The gas jets had been turned on, and the flickering flames danced from inside the brick-lined firebox.

He watched the rising flames consume a DVD case. Patas then placed a DVD on the tiny inferno and the room filled with even more vile fumes, as if the devil himself had oozed from the flames.

"What the hell are you doing?"

Patas jumped at Ethan's presence. She rose to her feet and folded her arms. "I know what's on the disc and have no desire to see it again. And I just made a decision. What happened in this house can never be seen by anyone ever again. I don't give a damn about it being important evidence." She pointed to Ethan's pocket which held the soiled napkin in the plastic bag. "What you have there is sick enough." She glanced at the curling remains of the blackened disc and the sparks rushing up the chimney. "No one needs to see this. I couldn't let that happen. This unspeakable act stays here. Only ashes remain."

Ethan's eyes softened as he looked at Patas. The DVD in his own hands grew heavy. He could almost feel it burning the flesh on his fingers. Although the rational side of his mind recognized that whatever the governor did to Kinsley couldn't have occurred in this mansion, the specific location did not matter, only the depraved and sickening act perpetrated on her. His earlier clarity grew stronger, and he knew Patas was right.

How could I ever have doubted you, Kinsley? I'm so sorry for everything I said… and did. Please. Forgive me.

Ethan tossed the case with the DVD inside into the fireplace. He grabbed hold of Patas's hand and said, "Time to go."

They walked across the master bedroom toward the door that led to the sitting room and the window which would take them to the fire escape. Ethan paused in the doorway and turned back to the fireplace. The last remnants of the disc disintegrated, and he imagined the digital images escaping their earthly bonds and freeing Kinsley from any further revelations of what she endured at the hands of the governor.

In his heart, Ethan now understood. Kinsley never had an affair with the governor. And on that last night, she had not taken her own life. The governor had put together the lie to make sure Kinsley could not reveal what had happened. Ethan didn't care about destroying any potential evidence against the man: he had no plans to go to the authorities.

Different reasons had earlier taken him to the Delta King. Now he would again plan to serve justice to the governor. He didn't need the gory details to drive him forward. He was getting used to taking matters into his own hands.

As they climbed across the roof and onto the fire escape, Ethan's mind registered that Kobe's barking had stopped, and except for a hushed conversation taking place near the mansion's side gate on Sixteenth Street, and the occasional sounds of late-night traffic passing by, the night had turned quiet.

In the distance, the door to Ethan's black Ford pick-up slammed shut and the engine sparked to life.

CHAPTER 22

(one year ago)

With white knuckles clinging to the steering wheel, Kinsley Galloway stomped down on the gas pedal and swung the Chevy Blazer onto the county road, heading east.

The day had started out on a bad note—typical of the last several months—and then things got a whole lot worse.

Kinsley had never been more afraid in her life. When she looked into Ethan's eyes before grabbing her purse and keys, she sensed a darkness bubbling up from the depths of his tormented mind. She didn't fear any physical reprisals; Ethan had never shown any tendencies for abusive behavior to either her or Corey. If he had, she would've ended this long ago. No, Ethan's own demons had always been directed inward. It seemed he couldn't break free and speak of what etched away at his soul. Since returning home from his last tour in Afghanistan, he had shut out the life they had together.

Kinsley racked her brain, going over every aspect of their disintegrating marriage. She agonized over what this relationship was doing to Corey. On occasion, he'd disappear for hours at a time, striding without purpose through the open fields and meadows surrounding their house, riding his bike down the county road into town, or spending the evenings holed up in his room; ears plugged, listening to music. Anything to avoid hearing the escalating arguments and accusations as his parents' marriage plunged into the abyss.

It seemed the more time they spent together, the more suspicious Ethan became about her activities whenever they were apart. A portion of the problem stemmed from their professional lives. Kinsley had worked in the public relations department at UC Davis for the last six years. When Ethan came home from Afghanistan, discharged from the Navy, he had taken a position with the university's campus security department. As the newcomer, he worked the graveyard shift. Their schedules rarely overlapped, so they spent little time together on campus, but Ethan managed to create incidents of growing embarrassment for Kinsley. At first his odd behavior was isolated, but when his outbursts accelerated and threatened her own relationship with the university, Kinsley decided to switch jobs.

She got a position at the governor's headquarters in Sacramento. She had little interaction with the governor himself as he spent a good deal of time working from his Malibu estate in southern California. She'd heard talk that the historic governor's mansion in Sacramento was being renovated and Governor Blackwell would one day reside at this location. If so, he would be the first governor since Ronald Reagan to live there.

Kinsley was hired by Governor Blackwell's chief of staff as an assistant to the press secretary. At first, leaving the university and getting this new job had tamed some of Ethan's hostilities. That turned out to be a temporary respite, and soon Ethan started questioning Kinsley's motives for leaving the university. He repeatedly accused her of having affairs and constantly challenged her whereabouts.

Tonight, as she started to do on a more frequent basis, she questioned her own shortcomings in dealing with Ethan's emotional issues. She knew he had periodic appointments at the Sacramento VA Medical Center, but he had refused her requests to join him. The medicine cabinet was filled with a litany of prescription drugs. She'd researched the ones she could identify in the university's library but came away more confused as to how they applied to his symptoms. Several of the prescription bottles were only labelled with a series of numbers and letters. Whenever she asked Ethan what they were for, he either stared at her without answering or told her to stop interfering.

Kinsley got nowhere when she'd attempted to contact the VA hospital directly. They told her that due to patient privacy, without Ethan's consent, they could not divulge any details of his treatment. She'd heard nightmarish stories about veterans being misdiagnosed, ignored, or lost in the inevitable bureaucratic ether of the government-run healthcare programs. At a loss, she didn't know where to turn to for help.

After storming out of the house, Kinsley headed into downtown Davis, but had no real destination in mind. Distraught, she pulled the Blazer into the parking lot near a Whole Foods Market and found an empty spot next to a battered pick-up with a Golden Retriever waddling about in between piles of junk in the truck's bed. She turned off the ignition and leaned her head against the steering wheel.

Not knowing how long she'd sat there, the fading engine ticks were replaced by an irritating series of screeches. Her head turned and she saw the dog in the pick-up truck pawing at a rusted watering can and staring at her. She twisted the ignition key and tapped the button to lower the driver's side window. The dog stopped scratching the can and tilted its head, letting a low whimpering sound escape from its graying snout.

Kinsley took a breath and smiled at the aging pooch. "Hi there, big boy."

This elicited a quick chuffing from the Golden Retriever. And what might've been a smile in return. They both gazed at each other, and a sadness overtook Kinsley; tears streamed down her cheeks. The dog leaned over a bundle of old newspapers and placed its head against extended paws.

An image of Chopper, Ethan's K9 partner, flashed through her head. Kinsley knew Chopper had died in Afghanistan saving Ethan's life. But that was all she knew. Like everything else that transpired overseas, the events surrounding Chopper's death remained a black hole. The more Kinsley tried to get Ethan to open up about his experiences in Afghanistan, the more isolated and distant he became.

Recently, Corey had talked to her about getting a puppy. He'd brought her an article showing how pets could help disabled veterans span the gap between the horrors of war and the difficulty in transitioning back to a normal life at home. Corey could be right. But at this point in their relationship, she didn't dare bring up such a topic.

Frantic about what to do, Kinsley made a desperate decision.

A short time after ending the phone call, she guided the Blazer onto the eastbound freeway toward Sacramento.

CHAPTER 23

The closer Kinsley got to her destination, the more conflicted she became about her decision. She had been surprised when Governor Blackwell took her call. They only had minimal interactions since she began working in his office, so when she explained who she was and what she wanted, she assumed he'd politely respond by telling her he'd ask someone in the Department of Veterans Affairs to look into the problem. And then hang up without giving her a second thought. She'd not been sure he would even recognize her name.

After describing her dilemma, the governor at first stayed silent, but then his voice took on a huskier tone, and he suggested they meet later tonight to come up with a suitable solution.

Kinsley glanced down and checked the address she'd scribbled on the back of an old envelope pulled from the center console. She passed the employees' parking lot for the California State Governor's Office and headed toward the historic district. She drove two more blocks and spotted the number for the governor's private residence—the upper floor of a converted warehouse on the outskirts of Old Town. This was where he stayed on the occasions when it wasn't convenient to fly back to his Malibu estate.

As directed by the governor, Kinsley parked in the space marked *Reserved for Official Use Only*. Before getting out of the Blazer, she stared up at the governor's residence and took a deep breath. Exiting the vehicle gave her a feeling of despair as she walked toward the building. The surrounding neighborhood was quiet. It seemed all but deserted to Kinsley, the sounds of the freeway barely penetrating her senses as she reached the outer gate securing the grounds.

She pressed the intercom button and responded to the disembodied voice. The harsh buzzer made her jump, and she almost missed the opportunity to push open the gate. She again flinched at the loud clanging as it snapped shut behind her. Her head twitched in all directions while her body spun about, startled by the suffocating feeling of the short, narrow path lined with dense shrubs leading to the front door. In another second, she would've turned and grabbed the bars on the security gate and screamed, but an overhead light came on and she heard the latch on the front door click open.

Kinsley's eyes widened and her jaw dropped.

"Ms. Galloway?"

Kinsley dumbly nodded her head. It took only an instant to realize that Anita Blackwell, the governor's wife, had answered the door. It should've put her mind at ease. She had felt awkward—and a little anxious —at the thought of meeting with the governor alone—not in his office, but in his home. His wife's presence should have alleviated the tension. But the way Anita Blackwell was standing in the open doorway with those glowering eyes riveted on her had the opposite effect.

Kinsley attempted a smile and fumbled for the right words. "It's good to meet you, Mrs…. ahh… first lady… ahh…."

Anita Blackwell smirked and reached out a hand, patting Kinsley's arm. "Call me Anita. We're all friends here, right?" She stood aside to let Kinsley inside the small entry cubicle and picked up a cocktail glass from the side table near the door. After taking a sip, she motioned toward the stairs to the main floor of the governor's condo.

Kinsley obeyed and headed up the narrow staircase. As she walked, she sensed Anita's glare, like a hot iron on her back.

When Kinsley neared the top, Anita said, "We do have an elevator, but you're young… and in decent shape. In fact, I'll join you. I could use a little exercise to get the juices flowing again."

Looking back, Kinsley watched the governor's wife take a larger sip from her cocktail and climb the stairs. As far as she could tell, the woman appeared steady and took each step without faltering. Surprising, since when she'd strode past her across the foyer, she'd detected a strong whiff of alcohol on her breath.

While Kinsley waited for the governor's wife to catch up, she glanced around. She was in a large central hallway with three wide corridors branching out from the space.

Holding the empty glass in one hand, Anita pointed with the other hand down the corridor to the left. "It's the last door on the right. The governor is waiting for you. I know you two have some serious business to discuss. I was about to get ready for bed." She waved a finger at Kinsley. "But don't you dare leave without giving me a chance to say good night. Please tell my husband to buzz me when you're done. We can have a quick nightcap together. Nick makes one mean martini. And don't you two start without me."

She watched Anita head down the back hallway. Kinsley sighed and couldn't get a grip on her brief encounter with the state's first lady. With even more trepidation than when she'd first exited the Blazer, she placed a foot forward and strode toward the governor's office.

Standing at the closed door, Kinsley listened. Music flowed from inside. Not loud, almost indiscernible through the heavy oak door. She raised her hand to knock and noticed a slight shaking of her fingers. She quickly made a fist and rapped twice. The music stopped and a voice responded, "Come in, please."

As she opened the door, the governor rose from behind a glass-topped desk and smiled. He motioned Kinsley to a sitting area at the far side of the office and slipped behind her to close the door.

"It's so good to see you again, Kinsley. You don't mind me calling you Kinsley, do you?"

Kinsley shook her head. "No sir, that's fine."

"I just got off the phone with a good friend at the Sacramento VA Medical Center, where your husband is being treated. And I'm pleased to say, I have good news for you."

Encouraged, Kinsley looked back at the governor. "Oh? Can I speak to the doctors?"

Governor Blackwell smiled. "Please, Kinsley, have a seat."

"Thank you, governor." Kinsley twisted around and saw a couch with two armchairs on either side, and a small coffee table in the center. She chose one of the armchairs and sat down, tugging her skirt to her knees.

"I think you should call me Nick. I prefer my friends use Nick, not Nicholas." She sensed the heat from his eyes as he stared at her legs. She gave an almost imperceptible nod. Keeping one hand against the skirt's hem, she placed the other hand to her neck, unconsciously covering her breasts with her arm.

"Relax, Kinsley. I'll get you a martini while I explain the good news to you."

"Ahh… thank you, but I really shouldn't drink, I have a long drive home and—"

"Nonsense, Kinsley. I insist. After all, we have a lot to celebrate. And I do think it's time we get to know each other better."

He was already walking toward her with a glass in his hand as she tried to protest.

She declined the proffered drink several more times.

In a harsher tone, the governor said, "Drink this, Kinsley." He held the glass close to her lips, stretched the other hand behind her neck, and edged her head forward. She tried to stand, but his hand clamped down around her shoulders.

"I think I better leave."

The governor squeezed his hand tighter and shoved the glass against her lips. The liquid slushed from the glass and slid down her chin. Swallowing a small amount of the stringent-tasting substance, she spit out the residual liquid and lashed out with her left arm, sending the glass crashing on the marble surface of the coffee table. As the drink slid down her throat, it made her cough and gag. Afraid and confused, she thought: *that was no martini.* She detected a bitter, medicinal taste in her mouth.

Kinsley thrashed out at the governor with both hands and tried to get up; but he pushed her roughly back into the chair.

"Your wife is right down the hall. If I scream, she'll be here in a second—so get your hands off me and let me go!" Her face heated up and a scraping dryness clung to her throat.

The governor's response surprised her. He began laughing and his hands gripped tighter, pinning her against the back of the chair. Figuring she had nothing to lose, she let out a loud scream. She jammed a knee into his groin, causing him to loosen his grip enough for her to twist out of his grasp. She sprinted to the office door and yanked it open.

Right into the barrel of a large revolver in the two-handed grip of Anita Blackwell.

Kinsley gasped, but instead of retreating, swiped at the gun.

An earsplitting sound filled the office.

Kinsley swore the heat of the bullet seared her left earlobe before an explosion of shattered glass answered the weapon's report. The crystal decanter on the governor's bar fragmented and the precious liquor rained down the side of the antique cabinet.

Before Kinsley could push Anita aside, she was grabbed from behind by the enraged governor. He yanked her back into the office. His wife marched forward, dropping the gun to her side and launching an open hand at Kinsley's cheek. The blow stung, taking away most of her fight. In a semi-conscious state, she felt the governor's hands clawing at her blouse. The fabric tore open.

Following an animalistic grunt, he growled, "We could have done this the easy way, you little bitch. But one way or the other—it's going to happen."

Kinsley cringed at a sharp prick in her arm and the burning sensation as the governor pushed the plunger on the syringe.

In the split second before the governor made his next move, Kinsley's eyes darted around the office. They widened at the sight of Anita Blackwell settling into one of the armchairs and letting her robe fall open. She wore nothing underneath, and the last thing registering in Kinsley's head was the rising flush on Anita's neck and breasts as her hand plunged between her legs.

She never comprehended the governor's actions as her shredded blouse fell to the floor and the skirt was ripped from her body. Her mind faded into a drug-induced stupor, and she tried to think only of Ethan and Corey.

Chapter 24

(present day)

After scrambling down the fire escape, Ethan and Patas took the porch steps two at a time. As they hurried across the grounds of the governor's mansion toward the carriage house, Ethan heard the roar of an engine starting and tires squealing. Ethan helped Patas up the wooden fence in the alley and pulled himself over in time to see his black Ford pick-up truck screeching to a stop. They both jumped in the back seat and Corey floored it.

When they reached the end of the alley, Corey barely braked, cutting the wheel hard and fishtailing the truck onto Fifteenth. Ignoring any red lights or cross-traffic, he made a beeline for the closest onramp to the freeway. After merging into the light late evening traffic, Corey settled down and drove west, keeping close to the speed limit and maintaining a watchful eye in the rearview mirror.

* * * * * *

Prior to Corey's dramatic getaway drive—while he was still rescuing Kobe from the fence post and arguing with the caretaker—Olivia Davenport flipped on the light switch and tossed the binoculars on the bed. She thrashed around the tiny apartment looking for her clothes while Mike Finley again tried to call Steve Casella on his cell phone.

"I'm gonna get down to the street and find out what the hell's going on with that boy and the dog by the gate to the governor's mansion. You see what Casella has to say—then join me."

Finley waved the phone at her. "It's a damn cell phone, and I can multi-task. So I'm coming with you."

Olivia shrugged and smiled. "At least retirement hasn't caused you to lose your smart-ass attitude."

They both finished getting dressed, and without any further discussion headed down to the governor's mansion. As they got closer to the Sixteenth Street entrance, they watched the caretaker checking the lock on the wrought-iron gate and muttering to himself. Neither the boy nor the dog was in sight.

"Excuse me, sir," Olivia said, approaching the man.

Startled, the caretaker looked up. He stared at Olivia and Finley. Finley noted his eyes lingering longer on Olivia.

"Good evening, miss." He tipped his cap and smiled, revealing tobacco-stained teeth.

"You're the caretaker at the governor's house, aren't you?" Olivia asked.

"Yes, ma'am."

"You all alone?"

He nodded. "For tonight I am. The wife and I both work here, but this evening she's in San Francisco visiting our daughter. Things are going to be slow around here till after the election. Millie supposed it'd be a good time for a short vacation. She's been wanting to visit the grandkid again. Four years old and growing like a weed."

"A bit earlier," she said glancing at Finley who had backed away, talking in hushed tones on his cell phone, "we heard a commotion. Is everything okay?"

The caretaker shook his head. "Sorry the noise bothered you, but it was nothing."

Olivia's head spun around to the sound of a fast-moving black pick-up truck careening across the intersection a block to the south. Finley looked up in time to see it disappear down the alley. Seconds later he heard brakes squeal, a door slam, and once again, the sound of tires ripping into the old asphalt caught his attention.

The noise faded, and he refocused on his phone conversation.

Olivia reached in a pocket and pulled out her credentials, holding them up for the old man to see. He glanced back and forth between the photo ID and Olivia. "I thought you looked familiar, agent. My name's Stanley. Been working at this old house since way before they started fixin' things up." He pointed toward the old carriage house. "Pretty soon now, Millie and I will be moving into that there building. Soon as the construction work gets done. Won't say we'll be missing the old modular dump we're staying in now."

Olivia placed the ID back in her pocket.

Stanley snapped his fingers and pointed a crooked index finger at Olivia. "Didn't you start working on the governor's detail earlier this week?"

She smiled. "You've got a good eye, sir. Bet you got some interesting stories to tell. Especially with the governor now living in the house."

Stanley placed both hands on the gate and leaned forward, giving Olivia a knowing smile.

"But for now, sir, what can you tell me about tonight's little incident? When I looked down from my apartment window, I saw what looked like a heated discussion with a young man—and a rather disturbed dog barking and lunging at you. That's why Agent Finley and I thought we'd stop by and ask you a few questions."

Finley looked up at the sound of his name. Stanley now had his eyes on Finley, wheels spinning, undoubtedly trying to guess exactly what he was doing in Olivia's place so late in the evening. It looked to Finley like Stanley gave him a slight turn of the head and a quick wink. Finley cast an eye to Olivia. In their rush to get down here she never bothered to straighten out her hair. Finley had no such problem, as his head was cleanly shaved.

Stanley looked back at Olivia and shrugged. "Not much to tell. I was sitting inside reading this new Dean Koontz novel. Scarier than hell. Seems this demon-like dog had—well, so when this damn barking started, I almost pissed my pants." He paused, lips turning up. "Pardon my... anyway, I flipped on the floodlight and headed outside to see what the racket's all about."

He tapped a hand on one of the wrought-iron pickets on the gate. "So I come running out and whaddaya know? This big, mean dog got his leash stuck onto this here picket and he's jumping and barking, like he was after the devil himself. And then I see this kid sprawled out next to that tree over there, and he's hollering and carrying on about his damn dog. Guess I got a little spooked with this crazy dog. Could be the Koontz book got the better of me. But the kid's dog sure did look like he wanted to rip out my throat."

"Did the boy say how the dog got inside the gate?" Olivia asked.

Stanley scratched his head and looked a little puzzled. "By the time we all calmed down... I never thought to ask the kid. I was just glad not to get bitten when I unlocked the gate so he could grab the dog and be on his way."

Olivia gave him a long, hard look. "Seems to me, you guys were going at it for quite a while."

"Well... several times I told him to beat it and tried to get back inside, but the kid kept asking me questions."

"What kind of questions?"

"I dunno." Stanley's face scrunched up. "Like he was wondering if anyone was in the mansion tonight. If I was all alone. Did I usually check out the house or only the grounds. Stuff like that."

"And you didn't find that a little unusual?"

"Jesus," Stanley stammered. "Hell... he was just a kid. Didn't think nothing—suspicious about what he asked. Thought he was a little nosy, that's all."

"Anything about the dog... look familiar?"

Stanley tilted his head. "The dog? Familiar? Hell, it was just a big, black dog. See them all the time." His eyes widened and he paused, holding up a finger. "But now that you mention it, I remember seeing a black dog, about the same size... pretty sure it was a German Shepherd too. One of the government agents had it with him almost every time he showed up to work. Why are you asking about the damn dog, anyways?"

Finley stuck the phone in his pocket and turned his head up looking toward the roof of the governor's mansion. He wrinkled his nose. "You guys smell that?"

Stanley shook his head. Olivia glanced around and nodded. "It's faint, but it kinda reminds me of melting plastic."

"Could it be coming from inside the mansion?" Finley asked Stanley.

"Don't see how it could. The place is empty. It's just me on the grounds tonight."

"Stanley?" Olivia said. "Why don't you get the keys, and we'll take a quick look inside."

Stanley squirmed and hesitated. "I'm not supposed to snoop around inside when they got it all sealed up like this. I could get in a whole lot of trouble if—"

Olivia gave him a sharp look. "Stanley? I'm going to pretend that you and Millie have never, ever taken a looksee inside on other occasions when it's been *'sealed up'* like you said."

Using her left hand, she patted the pocket with her credentials inside and pulled back her jacket to reveal the outline of a shoulder holster.

After opening the gate, Stanley turned and walked away. "I'll go get those keys for you, Agent Davenport. Meet me by the front door."

Finley recalled the image of the black Ford pick-up truck screaming down the alley. As Stanley disappeared inside his temporary quarters, Finley caught up to Olivia and said, "I doubt anyone's still lurking around inside."

She nodded. "But let's see if we can find out what the hell they were up to."

CHAPTER 25

Following a hasty but thorough examination of the governor's mansion and making sure the caretaker wouldn't be reporting this little incident to anyone else, Olivia and Finley returned to her apartment.

Finley brought Olivia up to date regarding his phone conversations. She needed to catch up with the rest of the governor's security detail at their next stop in Seattle. Finley opted to tag along and stay in the background until they got more answers. As they drove Finley's rental car to the airport, Olivia grilled him again about the new information he'd uncovered on the suspected sniper aboard the Delta King riverboat.

They bypassed the main entrance to Sacramento Airport and headed to the general aviation area where they boarded an agency jet for the short flight to Seattle.

"Okay," Olivia said. "Let's go over this one more time." She leaned a tired head against his shoulder as they settled back in the plush leather seats.

Finley sighed. "I'll kick things up a notch in the morning and see if the president can rattle heads at the Pentagon. So far, I've been getting the runaround. My sources are waving the national security card and claiming that for all intents and purposes the fingerprints you found on the Delta King belong to an unnamed Navy SEAL—who doesn't exist."

Olivia turned to Finley. "You think the president can get those files released? I don't give a damn what kind of shenanigans he might've been involved with in a former military life. My interest lies in the connection this guy may have to Governor Nicholas Blackwell."

"The Pentagon officials tell me I can threaten all I want. But even the president's hands may be tied on this one." Finley stroked Olivia's neck. "I'd love to be there when they tell President Tyler Griffin that the identity of your so-called sniper is on a need-to-know basis, and he does not have a need to know."

"That's why, Mike, you should never have retired in the first place."

He grunted. "But in the meantime, based on what Steve Casella said before getting on his flight, Catori Torrence can tell us a lot more about Kobe's new owner. And the way he sounded, brought back memories of my previous encounters with his young Native American friend. Can't wait to show Catori a photo of the rifle stock you found on the riverboat."

"Here we go again. Like you always say: if you want to trust in coincidences, you might as well believe in the tooth fairy." After a slight pause, she added, "But I'm ready for one over the top—mind boggling—conspiracy theory. It's been way too long."

"So far you got a jihadist, a custom rifle, and the fingerprints of an ex-military sniper who's probably in possession of Anson Kostelecky's dog."

"Don't you think that kid with the dog is a little young to be a Navy SEAL?"

Finley shot her a look, and she added, "Can't Steve give you any more info about this guy?"

"He implied that Catori could be much more helpful. Besides, Steve and Edie were just about to board a flight to D.C. to join up with the president for his final rally appearances. He cautioned me about distracting the president, since this is the last week of the campaign—and it looks like a very tight race."

"I've seen the latest polls, and I don't get it. Blackwell has shown strong gains. What the hell is wrong with people?"

"Not everyone is in a position to be privy to the facts. Speaking of which, there's way more going on here."

"No kidding, Mike. Time's running out, and if we screw this up, the American voters may get a narcissistic maniac as their next president."

Olivia cursed under her breath and buried those thoughts. "What kind of information can you expect from Catori?"

"Steve said she took all the potential buyers' paperwork for this next litter with her back to Idaho to review. Including your guy's application form."

"But if he already brought Kobe home, why take his application along with all the others?"

Finley shrugged. "Maybe he still wants a puppy too. Who the hell knows. But if I know Catori, she'll have a lot more insight than whatever's written on any piece of paper. Unfortunately, we'll have to wait till she returns from her retreat on the reservation. According to Steve, Catori and her brother run a youth outing twice a year. They take a bunch of Native American kids from the Kootenecti Reservation on a wilderness experience. Supposed to help them learn about their tribe's cultural origins. And Catori doesn't allow any contact with the outside world—so no cell phones or internet."

Olivia shivered and snuggled closer. "From the stories you've told me about this young woman, she doesn't need a cell phone or the internet to communicate with the outside world."

"Exactly why we need to speak to her," Finley said, and then hesitated before asking, "and if it turns out the guy they gave Anson's dog to *is* the sniper on the riverboat? What's our next move?"

"*Our* move? Sounds like we're a team again. Too bad about your retirement plans."

"Yeah, but you still didn't answer my question."

Olivia sighed and buried her head on Finley's chest. She yawned. "All of a sudden, I'm feeling tired. It's a short flight. I think I'll catch a quick nap."

Chapter 26

Olivia and Finley landed at Sea-Tac International Airport and took a cab to a hotel in Seattle. Two floors of the Westin Seattle had been reserved for Governor Blackwell, his staff, and the security personnel. Finley checked them into a room one floor below the governor's entourage. Olivia hopped in the shower and then caught several hours sleep before reporting in to the agent-in-charge. She told Finley she'd be tied up all day helping to finalize security operations for the governor's appearance at the Seattle Aquarium.

After Olivia left, Finley fidgeted in the room for about twenty minutes before deciding he needed to make something happen. He grabbed a cab back to Sea-Tac.

En route, he placed a few key phone calls. By the time the cab dropped him off, an agency jet had been fueled and readied for takeoff. He was beginning to see how much he missed these perks during his short stint with retirement.

In less than ninety minutes, Finley sprinted down the Gulfstream's steps and hustled over to a waiting helicopter at a small airport several miles north of Coeur d'Alene, Idaho. The closest available helicopter had been a US Border Patrol Bell UH-1 with a bright white fuselage and *CBP* printed in bold letters on both sides. Following instructions, the chopper's pilot had already contacted the tribal police headquarters on the Kootenecti Reservation and got the coordinates for the youth outing at a remote site on the reservation. Catori Torrence's brother, Paco, was a detective on the tribal police force and in charge of the event.

During the short flight to the designated wilderness area in the heart of the reservation, Mike Finley remained mute on the breadth and purpose of the mission. The pilot prodded and pleaded to no avail. He tried to flatter Finley, repeating the overtold stories passed around by agents at the Kingsgate border crossing facility regarding Finley's legendary role in rescuing First Lady Alison Griffin in a daring siege on the Canadian side of the border. The pilot had only recently been assigned to the Kingsgate post, but it was a hot topic among the old-timers since his arrival. He even had the opportunity to hear a firsthand account by the sole Canadian involved in the raid. The pilot had ignored about half of the embellished yarns of the young Canadian Mountie but still considered the mission to be over the top.

Finley avoided any meaningful conversation and stuck to small talk about the Seattle Seahawks and the passing scenery in the Idaho panhandle. Calm and collected on the outside, as the Huey skimmed over Lake Coeur d'Alene and the rugged landscape of the Kootenecti Reservation, he recalled his first of many encounters with the enigmatic Catori Torrence. He imagined—no not imagined—he was positive: if not for this young Native American woman, potentially thousands of citizens, himself and the first lady included, would have died at the hands of several different terrorist plots.

"So, is this what it's like being retired? Must be nice getting chauffeured around by an underpaid federal employee. I had nothing important going on today anyway. Who's interested in a Canadian slipping through the net to shop at Walmart?"

Hearing the words through his headset, Finley glanced at the pilot and smiled; not taking the bait.

The pilot smiled back and raised his eyebrows. "Well, sir. I hate to cut this chat short, but our landing spot is coming up."

As soon as those words left the pilot's lips, the helicopter banked hard to port and began a gut-raising freefall. After suffering two additional sharp directional changes and several aircraft attitude corrections, Finley watched a dense grove of trees magnify in the cockpit's window, seconds before the pilot slid the craft onto an almost invisible clearing near a shallow streambed.

As the blades spun down and the dust settled, both men took off their headsets. Finley took a breath and extended a hand toward the pilot. "I didn't catch your name... but thanks for taking it easy on the landing. Usually the pilot is wearing my last meal by this point."

The pilot stared at Finley's hand and gave it a quick shake. "The name's McCarthy."

Finley nodded and said, "Look, son. You don't wanna know anything about this trip. When you get back, there will be no log—nothing. Consider this a personal favor for the president. I'll make sure he gets your name."

"Yeah, right. You're worried I'll hightail it outta here once your foot hits the ground."

Finley exited the helicopter and had gotten about twenty feet when a man appeared out of a dense stand of Ponderosa Pines. He looked to be over six feet tall and wore a heavy red plaid flannel jacket that did little to hide the holstered handgun strapped to his belt. His dark, rugged face exuded confidence. He strode directly toward Finley. A large splitting maul rested on his shoulder, the sunlight gleaming off the honed edge of the blade.

Finley glanced back at the pilot.

McCarthy waved and said, "Good advice. I'm not really here. I know nothing about this little excursion." He reached into a tattered leather bag and pulled a hunting magazine to his face.

CHAPTER 27

When Finley turned away from the helicopter, he stood face-to-face with the imposing shape who'd materialized from the forest. The man stared back and forth between Finley and the helicopter, obviously reading the border patrol insignia on the fuselage. He kicked the dirt and placed the splitting maul on the ground, leaning against the handle. "Jesus H. Christ. Don't you think you guys are a little far from the border? I'd say you're way off the reservation—but here you are—right in the middle of *my* reservation."

His eyes riveted into Finley, who stood his ground and matched the man's bravado.

"Not only is this the sovereign home of my people, but it's also my jurisdiction."

The man tweaked back the front edge of his jacket, giving Finley a better view of his holstered service revolver and the opportunity to see the badge fastened to his belt. He shrugged. "Unless the feds have changed the rules again, I'd argue that this is my land, and you all are the illegal aliens. The way I see it, if anyone's trespassing, it's certainly not me."

Finley raised a hand and spoke, "Why don't you calm down, sir. We're not here to cause you folks any trouble, but—"

A sudden string of barks shot from beyond the tree line and cut off Finley's words. When he looked over the man's shoulder, he saw a large white dog charging toward him.

The man stepped aside and mumbled, "This is going to be interesting."

Finley's eyes opened wide. He knelt down as the dog stopped inches from him and rolled over on its back. "Well, I'll be… Amber. How ya doin' girl?" He scratched the dog's belly while keeping an eye on the imposing stranger with a badge and a gun. Finley hadn't seen Steve Casella's white German Shepherd since she helped locate the kidnapped first lady in the investigation leading them across the Canadian border.

"Hello, Mike."

Finley's head twisted in response to the voice of Catori Torrence. He gave Amber a final pat and stood up to greet her.

She closed the distance and embraced Finley, planting an affectionate peck on the cheek. After releasing him, she turned to her brother. "Paco. What are you trying to do?"

Paco Torrence stared at his sister and pointed to Finley. "You know this guy?"

Catori let out a breath. "Of course. This is Agent Mike Finley. Jeeze, Paco. I've got pictures of him, along with Steve, Edie, and Amber plastered all over my living room wall."

She punched his arm playfully. "And you call yourself a detective? Don't tell me you don't remember the photo where I'm standing next to Mike in the Oval Office with President Griffin?"

Paco shrugged and wiped a hand on his trousers. He extended it toward Finley. "Nice to meet you, Agent Finley." He smiled. "Didn't mean anything personal by my previous attempt at hospitality. Never did trust it when the feds show their faces. Especially when one of those fancy white birds stirs up the neighborhood." He pointed to the helicopter, but McCarthy kept his head buried in the magazine.

Finley nodded. "No offense taken. There's a lot of that sentiment going around." About to continue, he paused and crooked his head toward Catori. "I may be mistaken, but you don't look surprised to see me."

She shrugged. "Must've recognized the helicopter. Looks like the same one that took us to Canada."

Finley smiled but remained silent.

"Come. We'll talk at the camp. I'm guessing you don't have a whole lot of time."

Finley looked back at the helicopter. McCarthy waved him off. "Don't worry, I'll wait for you to get back."

Finley followed Catori and Paco.

Catori said to Paco, "Send one of the kids with some hot soup for the pilot. There's a chill in the air. Winter will be here before you know it." She glanced at the light jacket Finley was wearing. "You look a little cold yourself."

He shivered. "It's been a while since I've experienced this damn weather. I can't figure out how you survive the winters."

"We go to teepee and smoke peace pipe around big fire. Eat buffalo meat," Paco said in a mocking tone.

"That works for me, as long as I'm not on the menu."

"Alright, children," Catori interrupted. "When we get back to the camp, make sure you behave yourselves. Remember, Paco, this camp is supposed to demonstrate to the younger kids the importance of our rich cultural history and how to interact in a modern world."

"That's exactly what we're doing." He put an arm around Finley's shoulder.

"Why in the hell didn't I stay retired?" Finley said, shaking his head. "Nothing but fishing... drinking... and—"

"And how are things with Agent Davenport these days, Mike?" Catori chided.

"Why don't you tell me? You seem to have all the answers."

Catori whispered, "That could be a little embarrassing."

Finley chose not to reply.

Arriving at the camp, Catori led Finley into a cozy cabin—not a teepee. A welcoming fire in the stone fireplace warmed him up as he eased into a chair near the slate hearth. Amber plopped down on the floor next to him. He pointed at the dog and gave Catori a questioning look.

"I asked Steve if I could borrow Amber. We like to add a little mystery to some of our more colorful legends." Her voice took on a mystical tone and she looked at Amber. "This creature—Coyott—she is the ghost of the ancient god of light."

Finley waved a hand at Catori. "Hey, young lady. If I've learned one thing in my entire career, it's if anything at all makes sense, it's the reality of your visions. Speaking of which… why don't you fill me in on Kobe, or more specifically, Kobe's new owner."

CHAPTER 28

Catori finished ladling out the hot potage. She picked up the two steaming bowls, each with a simply carved wooden spoon protruding over the turned edges and handed one to Finley. His stomach growled and he licked his lips. The rich, brothy aroma had bombarded his senses from the moment he'd entered the cabin.

Catori sat cross-legged on the floor in front of him; her back to the fire. Amber's head reared up, scanning the air with her snout, and homed in on the potential prize.

"Sorry, girl, you already scoffed down a sample of this at breakfast. Too early for your dinner."

The dog whined in response to Catori's words but settled her head between her front paws. The tip of her snout still twitched. In a matter of seconds, soft, soothing snores added a pleasant framework to the cozy scene.

"This is delicious, Catori. I'd ask for the recipe, but I'm not sure I want to know which species you sacrificed for this concoction."

"Wild turkey," Catori said, laughing. The mention of possible prey in the vicinity elicited a quick ear pricking and head turn from Amber.

Holding the bowl in one hand, Finley reached inside a pocket and pulled out a folded paper. Catori placed her bowl on the hearth and took it from him. She unfolded it and glanced at the photo: a close-up shot of an image carved into the gunstock of the sniper rifle found in the stateroom on the Delta King.

Finley watched Catori. Her face remained neutral as she stared at the photo. When she looked up, she nodded.

"I've been following the recent headlines about the events that took place in Sacramento."

"Do you think it's possible that the man who left this rifle on the riverboat is the same man who has Kobe?" Not waiting for an answer, he added, "We need a name, Catori. The Pentagon has been giving me the runaround. Steve suggested I talk to you. He said you might have the details of this guy and his family." Finley paused and added, "Although my gut tells me Steve knows more than he's letting on."

She shrugged. "Very little escapes his scrutiny. But, for the record, Mike, what makes you think we gave Kobe to the man you're looking for?"

"Olivia thinks she recognized Kobe causing a scene outside the governor's mansion last night. And when I spoke to Steve... well, that's why I'm here."

Nodding again, she handed back the photo. "I may be familiar with this."

Finley's eyes widened. "You've seen this rifle?"

"No, not the rifle, but I've seen a similar image—like this one—a dog profiled with the Navy SEAL emblem." She pointed to the picture. "It's beautiful."

Finley wanted to prod her further, but he held his tongue.

"Let me ask you a question, Mike." She proceeded without giving Finley a chance to respond. "With all the resources at your command, does it surprise you that you've failed to identify your subject?"

"To be honest, the lack of cooperation from bureaucrats in the federal government is par for the course. I've been dealing with these morons my entire career. But…."

"They want you to believe this man does not exist," Catori said quietly.

Finley pursed his lips. "It's only a matter of time before the president can make something happen. But with the election so close, it's important to sort through this whole mess before the country votes."

"Ethan Galloway," she said without preamble. "His son's name is Corey. When they came to the kennel, there was a young girl with them. They called her Patty. But that wasn't her real name. I presume you can surmise her true identity."

Finley's face scrunched up. "The intern who tried to kill the governor the same night they found this sniper rifle on the Delta King?" He shook his head when Catori shrugged. "This is way more complicated than I thought."

"No, it's not, Mike." Catori sighed and covered her face. "If you and Olivia Davenport are on the case, you'll chronicle those details by good old detective work. Like most of this seemingly confusing situation."

Pointing a finger at Catori, Finley asked, "Why Galloway? What made you contact him after Anson Kostelecky was killed and Steve got Kobe back?"

"Perhaps this is all a big coincidence."

"Right. And Amber is an underachieving big white German Shepherd."

"Shhhh… do not awaken the ghost of the ancient god of light."

Amber rolled over on her back and moaned.

"Let's not argue semantics," Catori said while reaching down and scratching Amber's belly. "There are many terms you can apply. Coincidence… fate… visions… legends. They are all one and the same."

"Leaving us… where?"

"My involvement started with Galloway's application to purchase a puppy from a future breeding at Mayacamas Shepherds. We received the completed paperwork about two months ago."

"Wait. So this couldn't have had anything to do with Kobe, because Anson Kostelecky was still alive two months ago."

"Right. On the surface, it all seems innocent. And typical for how we screen potential buyers. We look at past experiences with other pets. What breed of dog they might've owned. What are the current family circumstances. What are their expectations in dealing with a new puppy."

"So Ethan Galloway wasn't looking to buy a trained K9?"

"On the contrary. I had to persuade him that Kobe was the right fit for him and his son."

"And your reason for doing this was…?"

"First, let's back up a step. From the way the original application had been filled out, it was clear that Corey, Ethan's son, had done all the work. Ethan just signed on the bottom line and wrote out the deposit check. The idea of bringing home a puppy appeared to be Corey's idea."

Catori paused to collect the empty soup bowls and held one up to Finley.

He waved her off. "No, I'm good. Thanks. But one thing. I'm still confused as to why you singled this guy out for Kobe. There must've been plenty of other people who were on this waiting list."

After setting the bowls in the sink, she returned and sat in a chair, facing Finley. "I'm getting to that."

CHAPTER 29

Finley checked his watch and looked at Catori. "Please do. I'd hate for my pilot to get antsy and takeoff without me."

She smiled and placed a hand against her temple. "My senses tell me you needn't worry about that. It's safe to say he's comfy for the moment."

She paused and closed her eyes. A brief image of a tattoo, peeking from the bottom of a sleeve, flashed through her head. She'd first seen it on Ethan Galloway's forearm at the Mayacamas Shepherds training center. And now Mike Finley had handed her a photo of the same image carved into a gunstock.

Catori shrugged. "At first, when Steve returned with Kobe after Anson Kostelecky died, it was as simple as my recollection of a particular story Corey provided on their application. He wrote about a dreadful incident that took place in Afghanistan. He explained that his dad, a Navy

SEAL sniper, was also a K9 handler. Apparently, his dog died during a top-secret mission, but Corey didn't know the details. So you see, Mike, this began as an ordinary coincidence. From all appearances, giving Kobe to Ethan Galloway made perfect sense. None of our other current clients have that kind of training experience."

Finley folded his arms and sat back, remaining silent.

"But when they showed up at the kennel, and I came face-to-face with Ethan Galloway, I got a strong sense of a darker, troubled side of this man."

"And you still thought it wise to give Kobe to him?"

She stared at Finley and tightened her lips. "I had no choice. And neither did Ethan. Kobe is somehow part of this story."

"So here's where you tell me exactly what's going on and save this old body a lot of legwork, right?"

With a wan smile, Catori said, "I'm afraid it's not that easy. What I experienced when Ethan Galloway reacted to Amber at the kennel was only what the man allowed himself to feel. Behind what he accepts as truth are dark shadows. Something's preventing him from seeing the reality of his past."

She reached out and touched Finley's hand. "Ethan's mind is broken. There are external forces cloaking terrible memories. Those influences are powerful, but Ethan's own trepidations are also working to block his past. For him to become whole again, he must make the unconscious decision to open up his mind and let all the memories—good and bad—flow back and restore his sanity. It's all woven together. Right now he's frightened to open his eyes to see the truth. He's like a blind man trapped in his own house, bumping into the amorphous familiarity of those memories."

Catori's hand pulled back, and her eyes squeezed shut. "A good part of this has to do with the military. The things he did as a SEAL. Whatever happened when he came home has been fed by the traumas of his past."

Finley spread out his palms. "So, you're saying Ethan Galloway suffers from PTSD as a result of his experience in the Middle East?"

"Yes—and no. It's deeper, more deadly." Her eyes popped open, and the tenor of her voice switched gears. "Did you know my brother was in the Army? Well, he's told me many stories about his buddies coming home and the problems they've had getting medical care. Paco sometimes exaggerates, but his complaints regarding the treatment of our veterans at many of the VA centers are valid and well-documented. The neglect and the incompetence perpetrated on our wounded warriors are horrifying. It's way too convenient for the system to ignore the roots of their problems. We've all seen this, Mike. Our boys are sent into the most vile, inhuman conditions imaginable and return home as shattered men who are given mind-numbing drugs by a system bent on sweeping the real problems under the rug."

She paused and swallowed hard. "But in the case of Ethan Galloway, I sense a much more sinister force at work."

Catori's eyes darted into Finley. "Tell me, Mike, why are his records sealed? Who doesn't want you to understand Ethan Galloway's past?"

When Finley returned to the helicopter, McCarthy was sound asleep inside. An empty bowl of soup and a portable propane space heater sat in the cockpit. Catori grabbed the items and gave Finley a huge hug. "Just let me know if I can help in any way." She paused and tapped the side of her head. "If anything new turns up, I'll give you a call."

"Make it easy on the both of us and use your cell phone."

She patted his cheek and strode back a safe distance as McCarthy fired up the Huey. She didn't move until the helicopter faded to a tiny speck and disappeared from sight.

The ground-shaking signature *thump-thump-thump* pounding from the powerful Lycoming engine was gradually surpassed by the internal beating of her heart, prophesying the impending storm about to break on the horizon.

CHAPTER 30

Ethan had been deliberately vague when he announced plans to drive to Seattle. He understood that based on recent admissions regarding his intent several nights ago in Old Town Sacramento, Corey could only be imagining the worst about his father. If he knew the rest of the story, Ethan assumed Corey would call in the authorities himself to stop his father from acting out his rage.

Those thoughts played a role in Ethan's decision to bring Corey and Patas along. Since escaping from last night's adventure at the governor's mansion, he wrestled with the truth about the real intentions of this trip. He told himself he only wanted to further his investigations into the depravity of the governor's behavior—maybe get a chance to go eye to eye with him.

If that happens—there's only one way it could end.

In the final analysis, Ethan struggled to come to grips with the intensity of his hatred toward Blackwell. At last he recognized his own faults in blaming Kinsley for consorting with this devil. Perhaps he was even more culpable than Governor Blackwell.

Why had it taken so long to see the truth?

The visceral reality of the discoveries at the governor's mansion confirmed Kinsley's innocence, a far different conclusion he'd imagined while waiting alone on the Delta King with his eye fixed on the crosshairs and his finger poised to pull the trigger. Only now did he recognize that since returning from Afghanistan, his entire existence had been a charade.

And at this moment, he was at a loss of what to do next.

The seating arrangement for the long drive from their home in Davis, California, to Seattle, Washington, reflected the changing dynamics since adopting his new canine companion. Ethan glanced at Kobe, who had acclimated to his new restraint harness in the front passenger seat. And from the reflections in the rearview mirror, Corey had few complaints sitting next to Patas. On occasion, Ethan overheard Corey referring to Patas as *'the suicide bombing Muslim bitch'*. But now, judging by the look on Corey's face as he spoke those words, they appeared more like terms of endearment.

Smiling to himself, Ethan thought that it only took one girl with a cute smile to challenge Corey's deep-rooted hatred for Muslims. Ethan knew that his own failures to adjust to civilian life after fighting for years against the manifestations of radical Islamic ideology went a long way in forming Corey's view of the world. Until recently, he hadn't given much credence to the sordid stories Kinsley's grandfather had repeated to a much younger Corey. Ethan contemplated whether or not it had been a mistake to ignore his son's Jewish heritage from Kinsley's side of the family.

Thus far, the drive had been uneventful. During several stops along the way, Kobe took advantage of the potty breaks to get some needed exercise. Ethan marveled at the playful and loving nature of the dog and how he was quickly becoming part of the family.

He recalled listening to Steve Casella's description of the intense training regimens Kobe had gone through, and his intended role as a multi-purposed K9 officer. The image of Chopper flew into his head. Ethan swallowed the lump in his throat as he glanced at Kobe. He said a silent prayer for his lost companion and reached over and scruffed Kobe's neck. The dog responded by stretching to the limits of his restraint, nuzzling Ethan's shoulder.

As they approached the Tacoma area, about an hour south of Seattle, Ethan veered the Ford from the middle lane and barreled down the nearest exit ramp. Corey, who'd been dozing, awoke with a start. "Dad? I thought we weren't going to stop again till we got to Seattle." He glanced at the exit sign they'd whizzed past, and his eyes darted around the surrounding area. "Are you stopping at this mall?"

Ethan's mind didn't register Corey's words. In fact, for a moment, he'd forgotten he wasn't alone. He'd been driving along listening to a country and western station and tapping his fingers in time to a Hank Williams, Jr., song when he'd absently read the upcoming exit sign. His brain froze and his hands turned the wheel before fully processing the info still bouncing inside his head.

"Dad?" Corey repeated a little louder.

That brought Ethan back from his thoughts, but he didn't respond for several seconds. The images in his head were still spinning as he tried to put the pieces together. He completed a sweeping turn and headed west on WA-16.

"Go back to sleep, Corey. We're not stopping. I just got an idea and we're taking a different route."

Corey shrugged and looked out the side window as they traveled across a suspension bridge spanning a narrow body of water.

For the next twenty minutes, Ethan's head reeled. He tried to decipher the almost forgotten pamphlet he'd come across at the governor's mansion after retrieving the soiled napkin now stuffed inside the Ford's center console. In the hall closet upstairs from the governor's office, he'd glanced at a Washington State Department of Transportation brochure with a ferry schedule for the Seattle area. Someone had scribbled notes in the margins and traced circles around a particular route to Seattle: the one originating at the Bremerton Transportation Center. At the time, he didn't pay much attention to it. Now he racked his brain for the details. They were locked deep inside, and no matter how hard he tried, nothing floated to the surface. That's why he'd reacted so vehemently when the exit for Bremerton came into view. That was his destination. Well, not his final destination. He intended to board the ferry to Seattle.

Now he needed a plan to leave Corey and Patas behind. He looked over at Kobe. The dog responded by tilting his head. Once again appearing to smile back at Ethan.

CHAPTER 31

From now until election day, Governor Nicholas Blackwell's schedule was crammed with last-minute campaign stops. After returning from their break-in at the governor's mansion, Ethan Galloway had located the candidate's next appearance.

Back home, when Corey earlier questioned why his dad picked this particular campaign rally in Seattle to intersect with the governor's party, Ethan had given his son a big smile and said, "I'm interested in what Blackwell has to say on climate change. And didn't you once say you wanted to visit the Seattle Aquarium?"

From Corey's expression, Ethan knew he hadn't bought any of that, so he simply said in a voice that left no room for confusion, "Get ready to go, we're leaving in an hour." He glanced at Patas with a tight smile. "All of us."

That conversation took place about fourteen hours ago. And after a long drive, Ethan closed in on his next destination.

Just before WA-16 merged with WA-3 north, Ethan pulled the Ford into a gas station. After filling the tank, grabbing some snacks from the food mart, and exercising Kobe, they got back in the truck and drove toward Bremerton.

Corey said, "I assume you're not going to visit some old Navy buddies." They were passing the sign for the Kitsap Naval Base when he made those remarks.

Ethan exited WA-3 and drove along the Sinclair Inlet waterfront, passing several remaining mothballed aircraft carriers and Naval vessels. Ethan parked in a lot near the Puget Sound Navy Museum. He checked his watch and looked across at the Bremerton Transportation Center complex.

When they'd stopped for gas, Ethan had grabbed a current brochure with the ferry schedule. This one, unfortunately, had no notes written in the margins, but Ethan had already committed to the plan.

He turned his head and faced Corey. "We're going to part ways for a bit. I want you and Patas to head back to the I 5 freeway and continue north to Seattle. We'll meet at the hotel." He reached into his wallet and pulled out a wad of cash. He placed it on the center console after handing Corey a sheet of paper with directions to a hotel he'd scoped out.

Corey stared at his father. Outside, vehicles continued to line up at the entrance to the ferry terminal. Ethan jumped out and dashed around the truck. He opened the front passenger door and released Kobe from his harness.

He was attaching the leash when Corey finally realized what was happening and scrambled out of the truck to confront his father.

"Dad, what are you doing? You practically ordered us to come with you. Next you change your mind and drive to Bremerton. And now—you're just going to wave goodbye and get on the ferry?"

Ethan nodded. His gut wrenched with an underlying tension he couldn't untangle. The one thing he did know, however, was that he couldn't let Corey or Patas get on board the ferry. Too dangerous. But he didn't know why.

Corey shook his head and pointed at Patas. He tried, "You do know my California driver's license is provisional, don't you? And one of the provisions is—I can't drive alone with a passenger who's under the age of—of—"

Patas climbed out of the truck and chimed in. "I think it's twenty years old."

"Right," Corey said, "and I'm probably not allowed to drive in Washington at all without an adult."

"Besides," Patas said, "my father wouldn't approve of me riding alone with a man in a pick-up truck. Not to mention checking into a hotel."

Ethan and Corey stared at Patas.

She shrugged.

Ethan smiled before motioning for them to step closer. He placed a hand on each of their shoulders and said, "We're not negotiating this. I need to do this alone."

Kobe barked three times and pawed Ethan's leg. He nodded and patted the dog's head. "When the ferry docks in Seattle, I'll walk over to the hotel. It's not far." He looked at Patas. "Get two rooms. After you check in, you can wait in the lobby. I can trust you guys not to go to one of the rooms and fool around, right?"

"Da—aad!"

Both Patas and Corey's faces turned bright red.

"Now get in the truck and drive. I want to see you heading for the freeway before the ferry departs."

Ethan watched Corey pull out of the lot. The truck disappeared around the corner before he led Kobe toward the walk-on ticket booth to buy a ticket for the next ferry to Seattle.

After driving two blocks, Corey pulled into another parking lot and stopped the engine. "We wait five minutes, ditch the truck, and then get on the boat."

Patas smiled. "I figured you gave in too easily."

Chapter 32

Not long after the owner of the automotive body shop in Tacoma, the private investigator who provided the design blueprints and photos for the project, and the courier who delivered the documents had been permanently eliminated, a new two-man team got to work. The task for these men was to further modify the 2006 Dodge Ram diesel pick-up already outfitted with the double-insulated 700-gallon stainless steel dairy tank and painted to match the fleet of transport trucks used by Puget Sound Creamery.

This next phase consisted of fitting the mounted dairy tank with a propane fill valve and wiring an electronic mechanism for detonating the concealed explosive charges fixed inside the tank's mounting brackets. They filled the tank with propane by transferring the liquid gas from the existing on-site 1000-gallon propane tank located behind the body shop. So as not to raise suspicion, the prepared tanker truck remained inside the shop until the night before the planned hijacking of the legitimate Puget Sound Creamery's dairy transport vehicle.

After dark, the two men drove the modified tanker filled with propane and explosives to an old barn set in a pasture behind an abandoned Christmas tree farm along the designated route from the Puget Sound Creamery to the ferry terminal in Bremerton. They waited inside the barn throughout the night and most of the next day.

As scheduled, the real dairy transport vehicle left the Puget Sound Creamery in plenty of time to catch the Seattle-bound ferry that sailed from Bremerton. When the vehicle rounded a sharp curve on an isolated stretch of the county road, approximately five miles from Bremerton, the driver hit the brakes. He barely stopped in time to avoid a two-car accident that blocked the highway in both directions. The narrow shoulders and sharp drop-offs on either side of the asphalt forced the driver to wait till the two cars could be moved out of the traffic lanes.

As he shut off the engine and climbed from the dairy tanker, the driver observed three men engaged in a heated argument. The driver checked his watch and calculated he'd still have time to catch the ferry if he could get the guys to move the cars to the side of the road. From where he approached the accident scene, he didn't notice any significant damage to either vehicle involved in the crash. In fact, when he got a closer look, no damage at all could be seen.

The driver tried to interrupt the argument by tapping one of the men on the shoulder. He was rewarded by the appearance of a pistol pointed at his head. They ushered him back to the dairy tanker and directed him to get into the passenger seat. He complied and received two bullets to his temple. The man with the gun returned it to his shoulder holster and sprinted around to the driver's seat as the other two men ran off toward the cars still blocking the road. Each one got in a vehicle and drove away in opposite directions.

The man started the dairy tanker and continued down the road for about fifty yards, where he turned onto the weed-covered old entrance to the abandoned Christmas tree farm. The whole incident took less than a minute.

As the dairy truck approached the barn, he punched down three times on the horn and eased the rig to the side of the gravel drive. A man pushed open the sagging doors, and the modified Dodge, identical in all exterior aspects to the incoming Puget Sound Creamery tanker, pulled out. It stopped long enough for him to jog over to the passenger side and get in. They waved to the man in the waiting truck and drove toward the road leading to the ferry terminal in Bremerton. The legitimate dairy tanker with the dead driver in the passenger seat was driven inside the barn. The driver closed the doors and walked back toward the county road, where he waited to be picked up.

CHAPTER 33

As he inched closer to the head of the line at the ticket booth, Ethan realized he had no idea if Kobe would be allowed on board. He breathed a sigh of relief after purchasing his ticket, and they handed him a list of instructions for traveling on the Washington State ferry system with a dog.

Ethan boarded the giant vessel with Kobe close to his side. The MV Walla Walla was one of the largest passenger ferries he had ever seen. Searching a ship of this size between now and when they arrived at the Seattle terminal—in approximately forty-five minutes—seemed like an impossible task.

And what the hell am I even looking for?

Another thought also occurred to him. He may not have the full forty-five minutes available to complete the search. His mind swam with frightening consequences, making it difficult to focus on the problem. He scanned the remaining lines of vehicles pulling onto the ferry, hoping to spot anything out of the ordinary.

From the far side of the terminal complex, one of the last waiting vehicles, a Dodge Ram diesel pick-up with a large stainless steel tank installed in the truck's bed pulled forward to the boarding lanes and proceeded toward the starboard gallery ramp. Two additional cars moved in behind it.

The throaty sound of the diesel engine had caught Ethan's attention, and his eyes followed the vehicle for several seconds as it entered the lanes of traffic, inching its way on board. He read the logo painted on the truck's door and stared at the large stainless steel tank until reflections from the sharp angle of the setting sun caused him to turn away from the momentary glare.

He reflexively pulled the leash tighter and Kobe whined. Something troubled him about the vehicle, but when he looked again it had already disappeared on the deck beneath him. Ethan listened to the automated announcements regarding their departure and glanced around at the immense size of the ship and the large number of passengers and vehicles on board. He closed his eyes, willing his mind to concentrate and not draw him into an old nightmare.

* * * * * *

As soon as the gates swung closed and the ferry pulled out of the terminal, the driver and passenger in the 2006 Dodge Ram diesel, both in starched white coveralls, exited the fake Puget Sound Creamery dairy tanker and headed to the closest staircase. In the narrow corridor, they greeted three men wearing maintenance uniforms. After a quick headshake the driver of the dairy tanker gave a thumbs-up to the three men and watched them walk off in the direction of the main control center in the engine room. The two men then climbed the stairs leading to the upper deck and the restricted stairway to the pilot house.

Due to the cold temperatures and frigid spray of saltwater pelting the bow, no passengers were wandering in the area surrounding the secure passageway. Both men stood next to the locked gate. One of them, with his back to his partner, scanned the vicinity while the other man punched in the stolen security codes. If for some reason that failed, they were prepared with ropes and grappling hooks to scale the final obstruction to their goal. None of that turned out to be necessary as the release latch snapped open with a resounding click, and they pushed back the gate.

Knowing there was no need to rush, they stepped deliberately up the stairs and knelt down alongside the wall to the pilot house. Before proceeding further, the driver pressed the button on his handheld. "You boys ready to party?"

The response came back almost immediately. "That's an affirmative. And by the way, don't concern yourself about the man of honor. We found him sipping his tea down in the sweat box."

Both men looked at each other and smiled. They knew he was referring to the ferry's captain. One less body to worry about in the pilot house.

The driver gave the nod, and they began to move slowly toward the door, making sure to stay below the level of the windows. Reaching up to the door's control panel, the driver entered the final codes required to gain access to the pilot house. Things could get messy if they needed to shoot their way in, but again it went according to plan, and the lock snapped open.

Using raised fingers, the driver counted down and yanked open the door. He veered right and his partner took five steps to the left. Both crouched below the panoramic windows. They each held silenced semi-automatic pistols aimed at the quartermaster and the relief mate.

The driver spoke to the quartermaster. "Take your hand off the lever and move back away from the panel. We wouldn't want any sudden movements to disturb the ride for your passengers."

The quartermaster took a step back as he eyed the emergency stop-engine button.

"You might get your hand on the button, but it won't do a bit of good. We've already commandeered the engine room and control center."

Waving with his weapon, he motioned for the relief mate to join the quartermaster. "Now gentlemen, please step back and face the wall."

They complied, and the driver grabbed the intercom mike. "We're ready to go boys. So relax. We've got some time before abandoning ship." He replaced the mike and walked away from the panel. His partner stepped forward and assumed the quartermaster's responsibilities.

The driver focused his attention on his two prisoners. "Take your jackets off and toss them on the chair." After they complied, he said, "They'll help us look a little more official in case a nosy passenger decides to peek inside."

He laughed and then sighed. "Since things are going so well, I'll save you from any unnecessary fretting about what this is all about."

Without any further explanation, he fired a single shot into the back of the head of each crew member. He picked up the jackets from the chairs and examined them for any blood or brain matter stains. Satisfied they'd not been soiled, he stepped over and around the spreading pool of blood seeping from under the bodies.

"Here you go, captain," he said tossing the smaller jacket to his partner.

"Quartermaster," the man muttered at his partner's error as he eased into the jacket. It fit perfectly.

The second and larger jacket was still way too small for the driver, so he tossed it on top of one of the bodies. He checked the ship's location on the GPS display. Deciding they were right on schedule, he pulled out an electronic device housed in a metallic case from his pocket and entered a coded series of digits followed by a time entry. When finished, he snapped the outer cover closed and placed the device inside one of the emergency storage chests.

His partner shook his head. "Do you think that thing is going to survive?"

"Just following orders as to what evidence to leave behind. The boss told me it will lead the authorities to a specific terrorist group. Either way, this will be one hell of a party. Let's hope our designated driver shows up on time."

CHAPTER 34

The Washington State ferry system is the largest in the United States and the third largest in the world. It carries over twenty million people and almost ten million vehicles annually. On average, approximately one hundred thousand people in the greater Seattle area depend on this mass transit system daily.

It is also the number one tourist attraction in the state.

The ferry fleet consists of several different-sized vessels. One of the largest configurations is the Jumbo-class. An example of this is the MV Walla Walla. It is 440 feet long and can carry 2,000 passengers and 188 vehicles.

The United States Coast Guard provides armed gunboat escorts for the numerous ferry routes on a random basis, following no specific schedules. The twenty-five-foot 450hp Defender-class Coast Guard vessels are equipped with M-60 machine guns and a number of assault rifles and shotguns. The sight of these fast-moving crafts approaching, shadowing, and crisscrossing the path of one of the ferries often alarms the uninformed passengers. Before notified of the intent of these formidable vessels, wary passengers fear a terrorist attack is imminent.

* * * * * *

The initial jolt of the MV Walla Walla pulling away from the Bremerton terminal for its forty-five-minute journey to Seattle, refocused Ethan's attention on the problem. But he still had no idea what to look for on board the massive vessel. And no plan for how to proceed—or if what he was looking for would be even found on this particular voyage or vessel.

At first, he wandered down to the auto deck and then up the ramp to the gallery vehicle level. The area was inundated with passengers leaving their vehicles and heading for the main passenger lounge. Ethan recognized the same Dodge Ram diesel with the stainless steel tank attached that he'd observed boarding the ferry. As he walked around the truck on the narrow ramp, the driver's door almost hit him when it abruptly opened. The driver exited. The man showed no indication that he'd seen Ethan and briskly walked away. He was joined by another man who climbed out of the front passenger side. They both wore white coveralls.

Kobe pulled Ethan toward the truck, but the reaction was brief. He read the sign on the tank and shrugged.

A dairy transport?

He stared back at the departing figures until they met up with several maintenance men in the stairwell and disappeared.

Since this whole mess started, he couldn't shake the feeling that his mind had become more... more... well, he didn't understand it, but old memories kept dancing into his head. They only stayed centered in his consciousness for brief instances, and then the fog returned, wiping out the images along with any possible meanings. This wasn't all bad; the recollection of Kinsley and the good days together brought him comfort. But even that had its downside, as it made him see how much of a screw-up he had made of their relationship.

Why didn't I see it? And more importantly—trust you, Kinsley.

Along with those bittersweet memories, other darker thoughts pounded in his head. These troubled him in a different way. He'd find himself focused on the crosshairs, poised to squeeze the trigger when—he'd hesitate. And then something made him finish the job. As those pictures crumbled into oblivion, the faces of countless targets dissolved into unrecognizable masks of death.

His thoughts drifted to the more recent act of flushing his meds down the toilet and the echoing warnings of his doctors about the dangers of not taking his pills. The possibility of that triggering his final descent into the abyss played in his head, but for the first time since his last tour in Afghanistan ended, he felt almost human again.

He shook his head and glanced at his surroundings. After leaving the auto deck, he had let Kobe lead the way and dumbly followed behind the dog. They'd walked through several sections of the main passenger deck, and it appeared Kobe hadn't come across anything suspicious. Then he considered the obvious problem. Although Steve

Casella had told him Kobe was trained to perform a number of specific exercises, such as chemical and drug odor recognition, bomb detection, search and rescue routines, and protection work, Ethan himself had no direct handling experience with Kobe. He didn't know any of the dog's alert indications or the commands to trigger the appropriate responses from Kobe.

Casella's main objective when he turned Kobe over to him was to allow for an adequate period of adjustment and bonding for the dog with its new family. As the owner of Mayacamas Shepherds, he had said he'd be more than happy to work with Ethan at a later date to familiarize him with Kobe's special skills and how to handle them. He also emphasized that, at first, he'd been reluctant about the prospect of allowing Kobe to be adopted into a civilian family, but at the insistence of his assistant, Catori Torrence, he had agreed to this arrangement.

Ethan had no trouble understanding how Catori Torrence could convince anyone to do almost anything. Back at the training facility, when Ethan's eyes fell onto the white German Shepherd, Amber, he'd lost all sense of reality, but somehow Catori guided him through the darkness.

And now, his eyes snapped shut and he relived those last moments inside the training center at Mayacamas Shepherds.

* * * * * *

Amber looked exactly like Chopper. Identical color and features, right down to the unruly cluster of raised fur behind the withers. And her gestures and movements were uncannily like Chopper.

Ethan's world crashed in around him, and he bolted from the stifling confines of the training facility. Once outside, he gulped up the crisp mountain air and staggered to the front of his truck. He placed both hands on the hood and took long, deep breaths, trying to calm down. He repeated to himself that all white German Shepherds look alike, and he was projecting Chopper's persona onto Amber.

But there was one thing he couldn't shake. When Amber entered the room and turned in his direction, her eyes penetrated deep into Ethan's soul.

He remained frozen with his sweaty palms plastered to the warm metal on the truck. The voice appeared out of nowhere. He never heard Catori or Kobe as they approached. When Catori spoke, she was standing close enough for him to smell a sweet and captivating aura emanating from the woman. More than an exotic perfume, it seemed to imprison the fear and distrust of his senses and cast his anxieties into a bottomless pool.

Catori whispered to him.

"Amber is not Chopper. Nor is Kobe meant to replace your lost companion. But Kobe can save you from your past. Your lives may depend on him."

Ethan lifted his hands from the hood of the truck and turned to face the young woman. When their eyes touched, Catori reached out, pressing a palm lightly to his chest.

She spoke again, and her voice sounded urgent.

"They do not have as much power as you think. They can only control what you allow. The truth… it is still inside you. If you want answers, no one can keep them from you."

* * * * * *

Ethan was now standing on the passenger deck of the ferry, pondering those last words. At the time Catori had spoken them, he felt a shiver deep in his heart.

He had sensed a hidden depth lurking behind her bright probing eyes. How did she know about his dog? He had meant to ask Corey if he had written about Chopper in the application to Mayacamas Shepherds, but so far hadn't gotten around to it.

Kobe's sudden lunges and sharp barks jerked Ethan back to the present. Before thinking, he responded, "Good boy, Kobe. What'd you find?"

Kobe promptly sat on his haunches and barked twice. Ethan's surroundings came into focus. They were next in line for the Walla Walla's café grill.

"What can I get for you, sir?"

"Ahh… we'll take a hamburger?"

Kobe whined and pawed the deck.

"Better make it a cheeseburger." He paused and added, "Hold the pickle and onions?"

Kobe barked once, head nodding.

Ethan paid and grabbed his order, leaving a generous tip for the giggling girl at the counter. They moved to a quiet corner, and Ethan unwrapped the burger, placing it on the deck for Kobe. As the dog gobbled up the food, Ethan murmured, "I'm gonna ask Casella if this is how he trained you. You get the reward before you've done the job?"

Kobe stopped chomping long enough to tilt his head at Ethan's words. Ethan pointed a finger at the dog. "Don't mess with me. I won't be fooled by that alert next time." He had trouble keeping the smile from his face.

Turning serious, Ethan balled up the wrapper and tossed it into a nearby trash bin. "Let's go, Kobe. Back to work." They completed another circuit of the main passenger deck, this time making a wide berth around the food court. Still not sure of what he was looking for, Ethan resumed searching the other decks. They proceeded to one of the stairways and Ethan headed up to the sun deck. Starting at the stern, they loosely zig-zagged across the center solariums and seating areas.

As they approached the side of the fore pilot house, Kobe pulled harder. Then the dog hesitated near the locked gate to the restricted stairs. With a quick upturn of his snout, he barked and pulled Ethan around the enclosed structure of the pilot house and down the steps onto the port side deck that extended above the bow. When Ethan saw the target of Kobe's actions, he shut his eyes and cursed under his breath.

What else could possibly go wrong today?

CHAPTER 35

Ethan stopped short and glared at Corey and Patas. They stood huddled against the railing, looking cold from the constant onslaught of the frigid, salty air and staring out at the rippling waves crashing across the bow.

At the sound of Kobe's barks, they turned around, not looking surprised at the sight of Corey's father. Corey attempted a weak smile while Patas pulled the jacket she'd borrowed from him tighter. She appeared to shrink deeper inside it.

A rapid movement in the water, about fifty yards from the bow, interrupted Ethan's outburst. Corey turned and pointed at the small vessel circling to the port side. It slowed as it reached the ferry's stern. "What's happening, Dad? What's that boat trying to do?" He paused, taking a closer look before the craft started to edge behind the ferry. His voice got louder and cracked. "I saw a monster-sized gun mounted on that boat."

Ethan took a breath. "That's the least of your problems. It's a Coast Guard escort boat. They sometimes follow the ferries. Serves as a warning for other boats to keep away, and it also acts as a deterrent—a show of force—against potential terrorist attacks...."

His voice slowed and faded as he scrutinized the waters of Puget Sound.

"What is it, Ethan?" Patas said, following his gaze.

Before answering, he turned to check the location of the craft they'd observed heading toward the stern, but it was now completely out of sight. "As a rule, they don't patrol with only a single gunboat...."

He shrugged, his eyes looking forward toward the Seattle skyline. The approach to the Colman Dock terminal was now visible off the bow. To the port side, he glanced at the Ferris wheel on Pier 57. He was quickly running out of time. But then again, he might be wrong and nothing was going to happen anyway.

Ethan checked his watch. If his hunch turned out wrong, there'd still be time to catch most of Governor Blackwell's speech at the climate change rally outside the Seattle Aquarium.

"I'm going to take one final look around the ship. After we dock, I'm heading over to the aquarium." He took a step closer to Corey and pointed a finger in his face. "Now listen. Like I told you before, I want you and Patas to take the truck and go directly to the hotel. Park it in their garage, check-in, and wait for me in the lobby. Then we'll discuss why you didn't listen to me in the first place. Can you do that?"

Corey bit his lip and looked up at his father. "Not exactly. We'll have to walk to the hotel because I left the truck at a parking lot in Bremerton."

Ethan glared at Corey with his mouth wide open. Before responding, he felt his body shift as the ferry began a shallow turn to port. When he looked ahead, the ferry terminal was no longer centered on the bow. As the ferry came around, he noted the large Ferris wheel now stood slightly starboard to their new heading.

In the distance—the Seattle Aquarium—dead ahead.

A cold wave spread down Ethan's body, locking him in place. Long lost memories swam to the surface, but this new reality pushed them back. The past would have to wait. He began processing the more recent images and came to a frightening conclusion.

CHAPTER 36

Kobe reacted with a series of barks and lunged away from Ethan, almost pulling him to the slippery deck. Ethan caught himself by grabbing onto the railing and wrapping the lead into a tight loop around his other wrist.

"Knock it off, Kobe," Ethan said and turned to Corey. "I'm beginning to think this dog enjoys dragging me around like an old ragdoll."

Kobe whined and pawed the deck. When Ethan glanced up toward the pilot house, he saw two men scurrying down the secure stairway and shoving the gate open. One of them yanked a crew jacket off his shoulders, bunched it up, and tossed it into a trash container. Walking briskly away from Ethan's position near the bow, the two men disappeared down the stairs leading to the main passenger deck.

Ethan tried another command on Kobe, finally getting the dog to stop pulling on the lead. "There's something damn familiar about those two guys. I'm positive I saw them getting out of a small dairy tanker down on the gallery deck." The forgotten image of Kobe pulling toward the truck popped into his head.

"What do you think they were doing in a restricted area?" Patas asked.

"Something tells me they weren't making a milk delivery to the crew members in the pilot house." He glanced over his shoulder. "And I doubt our new heading is taking us to one of this ferry's regular stops. I'm going to follow them and see what they're up to."

"Maybe that's why the Coast Guard boat showed up," Corey said.

As he finished those words, several long blares echoed in the distance off the port side. They looked toward the setting sun, and the shapes of at least a dozen small vessels emerged from the misty air that hugged the surface of Puget Sound—speeding toward the errant ferry.

"Let's hope that's the rest of the cavalry coming to the rescue," Ethan said as he sprinted after the two men. Over his shoulder, he added, "Follow me, but don't get too close."

He acknowledged that standing near the bow wasn't the best place for Corey and Patas to stay, but with the alarming thoughts spinning in his brain, he could just as easily be leading them toward a worse nightmare.

Kobe remained in the lead, but he responded to Ethan's commands. His pulling was less forceful, and he no longer barked incessantly. They entered the main passenger lounge and paused near the aft seating section. Ethan spotted the two men in white coveralls as they passed the cafeteria and entered the corridor near the elevator, heading for the stairway to the lower decks.

He could see that although they moved with purpose, they tried not to garner any undue attention. Ethan glanced around at the gawking passengers and realized Kobe's actions were triggering a greater concern. He moved forward at a more cautious pace. As he approached the passageway where the men had disappeared, he turned and saw Corey and Patas about thirty feet behind. He considered telling them to stay back in the main seating area but decided it might be better to keep them in sight.

Kobe began straining again, his whines and growls returning with a vengeance. Ethan peered down the staircase and saw the two men stepping onto the main auto deck. Another group of men handed them life jackets and pointed to the stern. Together, they all donned the bulky vests and darted around the parked vehicles. They no longer tried to appear non-threatening and started shouting at passengers to get out of the way. Pistols waving in the air reinforced their demands.

As Ethan drew closer, he heard several of the men screaming taunts in Arabic, accompanied by familiar, loosely translated English phrases consistent with the world's view of Islamic terrorists. In the heat of the moment, Ethan's mind strained to remain focused on his immediate task, but he couldn't ignore the fact that he'd never pegged these guys as religious fanatics. Something seemed off—but he filed those thoughts away for a later time. Right now, determining motives didn't appear very important.

With Kobe yanking him forward, they closed the gap. The first of the men to reach the stern ripped down the barriers and signaled toward a lone Coast Guard gunboat keeping pace near the outside of the ship's wake. For the moment, Ethan concluded the cavalry had indeed arrived. He anticipated a gunfight if the Coast Guard attempted to board. He needed to distract the terrorists—and save the more precise jihadist labelling for later.

Before he could act, one of the terrorists turned his weapon on Ethan and sent a volley of silenced shots in his direction. He dove below a nearby Honda Civic, jerking Kobe to his side. By instinct, he reached for his M11, forgetting Corey had convinced him to lock it in the Ford's glove box when their journey north began. The weapon never crossed his mind until this moment. With the truck abandoned in Bremerton, his options became more limited.

Ethan didn't see Corey and Patas but shouted for them to get back up the stairs. He lifted his head and turned in time to watch Corey grab hold of Patas and pull her into the stairwell.

Ethan ducked down again as another round of gunfire shattered the rear window of the SUV behind him. After several seconds the shooting stopped, but people screamed as panic escalated. Luckily, many of the vehicles remained empty, since the passengers had not yet returned from the upper decks.

Ethan crouched further down and inched his way to the passenger side of the Civic. He placed a hand on the front bumper and eased his head out. None of the terrorists were looking in his direction. But instead of firing on the trailing vessel, he could see one of the men motioning to the others. One by one they jumped from the stern and into the foaming waters where they were scooped up and onto the Coast Guard gunboat.

It was then Ethan realized that the fleet of Coast Guard vessels they'd observed from the ship's bow couldn't have gotten here so soon. This was the boat they'd seen earlier. It had been a decoy. Part of the plan to get the terrorists off the ferry.

And that confirmed his worst suspicions.

Ethan stood and gazed around the auto deck. His eyes homed in on the dairy tanker parked on the gallery level. Kobe let out a series of barks and pulled free from Ethan's distracted grip. He bolted toward the stern, targeting any remaining terrorists before they jumped. The driver of the dairy tanker was the last man standing. He turned at the sight of the charging black dog and reached for his weapon. The pistol's silencer hung up and snagged in the holster. Rattled, he scrambled to yank off his utility belt. As he got it free and extracted the weapon, Kobe's teeth ripped into the belt and pulled. When the belt dropped to the deck, Kobe spun around, poising for another attack. The man fumbled with the weapon, reflexively lifting a leg in a defensive move to kick out at Kobe.

Kobe latched onto his boot and wrenched the man down. Landing on his back, he succeeded in holding on to his weapon and leveled it at Kobe as the dog dragged him across the slippery deck.

Out of nowhere came a blood-curdling scream and Ethan slid over the wet surface on his back, one leg arched up and out. On impact, the man screamed out in pain and the pistol slipped from his grasp, skittering over the stern and into the water. The momentum sent them both teetering closer to the stern, inches from plummeting off the slick deck.

Kobe bit harder, but the man's boot slipped off his foot. At the last second, Kobe's jaws grabbed onto the back of Ethan's jacket. Ethan stopped wrestling with the man. Slowed by Kobe's action, he grabbed hold of a mooring line dangling near the stern. He watched the driver of the dairy tanker dive over the edge and hit the water.

After several seconds, he burst through the surface and gasped for air. Men on the trailing vessel plucked him from the churning water. The craft veered off to port as its powerful engine throttled up. Gaining speed, it moved away from the ferry and headed deeper into Puget Sound.

CHAPTER 37

The scene at the Seattle Aquarium had settled down after hours of prep work to secure the building and the surrounding waterfront for the governor's appearance at this evening's rally on climate change.

Earlier in the week, crews had assembled a stage and a large seating area on the pier adjacent to the aquarium's main building at the northern edge of Waterfront Park, with Puget Sound as a backdrop. The governor would address the crowd and then attend a fund-raising tour of the aquarium, followed by a private dinner.

The rally had been scheduled to start ten minutes ago.

"Where the hell is Governor Blackwell?" Olivia Davenport asked the governor's head of security, Victor Petricello. She had been sent down by the agent-in-charge. Since the secret service detail had joined forces with the governor's private security team, the agency's staff had been met with resistance every step of the way.

Petricello held up a finger as he turned away and spoke into his cell phone. "Yes, governor. I've informed the committee. We have the campaign video set to go for the crowd while we're waiting."

After ending the call, Petricello spun back to face Olivia. "Agent Davenport. That was the governor. There's been an accident on the interstate, and he's stuck in a massive traffic jam. A tractor trailer sideswiped a school bus. There's talk of one fatality and a number of severe injuries on the bus."

The image of hurt and dying kids took the steam out of Olivia's irritation. "My God, that's awful." She swallowed and tried to refocus. "Why is Blackwell riding alone? He should've been part of the service's motorcade from the hotel."

Petricello shook his head. "The agent-in-charge received the memo earlier today. The governor needed to meet with an important donor in Redmond."

"You know, Petricello, if your guy gets to the White House, things will be a lot different. The secret service will be in charge—and you'll be out of a job."

Olivia expected a snarky comeback, but instead Petricello looked nervous. In spite of the chilly weather and the fog rolling over the Seattle waterfront, she watched him wipe a bead of sweat from his forehead and steal a hasty glance at his watch.

"I understand things will be different, agent. Now if you'll excuse me. An emergency meeting's been called, and I need to return to the Westin."

Olivia didn't get a chance to respond as she watched Petricello charge off toward a waiting SUV. He jumped in, and she listened to brakes screech and horns blare as the vehicle cut into the heavy Alaska Way traffic and sped off. Before she could process his bizarre behavior, Olivia's handheld sparked to life, spewing frantic messages from other agents on her detail. She joined several colleagues as they jogged to the south side of the pier.

One of the agents pointed at a large ferry running parallel to the Seattle waterfront. It was heading toward the aquarium. Farther out on the water, piercing the wrapping layers of fog, she saw a fleet of Coast Guard gunboats fast approaching.

While the agents got busy and started evacuating the aquarium and adjacent waterfront, the image of the governor's head of security running toward the waiting SUV stuck in Olivia's head. That, and a tardy governor, conveniently caught in a traffic jam.

Don't start thinking like Mike. It's just a coincidence. Or maybe two coincidences. Not a conspiracy. No way—even someone as sick as Blackwell—could not be a part of—

She looked south at the approaching ferry, now much closer and looming larger than life. She shook her head.

What the hell's going on?

Olivia's cell phone rang.

She took the call.

"Mike? Where the hell are you?"

CHAPTER 38

Ethan looked to the west where a fleet of Coast Guard vessels closed in on the ferry. Two gunboats near the rear changed course and intersected a path with the escaping boat carrying the terrorists. He gauged that the rest of the fleet might have time to board the ferry and prevent it from crashing into the aquarium, but Ethan's intuition cried out—telling him the terrorists had something else up their sleeves.

Kobe finally stopped barking as Corey and Patas rushed to Ethan's side and helped him back to his feet.

"You never told me you were a ball player, Dad. What an awesome slide."

"To tell the truth, I was terrible at baseball. The one time I tried a slide like that—it was into first base—and I broke my leg—in two places."

"I'm not much of a sports fan," Patas said, "but I don't think you're supposed to slide into first base."

Kobe barked again, catching Ethan's attention. When he turned, he saw Kobe sitting in front of the terrorist's discarded utility belt. Ethan reached down and picked it up, immediately noticing a key fob clipped to one of the chrome rings. After snapping it off, he smiled and ran to an emergency locker along the wall. He grabbed three life vests and tossed two to Corey and Patas, fitting the third one on himself.

"Put those on. Then go flag down some crew members. Tell them to check out the pilot house and control room. Make sure they understand what's happening."

"But what *is* happening, Dad?"

Ethan grimaced and said, "Just tell them to assist the Coast Guard in boarding the ship. I think they can work out the rest."

Ethan struggled with how to keep Corey and Patas safe. He reasoned that if he could finish his job, they'd be safer on the ferry. "After doing that, get up to the bow and keep an eye out in front of the ferry. If it looks like it's not going to stop in time, run back down here and jump off the stern deck. But wait till the last second. I want you as far as possible from this part of Puget Sound."

"But where're *you* going to be?"

He shook the key fob in his hand. "Seems the driver left without his ride. I'm making one final delivery." He turned to Kobe. "Let's go, boy."

With a last look at Corey and Patas, he added, "Remember, we're meeting at the hotel after you get off this damn boat."

Ethan ran along the side of the main auto deck and onto the ramp to the gallery level. When he reached the dairy tanker, he pressed the key fob and pulled open the driver's door. He took one more look at Corey and Patas, who hadn't moved a muscle.

"Now! Go! What didn't you understand?"

He watched the two kids, at first barely moving, pick up speed. He heard Corey shouting at crew members before disappearing up the stairway. As he grabbed onto the hand strap and tried to jump into the truck, he came face-to-face with Kobe in the driver's seat.

"Move it, smartass. *I'm* driving."

The dog grudgingly complied, and Ethan slid behind the wheel. The task made more difficult by the bulky life vest. He took in a deep breath and listened to the escalating sounds as people darted about the auto deck, not knowing where to go or what to do. The crew was fighting a losing battle in trying to restore any semblance of order.

He noted several crew members with portable radios rush to the opposite side of the auto deck. They opened a storage container and hastily pulled out mooring lines and cases of emergency supplies. So far no one was paying attention to Ethan or the dairy tanker. His next move would change that. He prayed the crew was now in direct communication with the approaching fleet of Coast Guard vessels and preparing to aid in their boarding.

That meant he needed to act now and not wait for the Coast Guard to take control of the ferry. Time was running out, and he didn't want to get bogged down in any red tape or prolonged explanations. He glanced at Kobe and shoved the key into the ignition.

"You wouldn't be smiling if you knew the plan, big boy."

Kobe tilted his head and Ethan swore the dog grinned back at him again. This habit was making him nervous.

After one final check to assure that no passengers were either standing nearby or seated in the two closest vehicles, Ethan jammed the gear shift into reverse and touched lightly on the gas pedal until the tanker truck inched back and nudged the front bumper of the next to last car in the gallery deck line. When the truck made contact, he pressed down and increased the engine speed, forcing the car backwards. The second impact jerked the truck harder as they struck the last vehicle in line.

Ethan gave a quick thanks to the owners of those vehicles for being energy conscious enough to purchase small, lightweight cars. They might not approve of his next move, which would result in a significant increase in pollution of the Seattle waterways, but at least they, along with the rest of the passengers and the attendees of the climate change rally at the aquarium, would live to file an official complaint. If Ethan failed in his mission, they'd be dealing with a lot more contamination.

With no more time for second-guessing, Ethan punched down hard on the accelerator. He heard additional grinding noises coupled with crunching plastic and screeching metal as the heavy truck pushed the two cars the remaining distance down the ramp and onto the main auto deck. The tanker truck had just cleared the ramp, when one of the cars twisted sideways and jammed into the wall. Stepping harder on the gas pedal resulted in more spinning tires and a rising cloud of burning rubber which obliterated the salty tang of the night air. Flipping the transmission into four-wheel drive added to the pungent smoke filling the cab.

Cursing, Ethan dropped the gear shift into drive and drove partway back up the gallery ramp. Like pulling teeth, the menacing crunches of tearing bumpers competed with the growing shouts from the crew who waved their arms in an attempt to stop the madman. He raised the window and locked the doors as several crew members grabbed at the door handle and pounded on his window.

"Get the hell away or you're gonna get hurt," Ethan shouted, stating the obvious. For a moment, his brain appeared to slip-slide to a different time—a different place—the inside of the truck's cab turned cold and dark.

"Not now! Please, not now. Please. I'm not gonna let you do this to me now. Please!"

With each word, his voice lowered and the cadence slowed. He took several more breaths and his vision cleared. Kobe licked his face.

Ethan swallowed hard and once again put the truck into reverse. He didn't ease back into the cars blocking his path. His foot slammed the pedal to the floor. Tires screamed and smoked. He hit the first one and it spun further around. The last vehicle in the line stopped the first one before the truck could push it completely aside. As Ethan pulled forward again, he glanced in the rearview mirror in time to watch the rear wheels of the last car drop off the end of the deck. In slow motion, it slid further back and then the front reared upward.

"Hi-ho, Silver. Away," Ethan muttered, seeing it drop straight down out of sight.

He turned to Kobe. "Last chance, Black Beauty." Without waiting for the dog to criticize his cinematic references, Ethan once again plastered his foot on the accelerator. This time the truck wasn't about to be stopped by any politically correct means of transportation. The remaining vehicle banged into the side wall after the final impact, its crushed body mingling with the unforgiving steel-plated partition near the stern.

Ethan kept his foot pinned on the gas pedal. The truck shot off the stern deck. It hit the water, and the heavy, propane-filled stainless steel tank pulled the rear of the truck down at a sharp angle.

The ferry continued forward as the sinking truck buffeted in its wake. Before banging his head against the steering wheel and the short-circuiting of the truck's electrical system, Ethan remembered to open both front windows. He heard Kobe give him his best whine as the cab descended below the surface and quickly filled with water.

A parting thought flew through Ethan's head as everything went black.

Here we go again, Patas.

Let's hope this detonator's not waterproof.

CHAPTER 39

Once again Corey failed to follow his dad's instructions. After trying to convince several crew members of the danger and assisting two elderly passengers, he clamored back down the steel stairway and reappeared on the auto deck in time to watch the dairy tanker careen down the gallery lane like a battering ram, swiping away anything in its way.

Catching up to him, Patas screamed, "Corey! What're you doing? Your dad told us to—"

She gasped and grabbed Corey's arm. "Oh my God. Your dad's still in the truck."

He nodded as they both watched it disappear off the ferry's stern.

"We've got to tell somebody, Corey. Maybe the crew can help."

Events ratcheted up at a furious pace. But to Corey and Patas, it all played out in agonizing, slow-motion. They had already gotten the attention of a few crew members and explained the situation they'd observed outside the pilot house. Soon they heard a series of orders shouted out. Next, the crew attached lines to the stern of the Walla-Walla.

A team of Coast Guard personnel boarded the ferry and began to take charge of the runaway vessel. Several passengers came out of hiding and relayed unbelievable accounts of the fleeing terrorists, the ensuing gunfire, and the maniac climbing into a truck and mowing down everything in its path until the fool backed it right into the water.

The pilot of the lead Coast Guard gunboat had witnessed a large truck dropping off the stern. It had disappeared beneath the surface barely thirty seconds before the gunboat fleet came around and aligned course with the ferry. By now the sunken truck was several hundred yards astern, and the Coast Guard had a more pressing problem. They needed to take control of the huge ferry before it rammed into the aquarium pier at the north end of Waterfront Park.

As they gained entrance to the pilot house and seized control of the engine room, the starboard side of the fast-moving Walla-Walla sailed abreast of the Seattle Great Wheel. Startled riders near the top of the Ferris wheel got a bird's-eye view of the unfolding drama.

After tensions on the ferry diminished, Corey and Patas huddled together, trying to blend into the crowd. Corey saw no benefits of identifying his father as the person who drove the truck off the back of the ferry. From this point on it served no purpose to provide the authorities with anything but the minimum cooperation. Corey was scared to death about his dad's well-being and wanted nothing more than for the crew to dock this damn ferry at the Seattle terminal, so they could get off and find out if his dad was okay.

Patas tried her best to ease Corey's anxieties. His rational side knew that his father's training had prepared him for a lot worse situations. But Corey still fought back the tears as they waited for someone to redirect the ferry back to the terminal and allow the passengers to disembark.

CHAPTER 40

When word reached Governor Blackwell that the so-called terrorist plot had been thwarted, he looked at his wife in disbelief. They were still stuck in traffic on Interstate 5. His chief of staff sat behind the wheel of the Suburban and relayed the incoming messages as quickly as he could. The governor and his wife were the only passengers in the SUV.

"This is a disaster," Governor Blackwell said. "We've already issued a statement specifying that an obscure offshoot of ISIS has taken credit for the attack. And by now, the copies of the alleged documents received by our office describing the intent to assassinate me should've been released."

Anita Blackwell slipped her drained martini glass into the cup holder. She patted her husband on the cheek and snorted, "Don't look so glum, darling. At least you're alive. And we can still make this work."

Steadman grasped one hand on the steering wheel, holding his cell phone in the other. He glanced in the rearview mirror at the desperate look on the governor's face and the glazed eyes of his wife.

He almost countered Anita's glib statement with: *And your insane stunt still got at least one kid killed in this staged bus accident, you drunken bitch.*

But instead, he said, "She's right, Nick. Since the aquarium and the waterfront remain intact, you can make a personal appearance and thank the authorities for their splendid work in responding to this potential crisis. This could be an even better way to get the point across that you'd make a better president than the current asshole in the White House. Our story hasn't changed because the phony jihadists failed. Anybody watching this whole debacle must know you were the intended target. The press releases can stay the same. What better backing can you have? The Islamic extremists are more afraid of you than Tyler Griffin. They'd rather have him in the Oval Office. That's one endorsement a presidential candidate could do without." Steadman paused and allowed a smile to spread. He turned and looked at the governor. "And with the appropriate leaks to the media, we might even convince the voters that Tyler Griffin himself colluded with the terrorists."

The governor nodded.

Anita burped and placed a hand on her husband's thigh. "What about leaking out that our own security staff provided key information to alert authorities of the imminent attack, allowing them to stop it? By the time the bureaucrats sort through all the bullshit, the election will be history, and Nick will be fondling every White House intern he can get his sticky little hands on."

Steadman remained silent but thought, *Jesus Christ, the bitch thinks better when she's drunk.*

The governor grabbed Anita's hand and whispered, "My God, Anita. You make me horny as hell." A little louder, he said to Steadman, "Tom, can't you get us out of this damn traffic? We're late enough as it is."

Although Steadman also caught the governor's hushed words to Anita, he responded only to the governor's second request. "Yes sir, I'll see what I can do." To himself he added, *You and your wife think that with only one dead kid on the wrecked school bus, they should've cleaned this up long ago.*

Anita got in the final word. "Nick, I don't give a damn how horny you are. I'm not drunk enough yet. And I get off better watching you panting over one of our little whores. Not to mention adding another DVD to the collection."

CHAPTER 41

Dropping from the stern of the moving ferry, the modified Dodge Ram plunged beneath the surface. The cold waters of the Puget Sound churned and bit at Ethan's body, striving to steal the sweet taste of life-giving oxygen. Kobe's anxious movements faded from his consciousness as the memory of another canine companion materialized inside his head.

The icy tremors of an imminent death melted away and Ethan's thoughts turned to a long ago, fateful night in Afghanistan.

As reality dissolved, his skin grew raw and sweaty. Pungent smoke and the cloud of spent ammo embraced him. His eyes stung from spatters of blood and foul gases. Using a tattered sleeve, he swept the grit from his face, forcing his eyes to confirm the nightmare.

The rifle dropped to the ground and his legs turned to butter. Crouched on his knees, he stared at Chopper's body. His pure white fur already streaked and embedded with dirt was now soaked in the blood spilling from a large rent in his belly.

The dog lay motionless.

Ethan's face twisted in anguish.

"Chief? We gotta move." Schlessinger's voice sounded distant and faint. "The extraction team's thirty seconds out."

Ethan remained still, his eyes glassy and cold.

Schlessinger placed a hand on Ethan's shoulder. "He's gone, buddy. Nothing you can do."

Ethan reached out his arm and lightly touched Chopper's ear.

The dog's eyes fluttered, and a low moan tumbled from his snout as rivulets of blood mixed with saliva and pooled at his neck.

"He's alive! I'm not leaving him."

Schlessinger sighed. "Man… man, Ethan. Look at him, Chief. He ain't gonna make it." He grabbed Ethan's shoulder harder and softened his words. "He's suffering. You go—join the guys waiting on the roof. I—I'll take care of Chopper."

Ethan's body stiffened, and for the first time he looked away from the dog. His head gave a slow shake. "Schlessinger. I want you to get moving—now. That's an order." He paused and added, "I'll be there in a minute."

"But—"

"I said that's an order. Now go! Time's wasting."

Schlessinger gave the team's leader a quick nod and hesitated at the base of the ladder. He turned his head one last time before clamoring up to the roof.

Ethan stroked Chopper's neck while whispering comforting words as he leaned in closer. He could see Chopper's life slipping away and could feel the pain radiating from the dog's mortal wounds. Chopper's eyes held a pleading glisten. His front leg pawed at Ethan's outstretched arm.

Ethan knew what needed to be done.

The tears washed away the remaining blood and grime from his eyes. He couldn't bear to look at his treasured companion. To be a witness to his suffering was too much. With no conscious decision, he sensed his other hand slide to his utility belt. The opening snap sounded louder than the approaching helicopter and the frantic shouts of his men on the roof. It pierced his heart. He withdrew the weapon, and knowing the safety was off and a round chambered, he brought it to the side of Chopper's head.

He whispered last words to the dog who'd just saved his life.

Ethan begged forgiveness.

As the blast echoed, he pressed his head against Chopper's body and let out a gut-wrenching wail. His hand still shaking, he turned the muzzle and jammed it to his own temple.

With eyes shut tight, his finger slowly squeezed back on the trigger.

Flip-flopping sounds rattled in his head. From somewhere in between the escalating thunder of the helicopter's engine and the buffeting down-drafting winds blowing through the opening to the roof, Ethan swore he heard a chuffing noise escape from Chopper.

He figured that wasn't possible. Then a more definite sound screamed from above.

"Galloway—You got ten seconds before this bird leaves your sorry ass behind."

* * * * * *

Ethan felt a tugging and ripping as the straps on his life jacket stretched from powerful jaws grasping—trying to get him to move.

As his mind transposed to the current situation, Kobe's barks filled his ears. Ethan coughed as the rising waters struggled to fill his lungs with icy fingers of death. He took a large, final deep breath of air. When the waters pushed the remaining air pockets from the Dodge's cab, he kicked open the truck door, and with Kobe at his side, he fought for the surface.

He forced the new-found images of Chopper's death aside. As his head burst through the surface and into the cool night air, he thought, *God help me when the rest of my memories return.*

Kobe yanked and barked, pulling the disoriented Ethan toward shore. Recovering to a degree—relying on his own instincts and years of training—Ethan swam and scrambled up the rocky embankment underneath a pier to the north of the ferry terminal. He sat back against one of the concrete pilings and watched the ferry still traveling in the direction of the Seattle Aquarium. Its speed appeared to slow, and he imagined the crew responding to frantic orders from the coast guard officers who'd by now boarded the ferry.

Kobe jaunted up in front of Ethan and licked his face. Ethan patted the dog's wet, matted coat and inhaled the briny scents radiating off his new friend. "We did it, boy." He glanced over the waters of Puget Sound, trying to estimate the location where the modified Dodge Ram had sunk.

No explosion.

The ferry and all aboard appeared safe.

Unfortunately, the terrorists escaped.

Drained and exhausted, Ethan fell into a rare and dreamless sleep.

He never heard the distant sound of the terrorists' getaway boat bursting into flames and incinerating seconds before the pursuing Coast Guard gunboats closed the final gap. Like the earlier fate of the others, someone had taken care of any potential plea-bargaining from the last known team members of the terrorist plot.

Much later in the night, Ethan stirred again but couldn't fight off the overwhelming fatigue. Kobe's head rested on his thigh. Ethan shivered from the cold night air, while the intruding fog made his wet clothes feel even more discomforting.

He responded to the lights and sounds coming from the Seattle ferry terminal to the south, and the moored Walla-Walla came into focus. Aside from the surreal light show propagated by the emergency response vehicles, the ship itself looked intact. When he glanced over his shoulder, he caught a glimpse of the distant plaza that surrounded the aquarium, and that too appeared untouched.

Ethan watched uniformed personnel usher the waning mass of passengers through the terminal's walkways. When he attempted to pull himself to his feet, his head grew heavy, and a dark curtain descended once again. He barely vocalized his last thoughts before oblivion struck.

"Thank God Corey and Patas are safe. Just a little more rest and we'll meet them at the hotel."

CHAPTER 42

After imprisoned on the Seattle-bound ferry for what seemed like an eternity, Corey and Patas disembarked the Walla-Walla, where it remained docked and guarded at the Seattle terminal. They slipped through the requisite inquiries without revealing any solid information as to their true identities. Once detached from the chaotic scene, Corey became frantic to find his dad.

They tried to calculate the approximate location of where the tanker truck had plunged into the chilly waters of Puget Sound. They began scouting out the areas north of the ferry terminal but getting near the waterfront proved difficult. The entire western sector of the city still crawled with local cops; often teamed up with state and federal officers. Every time Corey and Patas wandered away from the main throngs of people, they elicited sharp stares from the patrolling authorities. As they got closer to the Seattle Aquarium, the crowds grew larger and more boisterous.

After a brief shutdown to divert vehicles from the vicinity of potential terrorist activities, the city's main north-south elevated highway that flanked Puget Sound was again snarled with traffic. This added a familiar, reassuring pulse to the Seattle waterfront. Dark, fog-shrouded shadows enveloped the street beneath the concrete stanchions of the heavily traveled Route 99 viaduct; contrasting with the bright tourist enclaves that dotted the pavement on the opposite side of the local thoroughfare.

"Let's head to the hotel like your dad told us to do. I'm sure that's what he expects. It's the first place he'll look for us," Patas suggested.

Corey nodded. "Good idea."

Patas hesitated before saying, "You should try giving him a call."

When Corey looked off toward the darkened waters of Puget Sound and didn't answer, she touched his shoulder and quickly added, "I'm sure he's fine, Corey. I know from first-hand experience that he's a fantastic swimmer... ah, but even if he doesn't answer... it could be because his phone got wet and...."

Corey looked at Patas's hand and shrugged. "You don't have to tell me. He's a SEAL. Been in a lot tougher situations than this. That's not it." He paused, a small smile forming. "Back in Bremerton, when Dad told me to drive the truck to Seattle, I stuffed the cash in my wallet and threw it in the center console along with my cell phone. And kinda forgot it all when we ran to catch the ferry."

Patas stared at him but remained quiet.

"So—this is all I got." From his pocket, he pulled the sheet of paper his dad gave him before getting out of the truck. He checked the address of the hotel. A small map on the back of the sheet included directions from the Seattle Aquarium, where they'd supposedly been heading before his dad switched gears. Corey glanced around and pointed to his right. They were about to cross the street when the crowd got so thick they could barely move in any direction but the natural flow of the bustling wave of humanity.

Shrill-sounding audio checks burst from loudspeakers set across the front of a temporary stage about a hundred feet ahead. Corey saw a wall of uniformed security personnel lining the perimeter of Waterfront Park and the main entrance to the Seattle Aquarium. Like cattle packed tight in a feedlot, the determined crowd herded Corey and Patas toward the stage platform that rose atop the weathered pier planks at the park's northern boundary with the aquarium complex.

Security barriers and somber-faced officers slowed the forward movement of the crowd, but not before Corey and Patas were close enough to identify at least one person standing on the stage: the California governor, Nicholas Blackwell.

Although Patas tried retreating, the packed mob prevented any hopes of escape. Patas's hand tightened against Corey's arm. He saw the frightened look on her face as the pressure of the masses moved them ever closer to her greatest nightmare. Struggling to shield her from the governor, he stretched an arm about her shoulder, and with the unintentional assistance of the crowd, held her to his chest. In the undulating waves of strangers pushing, cheering, shouting; he swore he could feel the pounding of Patas's heart reverberating right through him.

The governor continued to speak, and they had no choice but to stay; all but crushed in place. Corey spotted something at the rear of the stage drawing Patas's attention. When his gaze landed on two humorless men, he realized one of them appeared to be pointing a finger in their direction and whispering into the other man's ear. The second man placed a handheld to his face, his lips moving feverishly into the mike. The first man leaned back and motioned to a woman. She stepped forward and Corey recognized her as Anita Blackwell, the governor's wife. Corey froze at the clouded expression that washed over her previously bored countenance as her eyes flung glacial shards at Patas.

Patas tried shouting at Corey, but the crowd's maddening din drowned out the words. With a strength he wouldn't have dreamed possible, she yanked him away from the stage, somehow prying, muscling, pushing through the crowd and toward the street. Bursting free from the last stragglers meandering in the fringes, Patas didn't stop thrashing. Corey helped calm her gestures but never hampered her retreat.

When finally liberated from the suffocating confines surrounding the stage, Patas's eyes darted around. She gasped and pointed toward the welcoming darkness lurking on the far side of the street beneath the rumbling stream of traffic on the elevated highway.

Corey grabbed her with both arms, spinning her toward him. His eyes, bulging and penetrating, begged the question.

"Those two men on the stage—behind Blackwell. One is his chief of staff. The other is the head of his private security team." She extracted herself from his arms and twisted away. "I'm sure they recognized me. And did you catch the glare from that witch?"

Reaching out and tugging his hand, she added, "Come on, let's go." Corey in tow, she darted across Alaska Way while braking motorists hit their horns.

With the relative solitude and darkness of a nearby parking lot affording them a hint of anonymity, Corey pulled Patas behind a red and white florist's delivery van. Holding her against the van's rear side panel, he craned his neck around the back. In the constant shifting and movements of the crowd, he saw nothing threatening— no guns drawn or nasty-looking men with handhelds or cell phones shouting orders.

Their temporary shelter was demarcated by regiments of antiquated light fixtures perched on slender cast-iron poles. The soft glowing lamps parted the foggy breaths, transforming them into the eyes of many cyclops. The condensing liquid running trails down the ornate posts appeared as tears foretelling a dark sadness on the horizon.

Turning his head to Patas, Corey's hand gently lifted her chin. "We're both a little jumpy. How's it possible for anyone to recognize you? When you worked at the governor's mansion, your head and face were covered." As he touched her cheek, a tear found its mark and moistened his fingertip.

Stammering, Corey said, "And after my dad cut your hair—well, I could hardly tell you were that same girl wearing a suicide vest who Dad pulled from the river." He shrugged in an attempt to ease her fears. "Now you're a real California babe. Once you lost those bedsheets, who'd ever mistake you for a radical Islamic terrorist?"

Patas sobbed and let out a stifled giggle at the same time. Her breathing slowed as she glanced around. Appearing more composed, her eyes scanned the jammed parking lot and grabbed Corey's arm. She pointed toward a nearby streetlamp. "Look. A payphone. Didn't think they still existed."

He nodded. As they headed toward the phone, Corey fumbled inside his pockets and turned to Patas. She jangled a small purse in his face. "Guess you're not carrying any loose change."

After listening to the coins registering the appropriate beeps, he punched in his dad's cell number. Several seconds later, his face tightened. "He's not answering, I'm getting the '*not in service*' message and it's switching over to voicemail."

He waited and said, "Dad?" He hesitated. "Hope you're okay." He shut his eyes and swallowed. "We're off the ferry but the whole waterfront is packed with police and federal agents. Can't get anywhere near the water. We're gonna head over to the hotel and wait for you. Can't check-in though… I sorta left my wallet…." He continued rambling. "… and my phone… that's why I'm using the—"

Patas interrupted him. "Don't forget to tell him about those men from the governor's office. His chief of staff, Steadman—and the security guy."

Corey nodded, holding the phone closer. "We were listening to Governor Blackwell give a speech outside the aquarium. Patas thinks one of his security guys and his chief of staff might've recognized her. I don't see how that's possible but—"

"Corey," Patas pleaded.

"Anyway, Dad," he said, glancing at Patas, "we got away from the stage without being followed. And I doubt they could've known it was Patas because of all the changes to her looks and her clothes. She looks so different than when you brought her home from Sacramento after she tried to kill—"

Patas tugged on his arm and gave him a look.

"So… like I said, we're heading over to the hotel." He paused again and said before hanging up, "I love you, Dad."

As Corey placed the handset back in the cradle, he heard Patas gasp.

"Well now, isn't that touching. Brings tears to my eyes. You should've listened to her." The husky voice grew louder and more threatening as the man took a step out from behind a parked SUV. The handgun pointing at them emphasized the seriousness of their situation.

In the next several seconds, two additional men emerged from the gloomy mist, each carrying handguns. All three guns were aimed at Corey and Patas. Although the swirling fog obscured the glow of the overhead streetlamp, Corey had no trouble reading the expressions on the faces of their assailants.

While the men focused on Patas, Corey slipped a hand in his pocket and let the paper with the hotel information drop to the ground. Still unnoticed, he used his foot to slide it out of sight, under the SUV.

The spokesperson for the team motioned for the other men to make certain that neither Corey nor Patas had any weapons of their own. He talked into a handheld while leading them deeper into the shadows.

The man spoke no additional words until headlights cut through the layers of fog. The black windowless van halted next to the group. Still silent, the man watched the newly arrived men secure handcuffs on Corey and Patas and shove them inside the rear section of the van.

Before the door closed, the spokesperson leaned inside.

A small dome light painted his face into a sinister sneer. "Just to set the record straight, son. As head of the governor's private security team, I make it my business to know every employee who comes even remotely close to the governor. While we make exceptions and accommodations for religious zealots, such as Ms. Patas Ta'anari, it certainly doesn't prevent us from requiring the photo ID to show her entire face. Without, as you say, the accoutrements of an old bed sheet to hide such a striking image. Granted, she does look a little different from her original ID badge, but that's why I'm paid the big bucks."

He turned to walk away but hesitated and spun back with an enlightened expression on his face. He pointed a finger at Corey. "Well, I'll be damned. It didn't register at first. What you said earlier. *It was your father.* He was the guy who pulled Patas out of the river. Might he be the same one who left something personal behind on the Delta King?"

He moved his head closer to Corey. "I didn't catch your name, son."

Corey started muttering obscenities at his captors, but then changed his mind and smirked.

Victor Petricello laughed. "No matter. We've got the federal government's crack secret service agents working on this one. And, in particular," he paused and licked his lips, "one hot-looking lady who's put herself on the case. So it's only a matter of time before they come up with your dad's actual identity." He nodded and raised a finger. "My intuition tells me Agent Davenport knows more than she's willing to share with the governor, but that's not important, because right now we're holding a better hand. Plus, I got a few personal sources of my own."

Petricello's eyes shifted toward Patas. He placed a hand on her knee and slid it several inches up her thigh. "Don't worry, Patas, I like my women a little older." This time when he turned away, he kept walking.

Before the doors slammed shut, Corey heard him say to his partner, "The governor's not done with this one. And from the look we just saw on his wife's face, he might be needing to share. Let's get these kids to their final destination."

CHAPTER 43

On the Gulfstream's return flight to Seattle, Mike Finley had contacted Olivia Davenport. Her voice sounded urgent when cutting him short and vowing to call him back. During their second conversation, she described the attempted terrorist attack on a packed Seattle-bound commuter ferry that sailed from Bremerton.

Preliminary reports released by Governor Blackwell's campaign manager stated that the governor was the intended target. The governor's chief of staff, Thomas Steadman, cited communiques from unknown sources that an ISIS-backed Islamic group had claimed responsibility. According to Steadman, this new terrorist organization had recently sworn to prevent Governor Blackwell from entering the Oval Office. Steadman alluded to uncovering information immediately prior to the planned attack that aided authorities in stopping the threat and saving countless numbers of lives. When pressed for further details, Steadman refrained from divulging anything until such time that compromises to national security could be minimized.

For the time being, Finley chose to stay focused on the original investigation and let others substantiate the governor's claims. With the information Catori provided, Finley directed local authorities to check out the Galloway homestead near Davis but found it vacant. In a follow-up at Ethan Galloway's place of employment at UC Davis, they discovered he had called in sick and did not report in for his scheduled shift.

As Finley's flight taxied toward a waiting black Suburban at Sea-Tac, he fielded the latest report originating from an observant local police officer in Bremerton, who sighted Ethan Galloway's black Ford pick-up truck parked in a lot near the ferry terminal.

Jumping into the SUV, Finley's head spun, trying to sort out the various pieces to the latest episode in this strange saga.

What the hell did Catori's bizarre message about Galloway's mental health add to all this?

Only days ago, Olivia Davenport had called Finley for a little assistance regarding a new assignment: investigating the suspicious death of her long-time colleague, Anson Kostelecky. President Griffin had personally chosen Olivia to replace Kostelecky's position as a security consultant for presidential candidate, Governor Nicholas Blackwell, and to continue with Kostelecky's covert assignment. Finley had not been too surprised by Olivia's request, since the president had given him a heads-up last week and wanted to make sure Finley was available if his expertise was needed.

Anson Kostelecky's undercover assignment had been to investigate the growing list of potential crimes stemming from Blackwell's political organization. There had been a myriad of antidotal evidence tying Blackwell's rising star to his wife's family connections and power-grabbing operations.

Until recently, Anita's father, Daniel H. Chauncey, had been the chairman of the California democrat party, giving him control over one of the nation's largest and wealthiest political organizations. Chauncey, a native Californian, had taken charge of his family's investment corporation at an early age.

Daniel's father, a well-known and colorful celebrity in statewide politics and fundraising schemes had died in a single vehicle auto accident on an isolated stretch of the Pacific Coast Highway, north of San Francisco near the family's coastal estate. Rumors pointed to an organized crime retaliation stemming from a series of money-laundering schemes associated with accusations of gun running and drug deals. Although Chauncey's oldest son, Daniel, had only recently graduated from the Wharton School in Philadelphia, he slipped enthusiastically into the old man's shoes. Instead of striking back against presumed enemies, he joined forces with them and expanded his father's operation into one of the most influential investment organizations in the world.

CHAPTER 44

At the end of a long and trying day, Olivia Davenport dragged herself back to her hotel room. Mike Finley, who had earlier showered and shaved, pointed her to the waiting jetted tub in the lavish bath. He got busy ordering room service, which arrived as Olivia stepped into the room snuggled up in a white cotton robe.

For several moments, they sat and enjoyed the solitude of an intimate dining experience. Finley picked up his linen napkin and wiped a nonexistent spec from his lips.

"Like you suggested," Finley said, his eyes aimed at the mountains of paper on the corner writing desk, "I'm going through those files on Blackwell's organization. How in the hell did the president expect Kostelecky to make sense out of all this working by himself? It would take half the FBI at least six months to figure out where to start."

Olivia glanced over to see the files he'd separated into two stacks. The one on the left, short; the one on the right, tall. "Let me guess, Mike, the files you've read are on the left?"

He stared at her before pouring them both additional cups of coffee. With a long night ahead, they chose caffeine over alcohol. "So far, I haven't even gotten to Nicholas Blackwell himself. But the Chauncey family—that's another story. Before the old man died in the accident, or if you're into right-wing conspiracies, got wasted, his so-called investment corporation was involved with a lot of shady business deals. Once Daniel Chauncey took over the operations, all the nasty accusations faded away."

"On the surface," Olivia said, "it appeared Daniel Chauncey cleaned up this father's act. He aligned the corporation with the more successful state politicians, and almost overnight became one of the most influential businessmen in California."

"And then what, all the family's enemies disappeared?"

Olivia shrugged. "Either Daniel knew how to play nice or was too important an asset to be challenged. Seemed he liked working behind the scenes. When he became chairman of the California democrat party, he was in an influential position to manipulate large sums of money. His corporation was one of the first to take advantage of the growing unrest in the Middle East and the implications for covert dealings with foreign governments. As you might guess, the powers in Washington couldn't openly fund certain operations involving the more nefarious foreign leaders and needed a means to divert large sums of money. Apparently, Daniel

Chauncey was quite talented in that regard. After the 9/11 attacks, he turned a profitable operation into a gold mine."

Finley topped off his tepid coffee with more steaming brew from the pot and gestured to Olivia who shook her head. After taking a sip, Finley said, "I know the president has teams of investigators looking into this type of subterfuge, in general, with most of those efforts leading to dead ends. But tell me, how the hell did this two-bit, low-life loser, Nicholas Blackwell, hook-up with the likes of the most powerful democrat leader in the state?"

"You shouldn't underestimate Blackwell. So far, every opponent he's faced made that same mistake. Look what happened to the last governor of California. Thought he was a shoo-in for reelection. But along came Nicholas Blackwell. And now—nobody can recall the previous governor's name. Blackwell has this knack. When he stands up in front of an audience, he can sell them almost anything. And when he gets caught in a lie—he twists it around until you believe everything coming from behind his high-octane smile. The inside story is that Daniel Chauncey identified Blackwell's potential. He looked beyond the path that was sure to take Blackwell either to jail or an early grave. Chauncey realized that while he could control the purse strings and manipulate politicians on a national level, he'd never achieve his ultimate goal— the White House. To be the most powerful man in the world. So I guess he decided to settle on the next best thing. To *control* the most powerful man in the world."

"What about all the innuendos: the scandals from Blackwell's early days, before he entered the national arena?"

"That's where Daniel Chauncey is at his best. He can make things happen. Any time Nicholas Blackwell appeared to be in major trouble, things magically transpired. As you know, Blackwell's most serious problems stem from his purported interests in all things female. Many of Blackwell's *acquaintances* seem to have met with unfortunate accidents."

Finley let out a long breath. "What the hell kind of father would let his daughter connect with a man like Blackwell? Let alone approve of their marriage."

Olivia's face broke into a smile, and she waved a dismissive hand at the files on the desk. "What I've read in those papers about the governor's wife doesn't do any justice to the real Anita. I've only met the woman once. I'll tell you this, Mike. They deserve each other." She stopped. This time waving her hands in front of Finley's face. "Wait. I take that back. She's sicker than her husband. And that's no small task."

She leaned back in her chair and folded her arms. "Nicholas Blackwell is your typical sexual predator. Anita fits into that definition as well. But on top of that, she's also one calculating, cunning bitch."

"Since I haven't had the pleasure of meeting the governor or his wife, I'll take your word for it." He paused to look at his watch. "But for the sake of expediency, how does any of this help with the present situation?"

CHAPTER 45

Mike Finley watched Olivia push her chair back from the room-service table. She stood up, stretching her arms and paced across the hotel room. The caffeine started kicking in and her body looked edgy—wired and ready to spring. He felt the same energy pulsing in his own bloodstream. It had been a long day, but it was nowhere even close to ending. At the moment, they had no clue as to how events tied together, but they'd been in this game long enough to sense that time was running out.

Olivia paused at the window, taking in the glittery lights of Seattle. She turned back to face Finley. "For now, let's put aside the history lessons and the governor's biography. I can't even process what the hell happened today."

Finley nodded. "I followed the governor's press releases and caught soundbites from his speech at the aquarium." He stood up and walked closer to Olivia. "My bullshit meter jumped into the ionosphere."

Olivia popped open her eyes and tilted her head but remained silent.

Finley raised a finger and began counting. "First, I find it difficult to fathom that any respectable Islamic terrorist organization could believe that compared to Tyler Griffin, Nicholas Blackwell would represent the bigger threat to the worldwide growth and eventual domination of Islam and the global implementation of Sharia law."

As his fingers flew up, he rolled out his arguments. "I called my old colleagues at DHS, and while they tend to agree that the logical target of the Seattle attack was the governor, they have no credible evidence that any radical Islamic group is responsible. And as far as the governor's claims of providing key information that allowed the authorities to stop the attack—that one's got every intel department scratching their balls—and whatever you females like to scratch—trying to determine the veracity of the story. Problem with getting those facts sorted out is it'll take a congressional committee months of stonewalling and grandstanding before it's all forgotten."

Finley stopped, remembering the recent confirmed attempt on the governor's life at the theater. "There's one thing that kinda puts a monkey wrench in these so-called fake news stories spouting from the governor's office: That little incident in Sacramento the other night where they chased a real suicide bomber off seconds before she could blow herself up in front of the governor."

As Olivia tried to respond, he punched an open palm against his forehead. "Damn! That reminds me about what Catori told me today."

"Right. I almost forgot. When you called earlier you said you got the name of the guy who now has Kobe. And it sounds like this guy could be the sniper on the Delta King. Our ex-Navy SEAL." She shook her head. "You got a home address and place of employment. But so far, no sign of him."

"Not quite. A local cop located the guy's truck in a parking lot near the ferry terminal in Bremerton."

"Bremerton? The ferry involved with this terrorist plot sailed from Bremerton."

"Yeah, so I've been told." Finley smiled. He hesitated while pointing to the sofa. "Why don't you sit down?" He waited for Olivia to settle in. "Back to what Catori told me about this guy. She described two other people who showed up at the kennel with him. He had a son. His description fits the kid we saw outside the governor's mansion with Kobe."

Olivia nodded. "I love it when I'm right."

"But here's the thing. There was also a young girl tagging along with them."

"And?" Olivia gave Finley a confused look.

"Well, according to Catori's description of the girl, while it didn't completely match the news reports or the photo you showed me, she implied that the girl might've been the suicide bomber from the theater in Sacramento: Patas Ta'anari."

Finley could see a kaleidoscope of changes flowing across Olivia's face. She started-stopped speaking several times. Finally, she sighed. "Mike, remind me again—what were the details on this guy with Anson's dog?"

"I forwarded you a text with all the particulars. Didn't you get it?"

Olivia opened her mouth and grimaced. She grabbed her phone off the bedside table and punched the screen, scrolling down her messages. Finley watched what looked like the sequel to the previous display of facial expressions. He heard her muttering profanities before diving toward the desk. She scattered file folders onto the bed; some winding up on the floor. This went on for a while. Several times, Finley almost interrupted, but held his tongue.

His eyes diverted toward the minibar, flirting with the idea of dampening the circulating caffeine with an alcoholic beverage, when Olivia let out a gasp and slammed a fist down on the desk.

"Ethan Galloway. And Ethan Galloway had a wife."

Finley looked sideways at Olivia. None of that did much to alter his concentration on the minibar. He checked out an interesting vintage of white wine and was about to ask Olivia if she cared to join him.

"Ethan Galloway was married to Kinsley Galloway. She died about a year ago. It says here she committed suicide, but the circumstances were considered questionable."

Finley paused with the corkscrew held in one hand.

"Guess who Kinsley Galloway worked for?"

Finley looked from the corkscrew to the bottle of white wine to Olivia.

"Kinsley Galloway worked for Governor Nicholas Blackwell. That's why her name showed up in these files. One of his many acquaintances—to suffer an untimely death."

Finley placed the corkscrew on the counter, slid the wine bottle back in the tiny refrigerator, grabbed four mini vodka bottles, and sat on the bed next to where Olivia had plopped herself down. He twisted off all four caps and handed two bottles to Olivia, making a silent toast. In unison, they downed the vials of the eighty-proof clear liquid.

CHAPTER 46

Ethan Galloway awoke with a start and found himself in a rickety, far from comfortable bed, his clothes almost dry. He had a brief recollection of gunfire aboard a runaway ferry, escaping from a sinking dairy tanker, and crawling onto dry land, but whatever followed those harrowing experiences, for the moment, alluded his consciousness.

Enveloped in a haze of alien shadows and disconcerting scents, Ethan's brain began to assemble pieces of discordant sounds. In recent days, this rousing modus had become all too common. One of the resonating echoes knocking on the inner partitions to the mired mess inside his head was a low growling tune that he could feel through the vibrations of the squeak-prone springs on the thin mattress.

"Shhhh... Kobe," Ethan whispered as he crept from the bed and leaned an ear against the door. Not the door leading to the hotel's corridor, but the locked door to the adjoining room. He heard muffled curses seeping through the thin crevices around the marred door frame. He listened to one side of a phone conversation, while other voices interrupted: declaring Room 204 empty; no signs of their intended target.

Ethan reached into his pants pocket and retrieved a hotel key. An old-fashioned, real key—not an electronic coded plastic card. It dangled from a metal plate stamped with the numbers: *204*.

Next, he crab-walked to the exit door and placed a hand on the knob. He looked around the dimly lit room. Except for the clothes on his back and the damp and doggy-smelling Kobe, he'd brought nothing with him. With his other hand, he reached up, turning back the deadbolt latch and unhooking the tarnished security chain.

He cracked open the door and peered in both directions, finding the stale, malodorous hallway deserted. Directly across from him, an emergency exit sign glowed faintly above the door to the stairwell. After one final look, Ethan urged Kobe forward and carefully pulled open the door. They scampered down the stairs, passing the entrance door to the lobby. An additional half-flight of steps led to an emergency exit into the alleyway behind the hotel.

Ethan glanced at the sign on the locking bar across the heavy steel door. It read *Emergency Exit Only. Alarm Will Sound If Opened.*

Without hesitating, Ethan leaned against the door. A loud clicking noise burst from the door lock, but no shrieking alarm followed. Ethan and Kobe dashed down the dark, narrow alley. When they reached the end, he glanced in both directions and headed east, away from the hotel's main entrance and brightly lit boulevard.

After several blocks, Ethan diverted into a public park and found a secluded bench away from any intruding lights. He watched the first signs of a graying eastern glow seep around the sides of a high-rise office building, beckoning in the new day.

Kobe climbed onto the bench and sat next to him. He chuffed and pawed Ethan's arm, possibly inquiring about the smile on his face.

Back in the hotel room, when Ethan had stared at the key taken from his pocket, it all came back in a flood of images. He tussled Kobe's neck. "You know, boy. We're both highly trained soldiers."

Kobe shook, his ears flopping against Ethan's palm.

"But that's not where I picked up that little trick."

Kobe pawed Ethan's arm again.

"I saw it done in a movie. Seemed pretty damn lame at the time. Who the hell would fall for something like that?"

Kobe tilted his head.

Ethan now recalled that when he arrived at the hotel there was no sign of Corey or Patas. But he made the decision to check-in. He had placed a fistful of wet cash on the counter. The hotel clerk eyed the soggy bills and smirked. He informed Ethan that paying with cash was perfectly acceptable, but he did need to run his credit card through because he operated a respectable hotel.

Ethan refrained from uttering any disparaging remarks. After a brief hesitation, he slipped his VISA card across to the man's sweaty hand. When the clerk informed Ethan about the additional non-refundable pet fee, he once more bit his tongue.

Using cash was a precautionary move anyway. Ethan didn't think the authorities had discovered his identity at this point. He wasn't paranoid—well, the VA doctors had included similar words in his diagnosis—but it didn't hurt to be cautious. After entering Room 204, Ethan immediately strode toward the door to the adjoining room. He heard no signs of life, except for the native rodent population. Deciding the odds were in his favor, he gambled that the hotel was not fully booked and more than likely the adjoining room was vacant. He put his credit card to additional use, and in less than a minute both doors stood open. Ethan switched rooms. Kobe got to work ridding the new quarters of any potential pests.

One part of his returning memory of the last several hours wiped the smile from his face. He leaned back on the bench, raising his head and letting out a long breath.

Where the hell are Corey and Patas?

His hand reached into the waterproof pocket inside his jacket and came out with a sealed plastic bag. He shook his head. Something else he'd forgotten. Opening the bag, he grabbed his cell phone, along with the battery he didn't remember removing from the device.

"For once, being paranoid is a good thing."

CHAPTER 47

Mike Finley and Olivia Davenport had decisions to make; so earlier in the night, the caffeine once again won over the vodka. They continued combing through the files and discussing their options while holed up in the increasingly claustrophobic room at the Westin Seattle.

About an hour before dawn, the call had come in and Finley gave the go ahead. But by the time Olivia and Finley arrived at the seedy hotel—it was over. They now stood in the cramped hotel room inhaling stale tobacco odors and untold years of human detritus drenched in a milieu of undefinable moldy wafts of slightly more primitive life forms.

Finley was surprised they got such a quick hit on tracking Galloway's credit card transaction only hours after identifying him as their lead suspect from the Delta King stateroom. He now listened to the finger pointing, the excuses, and the blustering. Ethan Galloway had been sloppy, but not stupid. The Feds had figured it out, but not until Galloway had disappeared into the waning night air like a phantom. The only telltale clue was the scattered clumps of black fur adhering to the once white, floral-patterned; now graying remnants of a bedspread scrunched up on the threadbare carpeting in the adjoining hotel room.

Finley stood ramrod straight in the center of the dank chamber while Olivia stared through the torn curtains out the sole window that afforded a dismal view of the brick-faced wall on the opposite side of the alleyway. With his cell phone stuck to an ear, he spoke in a resigned voice after listening to updated reports on Galloway's abandoned pick-up truck in Bremerton and Galloway's house in Davis.

"Well that's something, I guess. Yeah, yeah. Get the warrants signed so there's no blowback. It's time we get lucky." In a louder voice, he added, "And possibly get on him before he splits again—leaving us with our thumbs up our asses. Let me know if anything else turns up at the guy's house. The Navy SEAL stuff confirms what I already got. No surprises. Another complication to deal with. Okay, good work. Keep me posted."

He placed the phone back in his pocket. Olivia stepped closer and said, "Time for another pick-me-up. The night's over and a new day's about to start." She grabbed hold of his arm. "Spotted a Starbucks down the street when we pulled up."

As she led Finley out the door, he said, "You're quite the detective, young lady. How did you ever find a Starbucks in Seattle?"

Finley stared into the Dark Roast Venti, looking for answers. He glanced around the bustling café, feeling even older than his years as he took in the self-absorbed millennial-driven chatter from the adjacent tables. Olivia remained quiet, and Finley detected a sullenness in her mood.

"Olivia?" Finley placed both hands around the green logo on the large container. "Galloway's military career may have nothing to do with his current motives, but the Defense Department wants us to believe he doesn't exist. We need to know what kind of baggage the guy's carrying. Could determine how he reacts when we confront him. It seems to me—whenever Ethan Galloway is close by—things tend to get interesting."

"What do you have in mind, Mike?"

Finley pulled out his cell phone, poised to press the number two speed dial. "I'm going to interrupt the president and ask him to make something happen with Galloway's files. Then—I'm on my way to Sacramento. They found a lot of paperwork from the Sacramento VA Medical Center at Galloway's house. And a bunch of empty prescription bottles in the trash. If the president can pull some strings, it might be possible for one of the doctors to give me a little insight into a man who doesn't exist."

Olivia looked skeptical. "What about patient confidentiality? Not to mention the Defense Department has redacted most of this guy's military life. Hell, we couldn't even get a real name from them."

"If I know the president, he'll use the national security card and get somebody to say something or he'll turn the Pentagon into a Walmart."

"That would at least be a first step in reducing our national debt."

"You wanna join me, Olivia? My finesse may not be sufficient to convince Galloway's physicians to speak out, and I might need some muscle."

She shot him a look and spoke slowly, as if putting together a plan of her own. "I've been AWOL from my cover assignment with the governor for way too long. Especially with these new terrorist angles. I don't want to raise any more suspicion than I've already done." She paused and then continued, "Right now it looks like the investigation into the terrorists on the ferry is hitting a wall. Seems everybody's turning up dead. I'm going to run down a few more leads here in Seattle before catching up with the governor at his next campaign stop."

Finley stared at her and reached a hand across the table, placing it on her arm. "You got something you'd care to share?"

Before she spoke, Olivia looked away and shrugged. "No, but I want to get closer to the governor. And I'm betting Galloway has a similar idea."

Finley sensed she had a more specific plan in mind but decided to let it go for now.

The expression on Olivia's face changed, looking more like her old self. "Mike. What about asking Catori to join you? From what you told me, she sounded awfully troubled by Galloway's mental health and how she imagined the VA doctors handled his case. She might be able to pick through the fog."

Finley nodded, smiled, and pointed a finger at Olivia. "Now that's what I'm talking about. Glad I thought of it."

CHAPTER 48

Sitting on the bench in a quiet corner of a city park in downtown Seattle, Ethan Galloway stared at the brightening morning sky. After a slight hesitation, he inserted the battery and powered up his cell phone. He held his breath and checked for messages.

"Damn," Ethan sighed. Nothing from Corey. There was one message received last night from an unknown number. He usually ignored calls he didn't recognize, but he decided to check this one out and punched the voicemail key.

"Thank God," Ethan murmured as he listened to Corey speak, along with Patas's comments in the background. The call log showed it had come in last night—hours ago. But there had been no sign of Corey or Patas at the hotel.

Beginning to panic, he almost forgot to shut down his phone. Once he did that, he automatically opened the back cover and yanked out the battery. He didn't think the phone had been on long enough to be a problem but decided to get up off the bench and stay mobile while he tried to determine his next move.

For the last several days he had struggled to maintain focus. At times his mind appeared sharp and functional, but then with no warning he lost concentration and his thoughts jumped to past incidents, blotting out the more immediate problems of the day.

"Keep it together, Ethan. Think it through," he murmured. Kobe stared up at him as Ethan led them out of the park and back onto the street. Although it was a Sunday morning, traffic had increased significantly since Ethan had escaped the confrontation at the hotel. He felt safer with the pedestrian numbers building around him at the start of a new day in Seattle.

Ethan grappled with the memory of Corey's words. If need be, he'd listen to the message again, but that would require powering up the phone. He could do that—but only if necessary.

"So they got off the ferry. No problems." Ethan knew that the terrorists' plans had been stopped. The bad guys got away, but at least none of the passengers had been hurt. He wasn't so sure about members of the crew. "Where the hell are you, Corey? You said you were heading to the hotel. Based on the time you left this message, you should've gotten there long before I did."

Now, not only was Kobe staring, but pedestrians started looking askance at him; most keeping their distance as he talked to himself. Deciding not to draw unwarranted attention, he continued processing Corey's message without additional verbal outbursts.

In his head, Ethan again tried to interpret what Corey and Patas had said. Patas sounded upset—and frightened. Corey had strived to downplay her concerns. Still, Ethan detected a wariness in his voice. If they had been close enough for someone from the governor's staff to spot them, it wasn't beyond the realm of possibility that a security person might've identified her. The changes made to her appearance wouldn't stand up to much scrutiny. He realized that at work Patas always had her face covered, but then he remembered that after getting her into his pick-up truck following their stint in the Sacramento River, he'd pulled a photo ID from her pocket. And Patas's picture had shown her without any facial coverings.

Ethan worked himself into a full-blown panic. If the governor's personal security team picked up Patas, there's no way in hell they'd turn her over to the real authorities. The governor had too much to lose if she got a chance to tell her story. They would stop at nothing to finish the job. They wouldn't care who Corey was either. He'd be just as dead as Patas.

Ethan knew he didn't have a whole lot of time. He needed to determine the governor's next scheduled appearance. Where would he go between now and election day? He'd turn to the internet and research the governor's itinerary. That's where he'd start. The quickest way to do that—power-up his cell phone and get to work. If he were careful, he could minimize the risk of any would-be trackers by keeping on the move and not leaving the phone turned on for any length of time.

The feds had his name and were following his electronic trail. The chances they'd soon latch onto his cell phone activity were pretty damn good.

CHAPTER 49

After a quick morning boost at Starbuck's, Mike Finley got his act together. The wheels of his Gulfstream hit the tarmac at Fairchild Air Force base, a few miles west of Spokane, Washington. After taxiing to a civilian-designated aviation building and picking up a second passenger, it immediately returned to runway five for the final leg of the early morning flight to the Sacramento area.

When Catori Torrence climbed the sleek jet's extended stairway, she turned and waved to the pilot of the CBP helicopter who had flown her to the base about fifteen minutes earlier. Walking down the G550's aisle, she approached the only other passenger on board and gave him a quick peck on the cheek before taking the facing seat across the table.

Finley had been staring out the window at the Border Patrol's UH-1 helicopter and the beaming face on the pilot. "McCarthy looks a lot happier than the last time *I* flew with him. Your brother too busy to try and shoot him down for trespassing at the camp? If you had cell phone service, we wouldn't have to keep dropping in unannounced."

"No problem. Paco's getting used to the government's big white eagle swooping in over the riverbanks. And the kids get a kick out of watching the chopper fly in. Can't say it does a whole lot for reinforcing the cultural traditions we've been teaching them." She shrugged. "McCarthy's smiling because he not only got a bowl of hot soup, but I gave him the recipe too. Says he's looking forward to his wife shooting a turkey and whipping up a batch for the family."

"Wife? The kid's married? I assumed he still lived at home with his mom and dad."

"Well… *the kid*, as you call him, also has two boys and a girl of his own. From what I gather, he's committed to building a self-sufficient lifestyle in case the government succeeds in destroying the entire infrastructure of our country."

Finley snorted. "Spoken like a trusted federal employee." He slapped a hand on the table. "And his wife gets to shoot his dinner before cooking it? The guy is a true Idahoan. Hey. You heard the joke about Idaho women, didn't you?"

Catori reached across the table and pinched Finley's cheek. "It's not a joke, Mike."

Finley nodded. "Hell, Olivia's a better shot than me… and she's from Philadelphia."

"When McCarthy picked me up, Paco hitched a ride to the tribal police headquarters in Plummer. McCarthy seemed okay with the little side trip… I hope it didn't cause a problem."

"Long as the kid's good with it," Finley said, studying Catori's face.

"Paco overheard McCarthy fill me in on your plans. That's how he got the idea to head back to civilization."

Finley's eyes narrowed. "As I recall, I never gave any details to McCarthy."

Catori winked and said, "That much was clear to me. I managed to deduce the main purpose of this trip and gave Paco the abbreviated version."

Finley nodded and Catori resumed, "Paco has a friend who works at the VA Medical Center in Sacramento. They both wrestled for the same team in high school. I think Dakota was a senior when Paco joined the squad as a freshman."

Catori paused, looking out the window. The jet banked sharply, and its rate of ascent slowed as they approached cruising altitude. "Paco called right before you landed at Fairchild. He spoke to Dakota. Dr. Dakota Wohehiv. He's interning in psychiatry at the VA."

Finley interrupted. "Dr. Wo… Wohe—what?"

Smiling, Catori said, "Dakota's patients call him Dr. Dak."

"I would've guessed—*Dr. Who*."

"Cute, Mike. Anyway, Paco figured—what with all the government red tape—even with the potential prodding of the president—a little inside help might speed things along. He expects that while you're waving the national security card to bully the staff, they'll hide behind patient confidentiality to keep you in the dark."

Finley's eyes opened wider, and he placed both hands on the table. "And the jury's still out on why the DoD is trying to reinvent his military record. So… is Ethan Galloway a patient of this Dr. Dak?"

"Paco wasn't too clear about what exactly Dakota's involvement was with Ethan, but he did say Dakota promised to make himself available to talk to us and would try to help in any way he could."

* * * * * *

The Sacramento VA Medical Center was located a short distance east of the city of Sacramento in an area called Rancho Cordova. The Gulfstream touched down at Mather Airport, a former military base about a quarter mile from the sprawling veterans complex. A local cab driver deposited Finley and Catori in the oval turnout adjacent to the hospital's main entrance.

Finley was supposed to check in with a bureaucratic liaison from the Department of Veterans Affairs. After paying the cab fare, Finley stretched his arms and sucked in a mouthful of the cool, crisp autumn air. He'd been to California's Central Valley in August and had experienced more than his share of the sauna-like nature of the beast in one of the nation's most prolific agricultural regions.

His eyes rested on a facility sign at the opposite end of the drive. When Catori started in the direction of the administrative offices, Finley called her back and pointed. "Let's do this my way."

Catori shifted her eyes to the blue-muraled sign. "Is this where I tell you that stepping on toes may not be the best medicine?"

"Nope. This is where you use your powers to tell me when I've stepped on the right toes."

Finley led the way, skirting around the typical drab-looking government structures, following the arrows, and winding up in front of the Behavioral Health Unit building. He held the door open for Catori.

"You have a name?"

"I've got lots of names, Catori. The president's office emailed official requests of compliance to every employee with any conceivable chance of ever interacting with Ethan Galloway."

Almost four hours later, the conference room door closed behind Finley and Catori after the director of the Behavioral Health Unit apologized to Finley for him having to travel to the VA Medical Center, when the same information he gathered could've been forwarded to him by an official military courier. In the spirit of cooperation with President Griffin's wishes, the director had arranged for staff physicians to meet with Finley and discuss the standard procedures in place for evaluating and treating veterans who exhibit signs of PTSD.

Following a string of unproductive meetings, Finley and Catori walked back through the lobby. He waved the package containing the identical redacted and edited documents he already had in his possession prior to making this trip. He sighed. "Well, it was worth a shot. Right now we're still trying to get a handle on what makes Ethan Galloway tick. The president warned me that if there is any cover-up involving Galloway's military record, it's going to require a congressional investigation to look into potential wrongdoings by the Pentagon."

Catori's phone buzzed as they exited the building. While Catori spoke in hushed tones, Finley paced the parking lot. She ended the conversation and called out to him, "Let's go back to the hospital's main entrance and grab a cab."

She headed off, reversing the path from earlier this morning. Struggling to keep pace, Finley said, "What's up?"

Catori climbed into the rear seat of the first cab in line in the taxi waiting zone. As Finley pushed in beside her, she gave the cab driver an address. When Finley placed a hand on her shoulder, she responded, "Trust me, Mike."

Chapter 50

The cab driver gunned the engine, driving around the VA hospital turnout and onto the street. He glanced in the rearview mirror and said to Finley, "She correct, sir. I take you best Mexican cantina in whole Sacramento area. My wife father—he top cook in kitchen." He reached into his shirt pocket and handed Finley a business card. "Tell them Alejandro bring you. They treat you extra good."

The lunch crowd had thinned by the time they walked into the restaurant. Finley's stomach growled in protest, responding to the rich aromas swirling about the bright, cheery dining area.

Catori patted a palm on Finley's stomach.

Surprised and embarrassed, he said, "You couldn't possibly have heard that."

She shrugged. "It doesn't take any special powers to sense the obvious."

"Besides," she whispered, placing a hand on her own stomach, "you may have a little competition." Her head darted around the room which looked about two-thirds empty. She grabbed Finley's arm. "Come on, Mike. This way."

Catori glided across the room, maneuvering the gaps between the close-spaced tables with a grace that Finley could only accomplish in his dreams. She targeted a booth in the far corner of the room; in a spot where the sun's rays glaring through the restaurant's front windows failed to penetrate. The rustic overhead lighting fixtures did little to illuminate the anxious face on the sole denizen of the booth.

The lone figure sat braced against the high-backed leatherette seat cushion, huddled into the corner, facing the breadth of the restaurant. A laminated grease-smudged menu stood propped on the butcher block surface of the table in such a configuration as to prevent anyone a decent view of the young man sitting in the booth.

Catori leaned across the bench seat, having to shimmy a knee on the cushion to get into position, and applied a chaste kiss on the man's cheek. Mission accomplished, Catori scooted around to the seat on the opposite side of the table and motioned for Finley to sit next to her.

In a modulated tone she introduced Dr. Dakota Wohehiv to Agent Mike Finley. Dispensing with formalities, the two men agreed on Dak and Mike.

Finley, taken aback by Dakota's slight, almost frail stature, blurted out, "So you wrestled on the same team with Catori's brother?"

A broad smile erased part of the angst on the young man's face. "Yes, but we were on the same team for only one year. I was a senior when Paco first started high school. And we became good friends."

"I'm assuming you didn't challenge each other for the same weight class?"

"Not even close. And until a growth spurt in my senior year, I competed in the lowest weight group."

Finley couldn't imagine a smaller rendition of Dr. Dakota Wohehiv.

Dakota peered over the table at the stack of files Finley had placed on the seat between him and Catori. "They give you those papers at the VA?"

Finley nodded.

"Learn anything today, you didn't know before?"

Finley glanced at Catori before answering. "No offense, Dak. But if I didn't have a clock and calendar on my phone, none of the bureaucrats at the VA Medical Center would've admitted to the time or day." He let out a long breath. "But that's nothing new. I've been dealing with government lackeys in D.C. for my entire career."

The waitress came and took their orders. She returned with three icy bottles of Corona. Finley watched Catori take a protracted swig and wipe her lips with the back of her hand. When he glanced at Dakota, he saw the young doctor carefully place the bottle on the cardboard coaster and dab his lips with a paper napkin pulled from the chrome dispenser.

Dr. Wohehiv, or Dr. Dak to his patients, cleared his throat, smiled at Catori, and with a sudden air of confidence, addressed Agent Mike Finley. "My specialty is psychiatry. The decision to go to med school came after the military rejected my application to serve. I was troubled by watching friends head off to fight our enemies. Many returning home in body bags. Or critically wounded; either physically or mentally—sometimes both."

He paused, and in a well-rehearsed-sounding monolog said, "My first choice was to practice medicine as a surgeon, but for obvious reasons, I chose psychiatry."

Knowing this was a prompt, Finley responded, "I'm not sure what you mean, Dak."

After a quick smile to Catori, Dakota said, "My name, Wohehiv, roughly translated, means *dull knife*."

"I can appreciate that," Finley said. "Based on the meaning of my family name, *fair-haired warrior*, I decided on a career fighting for my country."

"Seems to me, Mike," Catori interjected, "you had no clue as to the translated meaning of *Finley* until I enlightened you about the legend last year."

He frowned and wiped a hand over his shaved scalp before turning back to Dakota. "Please… go on."

"As you know, I'm currently interning here at the Sacramento VA Medical Center. A staff member in the Behavioral Health Unit. One of our major and most challenging tasks is to work with the large number of returning vets who show signs of post-traumatic stress disorder, or PTSD."

He sighed. "We doctors at the VA take this seriously, although I understand the public considers the federal system has been acting with neglect and incompetence, while determined to sweep many of the medical issues of our brave soldiers under the rug." Dakota momentarily lost his focus and then nodded. "So when I got my assignment to work at the Sacramento VA hospital, I was excited to learn about an innovative pilot program. From what I'd been told, there were only a handful of medical centers in the entire VA system incorporating this experimental approach to PTSD patients. And now, I believe we are the only one remaining."

"And Ethan Galloway was a part of this program?" Finley asked. When he looked down, he was surprised to find his bottle of Corona drained and his plate empty. He decided not to order another beer just yet.

"Yes. And as far as I can determine, he is still enrolled in the project."

"Can you be more specific about this treatment and what impact it could have on Galloway's behavior?"

Dakota hesitated. His head jerked up and his eyes darted around the restaurant before settling on Catori. "As a physician, patient confidentiality is important." He shrugged and looked at Finley. "Words I am sure you've heard over and over again since you arrived at the center this morning."

Finley looked at Catori and then back to Dakota.

Again, Dakota turned to Catori, his eyes softening. "I hadn't spoken to Paco in several months, so when he called me earlier today, I was pleased to hear from him. I listened to his story with great interest. Based on how you are involved with Ethan Galloway, Catori, and what I've learned about this particular program, I have a moral obligation to tell you what I know."

Dakota raised a hand to a passing waitress and signaled for three more beers. No one objected. By the time the next round of drinks arrived, he had made good headway into explaining the basic tenets of the experimental PTSD treatment program.

"So, if I get what you're saying in regard to this memory modification technique," Finley said, "for it to be most effective, it requires the treatment to start close to the event in question."

Dakota nodded his approval. "Exactly. But for our soldiers returning home from the battlefield, most don't show symptoms until much later. Perhaps months or years after the initial trauma took place. When I questioned Dr. Kumar Chakraborty, the founder of this program, about this he… well, it's safe to say he did not take kindly to my criticism."

"Dr. Kumar Chak… Chakra… whatever. Wasn't he the same narcissistic bastard who took charge of the meetings this morning?" Finley asked Catori.

She nodded and turned to Dakota. "What happened next?"

"At first, the awkward encounter appeared to blow over. But several days later I received a new assignment. They transferred me to a different section. One using a more traditional approach: group therapy sessions and the usual regimen of pharmaceutical interventions."

Finley leaned forward. "Exactly how many patients are enrolled in *Kumar's* pet project?"

Dakota held up a single finger. "Right now, it's Ethan Galloway."

Finley exhaled. His head was spinning. His guts churned, sending out warning signals he couldn't decipher, but leaving an acidy bite that dwarfed the recently swallowed burritos now roiling in a sudsy sea of Corona.

All of a sudden, the booth felt stifling. Finley turned away from Dakota and Catori, eyes flitting around the restaurant. He tried to unravel what he'd heard and focus on how any of it related to Olivia's investigation. Was Galloway just another PTSD statistic; a misdiagnosed and mistreated vet trapped in a bureaucratic nightmare of incompetence? Part of a failed experimental government project? Was the VA neglecting the warning signs of a disassembling brain and allowing Galloway to fend for himself in an imagined world inside his head? Or was he part of some insidious plot orchestrated by a clandestine military operation?

Collecting himself, Finley kept those thoughts inside and motioned to Dakota.

"For days after being dismissed by Dr. Chakraborty, I considered my options. Finally, I decided to confront him. When I got to his outer office, the room was empty; his secretary had already left for the day. I knew Chakraborty was still inside. I heard voices coming from his private office. After getting this far, I figured if I didn't confront him now, I'd lose my nerve. So I marched up to the closed door, but when I raised my hand to knock, the words I overheard gave me pause, so instead I leaned in closer and listened."

CHAPTER 51

Mike Finley, intent on understanding Dr. Dakota Wohehiv's story, noted a tightness building on the young doctor's face, as if he himself were suffering a trauma similar to his patients.

"I almost forgot," Dakota said. "As I listened to the conversation taking place behind the closed door to Dr. Chakraborty's office, I glanced down at his secretary's desk. The appointment calendar was still open. According to the last entry, Chakraborty had two visitors with him. They were from the Department of Defense: more specifically, the DSI." He looked up at Finley. "That's the—"

"Department of Special Investigation," Finley said for Catori's benefit.

Dakota continued, "I heard one of them mention the name *Ethan Galloway*. And that ratcheted up my interest.

Chakraborty was trying to placate the two men—persuade them he had everything under control."

Finley asked, "When did this encounter take place?"

"About two weeks ago. The men pressed Chakraborty to stabilize Galloway's level of conformance—or more drastic measures would be needed. They said since Galloway was the primary test subject, the resource with the longest time span and the highest number of displacement episodes recorded, any breakdown in his treatment could jeopardize exposure of the entire failed operation and threaten a lot of careers."

Dakota checked his watch and glanced toward the door.

"From the tone of the conversation," Dakota said, "it was clear the two men had made their point and given Chakraborty an ultimatum. I heard them getting ready to leave, so I ran from the outer office as quickly as possible. After reaching the corridor, I hurried around the corner and into a tiny alcove where I sat down on a cushioned armchair. My face was hidden behind a medical journal when the two men in the office strode by speaking in hushed voices."

"What did you do next?" Catori asked.

"Before I had the chance to make up my mind, a code sounded over the PA system requesting Dr. Chakraborty's immediate presence in suite two of the E.R. I peeked around the corner just as he exited his office heading toward the staff elevator. The next thing I knew I found myself standing by his office door, trying to turn the knob."

Finley shook his head. "I trust that a man like *Kumar* would never be careless enough to leave his private office door unlocked."

Dakota shrugged. "And you'd be correct in your assumption, Mike." He looked at Catori. "But I haven't forgotten several tricks I learned from your brother. And those cheap government locks aren't very secure. In a matter of seconds, I had the door open and was standing behind Chakraborty's desk. In his haste, he left Galloway's file on top. I scanned through the papers and found the same redacted nonsense you've already seen. I knew Chakraborty must have the real version somewhere, but that's not what I saw on the desk."

Dakota's eyes scanned the restaurant again and he lowered his voice. "But those DSI guys left him some new information. Under the folder was a single sheet of paper. I made a copy. Maybe you can make more sense out of it than me."

Dakota reached inside his jacket pocket and pulled out a folded piece of paper. He slid it across the table to Finley. After a quick handshake to Finley and a peck on the cheek to Catori, Dakota slid out of the booth and scurried across the restaurant, disappearing through the door and into the warm California sun.

CHAPTER 52

Corey Galloway's head started to clear, but when he tried opening his eyes, only darkness surrounded him. He had no idea of the time, or where they'd taken him and Patas. After handcuffed and tossed in the back of a van, one of the men had stabbed a needle in his arm and everything turned black.

He wiggled his hands and realized the cuffs were gone. When he attempted to shift his body, he was surprised to find no restraints of any kind. He leaned forward and set both hands on the floor. Propping himself to his knees, he tried standing up. Hit with an overwhelming wave of nausea, he cupped his hands to his mouth and dry-heaved until the galaxy of shooting stars in his head winked out, and he wound up splayed and unconscious on the floor.

A dim sound scratched the void and grabbed a thread from the shadows. Corey struggled to focus and caught a glimpse of recognition. The mellow sounds coalesced into a familiar voice. This time his consciousness settled on a welcoming brilliance, and Patas's soothing words as she cradled his head on her lap, repeating his name.

He took several shallow breaths. With Patas's help, he moved to a sitting position next to her. For the moment, he made no further attempts to stand. After gazing at Patas and making sure he was no longer dreaming, his eyes scanned the chamber, which was now bathed in light.

The room, about twenty feet square, contained a king-sized bed with blankets and sheets in a rumpled pile. A small table was turned on its side next to the bed; otherwise, the room was bare. The walls, about eight feet high, consisted of light brown rough-hewned vertical wood planks. The tiled flooring, cold and damp to the touch, had an intricate mosaic pattern with muted earth-toned colors. On one wall, he saw two small rectangular windows near the ceiling. They appeared shuttered from the outside, precluding the penetration of any natural light. Assuming it was daytime. Several recessed fixtures running along the center of the ceiling provided a bright, almost harsh, illumination. Opposite the high-mounted windows stood a dark oak-paneled windowless door, anchored and hinged in a heavy wooden frame.

"I heard you trying to stand. I was awake but afraid to move. Several times I called out, but—"

Corey finished Patas's sentence. "I puked and passed out."

"I discovered the handcuffs were gone, and I wasn't restrained but got dizzy whenever I moved—so I waited till my head stopped spinning."

"Good thinking. I'll try to remember that the next time we're handcuffed, thrown in the back of a van, and drugged."

Feeling near human again, Corey pushed himself up to his feet. He stood motionless, waiting for a repeat performance, but he found that he could move one foot in front of the other without getting sick.

He pointed to the messy bed and overturned table. "Looks like maid service in this place leaves something to be desired."

"My fault." Patas stood and clasped her hands. "When I started to explore in the dark, I stumbled onto the bed… and sorta freaked out. I flailed around till I fell onto that table and knocked it over." She shrugged. "After calming down, I felt my way along the walls until my hand bumped into the light switch."

Corey nodded and began walking around the room. He first checked the door, confirming it was locked. Next, he reached up toward the windows and determined they afforded no practical means of escape.

Discouraged, Corey leaned against the wall and slipped to the floor. Patas took several tentative steps forward and sat down next to him.

He shut his eyes and then heard her say, "Who's Saba?"

He turned with his mouth open and his eyes blinking. "W—what?"

"Saba. You yelled that name while your dad carried me into the house after I tried running away. Why would Saba want to kill me?"

He stiffened and his body shrank from her. His eyes narrowed and the words came out before he could think. "Saba was my great grandfather. On my mother's side." He gave Patas a tight smile and continued, "Before bringing his family to America, he fought in the Israeli military. Against the Palestinian invaders. All the Muslims in the Middle East want to destroy Israel. And now they're trying to do the same thing in America. My dad fought in Afghanistan to stop Islamic terrorists from taking over the world."

"So, you're Jewish?" Patas said with a wry look.

"Half. My dad's family is Methodist. You got a problem with that?"

She smiled and shook her head. "But you seem to have concerns with me being a Muslim."

Confused and shaken, Corey looked up and let out a long breath. His eyes stopped on a tiny, dome-shaped protrusion in the center of the ceiling. Its color matched the adjacent materials but possessed a slight opaqueness.

With his face darkening, Corey pushed himself up and stood beneath the object and raised his middle finger, mouthing the associated expletive.

Patas covered her mouth and exclaimed, "Oh! You think someone is—"

With a loud clank and an agonizing screech, the oak door swung open.

CHAPTER 53

Corey and Patas flinched. He pulled her to his side and stepped forward, trying to shield her.

Victor Petricello strode into the room and moved to the left. His weapon was in plain view but secured in his shoulder holster. A second later Anita Blackwell filled the doorway, the glaring lights making her appear more ominous than the governor's hostile security chief with a gun.

Cold droplets of sweat trickled down Corey's back as he stared at the governor's wife. He watched a dark shadow ripple across her harsh features, but a moment later Anita Blackwell's lips curled into a small smile as she stepped inside.

She looked past Corey and nodded at Patas. "This is the first time we meet in person. The video didn't do you justice. Nicholas seemed to enjoy himself though. Sorry I missed it."

She turned to Corey and the cold sweat evaporated as his skin crawled with a burning heat. "Victor's done a little digging—assisted by a well-paid source in Washington—and found out you're a Galloway. Kinsley Galloway's little boy. Did they tell you I had the pleasure of meeting your mother? But never did have the opportunity to really get to know her. So unfortunate. To die so young. She was in such a state that night."

Anita walked over to the bed. She pushed the heaped covers aside. After sitting down on the edge of the mattress, she gestured for Patas to come closer. Corey wanted to hold her back, but Patas gave a slight shake of her head and took a step forward. He could see her resolve falter; and her eyes dropped down, failing to return Anita's glare.

The governor's wife frowned. "For a pretty young lady, I'm disappointed in the pitiful wardrobe selections you seem to choose." She shook her head. "I've seen the video of you wearing that ridiculous *Muslim* outfit. And when Nicholas got done with you, the formless sheets looked even worse."

She rose from the bed and circled Patas, her eyes acting like knives.

"I don't fancy your current choice of clothing either. Much too masculine. Why don't you slip out of those jeans?"

"Stop it!" Corey cried out.

Steadman raised a hand for Corey to stay put and, at the same time, lifted his weapon from its holster, holding it at his side.

Patas raised her head and faced the governor's wife. A lone tear trickled down her cheek, but she made no attempt to stop it. Keeping her gaze on the despicable woman, Patas lowered a shaking hand to her waist and yanked the brass buckle. Thumbing open the button, she slid down the zipper and the loose-fitting jeans tumbled to the floor. She lifted each foot from the gathered material and kicked Corey's old jeans aside.

Anita leaned forward and scraped her polished nails down Patas's thigh. Corey swallowed a lump and closed his eyes at the advent of tiny welts trailing behind the clawing fingers.

Anita chuckled and squeezed a palm against Patas's backside. "Hard to appreciate your butt when it's lost in those baggy briefs." She looked down at the jeans strewn on the floor, back to the shirt Patas still wore, and turned to Corey. "Are these *your* clothes?"

Corey narrowed his eyes but remained silent.

"What else have you two shared?"

Corey's head swam with unbidden images of his mother. The troubling times between his parents after his dad returned home from his final stint overseas. The harrowing sounds of the bitter argument on the last night he saw his mom. The haunted look on his father's face when he spoke those words: *Corey… your mom is dead.*

A final burst of jarring thoughts rained down from within and formed a startling revelation.

"Why don't you leave her alone—you sick old bitch."

Patas's mouth dropped open.

Anita Blackwell didn't flinch. Instead, she threw back her head and let out a blood-curdling laugh. When she settled down, she glanced around the room and shrugged.

To herself she mumbled, "We talked about installing a minibar. Pity it hasn't been done."

Anita moved away from Patas and sat back on the bed, near the footboard. Looking at Corey, she said, "I didn't take you for the jealous type, but perhaps you want her all to yourself."

She patted a hand on the mattress and winked at him. "I've left you two plenty of room." To Patas she said, "Would you please unbutton your flannel shirt. It's *so* not feminine. Don't you agree, Corey?"

He closed his eyes. "Stop it. Please… stop it."

Patas finished unbuttoning the shirt and placed her arms across her breasts as the fabric dropped open, exposing the smooth olive flesh on her stomach.

"Corey," the governor's wife purred, "she's all yours… at least for now." She wagged a finger at him. "Leave a little for the governor. Once this damn election is over, we're going to celebrate." She looked back at Patas. "It's an honor to be ravished by the president-elect. You must've known this day would come. That's why you were so determined to live."

She prompted Corey. "I want you to step up behind Patas and slip the shirt off her shoulders. Let's get a better look at the rest of her undergarments. Unless you're kinkier than I thought, I'm guessing the bra peeking out behind Patas's modesty doesn't belong to you. Perhaps it's your mother's?"

Corey's body tensed and then started to shake. "Shut up! Shut the hell up and leave her alone!"

Anita's face hardened and she glowered at Corey. "I'm not telling you again. Get to work."

Patas shifted her head toward Corey. She whispered, "It's okay, Corey. It's okay. Do what she says."

Corey's eyes filled with tears, quenching the rage fighting from within. He took a half-step in Patas's direction. With an agonizing scream he switched course and lunged at the governor's wife.

Steadman must've sensed what was going to happen. As Corey's hands swiped at Anita's neck, the butt of Steadman's pistol smashed down on his head. Corey's body sagged and slumped to the floor at Anita's feet.

CHAPTER 54

Ethan Galloway's mood darkened as the day wore on. He searched the internet, combing through any articles on Governor Blackwell that might provide clues as to the whereabouts of Corey and Patas. He'd easily obtained the governor's scheduled appearances for the final run-up to election day, but Ethan didn't believe he'd conceal the kids anywhere near his public events. The need to keep on the move and constantly remove the phone's battery in between short search intervals made his digging more complicated.

Having Kobe with him limited the options on where Ethan could go. When the charge level on the battery became critical, he sequestered himself at a quiet sitting area inside a hotel lobby, plugging the phone's charger in an outlet behind a potted plant. For a while, he took advantage of the hotel's free Wi-fi service and resumed checking out data on Governor Blackwell. He'd done an exhaustive search of properties owned by the governor and his wife. The list proved long, and he had no way of knowing which locations to eliminate or if additional properties were titled in ways to avoid public scrutiny.

Frustrated, Ethan leaned back in the cushioned armchair. A sudden thought hit him, and he let out a sigh.

"You freakin' idiot."

He said the words loud enough for several guests seated nearby to get up and move to the opposite side of the lobby. Ethan didn't have to look at himself in the mirror to conclude that the current state of his wardrobe did little to help him blend into any upscale hotel environment. Time to move on before he garnered any more attention that could alert the hotel's security personnel.

He yanked the charger out of the wall outlet and grabbed Kobe's leash. "Let's go, boy. There's somebody I'd like you to meet."

Ethan exited the hotel and walked a short distance before stopping in the small vestibule of a boutique bookstore. He pulled out his phone and tapped in an address on Google maps and studied his proposed route. He checked his bearings by noting the street signs at the nearby corner; then removed the phone's battery and marched off to his intended destination.

"Two can play at this game," he muttered to Kobe. "They might be homing in on our location, but they'll need a visual for our next move. For now, no more electronic tracking. We're going to visit an old friend in person. And he might have a few tricks to help us out."

Chapter 55

Mike Finley looked around the nearly deserted Mexican cantina and tapped his fingers on the folded paper left by Dr. Dakota Wohehiv. Pursing his lips, he glanced at Catori and picked up the paper. After flattening the unfolded document on the table, he stared at it long enough for Catori to nudge his shoulder. He slid it closer so she could get a better look.

"I'm seeing more letters than a can of alphabet soup. But what's it all mean, Mike?"

Finley sighed, pressed both hands to his face, and rubbed his eyes. "More like we're about to open up a can of worms."

She looked puzzled and repeated the question.

"To add to your confusion, I'll give you three more letters: *CYA*."

"Since this looks like a government document, I guess I'm not surprised. But exactly whose ass needs to be covered?"

"Although the various intel organizations use different protocols and equipment to circumvent the minimal legal requirements to violate a citizen's right to privacy, I'm positive this document represents the DSI's initial filing to obtain a court order to track and download data from Ethan Galloway's cell phone. And look at this date." He paused, tapping a finger on the upper right corner of the sheet. "According to Dakota, the meeting in Dr. Chakraborty's office at the VA Center took place two weeks ago. This document indicates a court filing back in March of this year—almost eight months ago."

Catori shook her head. "I'm not following."

"Okay. First, there are several technologies available to track locations, cell phone calls, internet usage, etc. The government no longer needs to subpoena cell phone carriers to obtain customer records. For years it's been possible to acquire surveillance information using equipment designed to simulate the carrier's cell phone tower and trick the user's phone into connecting to it. We can also hack into a cell phone and insert Trojan software, which remains dormant and undetectable until we activate it."

Catori reached into her pocket and pulled out her cell phone. After studying it for several seconds, she pressed the power button to shut it off. She looked up and smiled at Finley.

"If it were only that simple. You may think that if you shut off your device, it can no longer be tracked, but that may not be true for several reasons. Depending on the operating system, the carrier, or the hardware itself, you may just be placing your phone into standby mode. Meaning signals are still emitted and picked up by cell towers which can be used to triangulate your position. This can all occur without the phone being hacked. Once the malware placed on the device is activated, we can simulate almost any condition we want. So while you think you're safe by powering off the phone, that's not always the case."

Catori nodded and flipped over her phone, placing it screen-side down on the table. She pressed the indents on the back cover and popped it off. Using her fingernail, she slid out the battery and set it down next to the open phone case.

"Can you hear me now, Mike?" She tilted her head and raised her brows.

Finley folded his arms and nodded. "That *does* work. But how many people go to all that bother?"

Catori mimicked Finley's actions, and said, "If I recall, didn't the NSA assure us they were not listening in on any private conversations?"

"Yes, they did *say* that. And for the most part, it's true."

"For some reason that doesn't make me feel all warm and fuzzy."

"There are specific guidelines required by the federal government to obtain a court order to allow for the insertion and activation of the surveillance software." He pointed at the DSI document on the table. "However, sometimes these legal avenues can be misused or forged or obtained after the fact. And if that's not bad enough, local authorities have much less stringent hoops to jump through when striving to invade your privacy. This is likely an example of one or more of the above."

"So, what happens next?"

Finley gathered up the document and shoved it into the file folder on the seat. He grabbed his wallet and threw down enough cash to cover the food and drinks, along with a generous tip. Picking up the folder, he motioned to Catori and headed out of the restaurant.

Finley's agitation ratcheted up while they waited for a cab to take them back to Mathers Airport and the refueled Gulfstream.

Catori interrupted his thoughts. "Are you saying the military is tracking Ethan Galloway's location and intercepting his phone calls and monitoring his internet usage?"

He turned to Catori, shaking his head. "Up until now, they probably didn't think it necessary. From what Dakota said, this Kumar character likely convinced them Galloway could be controlled."

Finley paused and cursed under his breath before continuing, "Goddammit, Catori. When I started making waves and tried to cut through all the bullshit preventing me from identifying Galloway's fingerprints—I may have signed his death warrant."

"But why would they want him dead in the first place?"

Finley put her question aside for the moment and concentrated on what needed to be done. "I'll worry about that later; for now I'm going to try and beat them at their own game." That was his excuse for stepping on any rights that Ethan Galloway had left. Although in his favor—he now had probable cause.

Catori shivered and held her arms against her chest. The California sun, even in the fall, should've kept her warm, but Finley noticed a decided chill run through her body. "Not sure what you've got in mind, Mike, but—could I tag along?"

Finley didn't say anything. He smiled and nodded.

Before they boarded their flight for the short trip to Seattle, Finley had made the necessary calls to set the wheels in motion.

CHAPTER 56

The distance proved longer than Ethan anticipated, and he grew anxious to get to his destination. Figuring he'd be safe for the moment, he attempted to flag down a cab. The first two drivers, after staring at Kobe, sped away without acknowledging Ethan. With Kobe crouched behind a wire trash container, the third cab pulled over in response to Ethan's hand signal. Before the driver spotted the extra passenger and had a chance to protest, Ethan wrenched open the door. Kobe jumped in first.

The driver smiled and said, "I had a German Shepherd when I was a boy."

Ethan nodded and recited a street name in Seattle's Central District. He gave the driver a house number about a block away from his real destination. In less than ten minutes they arrived at a residential section near Lake Washington. He paid the driver, who never questioned the damp bills handed to him. As he pulled away, he saluted Ethan through the open window and called out, "That's a great dog you got."

Ethan waved and started walking. After the cab disappeared around the corner, he crossed the street and headed in the opposite direction. When he got to the correct street number, he paused and gazed up at a Tudor-styled home tucked back from the road and shielded by dense, mature landscaping. A large, concrete-walled garage with a set of six wood batten doors formed the right-side border of a formidable stone retaining wall. Ethan climbed the slate steps of the path leading to the main residence, admiring the house's rich, brown boarded framework and pale-yellow stucco. His eyes shifted to a small security sign next to the walkway that informed visitors the premises were guarded by a renowned security company. This caused Ethan to chuckle. When Kobe shot a glance in his direction, he whispered, "I'm sure this place is protected by a much more sophisticated system than any of its neighbors."

Before Ethan had a chance to place a foot on the first porch step, the front door flew open. Kobe lunged, but Ethan had been prepared and brought him under control.

"Chief! You old son of a bitch. I had to double-check the monitors. Thought I was having a flashback—seeing your ugly face materialize on the screen." The man took one step forward onto the polished wood-planked porch deck. Although his head stayed fixed on Ethan, his eyes constantly swept the perimeter. Ethan noted that his right hand never strayed far from the open front flap of his jacket and the telling bulge of a handgun strapped to his belt.

"Hey, Schless. You're losing your touch. Looks like I got the drop on you." Ethan smiled at his old SEAL teammate.

Archie Schlessinger raised his brows. "Perhaps Chief, but I wanted to be certain the cab driver didn't double back and follow you. Your moves looked kind of obvious to any trained observer."

"Damn," Ethan sighed and walked up the steps. He held Kobe on a tight leash, feeling the throbs of the dog's bays telegraphing up his arm.

Schlessinger knew not to stare at the dog, and he turned his body to the side as Ethan guided Kobe up the stairs. Ethan watched him slowly move his hand away from the holstered weapon and slide it to his side, letting Kobe sniff the closed fist.

Kobe let out several tentative woofs and pawed Schlessinger's leg. Ethan's former SEAL teammate kneeled down in front of Kobe and tussled the dog's neck while he got his ears cleaned and his scalp nipped.

Schlessinger stood up and motioned for Ethan to go through the doorway. From inside the foyer, he took a final look outside and closed the door. Ethan heard the locks engage and watched the ex-SEAL activate the security system by entering a series of digits on a keypad next to the doorjamb. His muscled frame blocked the finer details of his actions. When he turned to Ethan, he shrugged. "No offense, Chief. Force of habit."

"Bullshit, Schless."

Schlessinger lifted his shoulders again and spread his hands out. His face softened and his voice turned throaty. "I would've lost the pool." His eyes pointed at Kobe. "The rest of the guys bet you'd get another dog. But they didn't understand what happened that night." He paused and swallowed. "I saw a part of you die along with Chopper. He saved both our lives—more than once."

Ethan nodded but couldn't find any words.

Schlessinger let out a long breath and patted Kobe's head. "But you did it. This is a good sign, Chief."

Ethan again tried to respond, but his throat felt dry and his tongue stuck to the roof of his mouth. He coughed and reached down to scratch Kobe's neck. Kobe looked up and tilted his head.

With the clock ticking, Ethan needed to get down to business. Schlessinger ushered him into what looked like the control center for a NASA space program. From a small refrigerator next to the multi-monitored computer station, he pulled out a couple of beers and motioned for Ethan to sit in one of the high-backed leather swivel chairs.

"I need a big favor, Schless, but you can't know the details. The less you know, the better off you'll be." He hesitated. "I—I'm sorry to drag you into this, but I ran out of options and—"

"Get over it, Chief. I don't want to hear any explanations. If not for you and your sidekick, I would've come home in a body bag. If they could've scraped up all the pieces." He handed one of the beers to Ethan. "Let's get to work."

Ethan rattled off a truncated version of what he needed and what he'd done so far. When he mentioned his cell phone usage, Schlessinger raised a hand and an anxious look spread over his face. Ethan pulled the disabled phone out of one pocket, the battery from another, and waved them at him.

Schlessinger's face relaxed, but he looked at the phone as if it could bite. Ethan shoved everything back in his pockets. Schlessinger turned to the desk and jotted down more notes, making sure he had the correct spellings on the names Ethan cited. He began working at the keyboard. Ethan watched the various monitors come to life. After about thirty minutes of exploring a number of databases Ethan didn't know existed, Schlessinger smiled, giving him a thumbs-up. He hit a key and one of the printers started spitting out paper.

Ethan stared at his old teammate. "This scares the hell out of me. No wonder I'm paranoid. If an ordinary citizen can get this kind of data, the feds must already be breathing down my neck. I'm surprised they haven't caught up with me by now."

"That hurts, Chief." He placed a hand to his heart. "I didn't earn all this by playing video games and sitting on my butt in Starbucks since getting out of the Navy."

"I'm just messin' with you," Ethan responded out loud, but thought: *What the hell happened to privacy in this country?* "So let me get this straight. About this location you've identified? As far as anyone's concerned, there's no obvious way to trace this to the governor or the governor's wife's family?"

Schlessinger shot him a look.

Ethan raised both arms. "No way it can be traced using ordinary means, is what I meant. And based on the tracking locations and patterns of Petricello's cell phone usage, you deduced the rest?"

He shrugged. "The likelihood of this being the target destination exceeds ninety-five percent. And with this information, finding the property specifics was a walk in the park."

Ethan stared at his friend. "I got one more favor to ask."

Schlessinger smiled and nodded. "Give me five minutes and I'll be ready to join you. I'm not sure exactly what the hell's going on, and it's obvious you omitted a few key facts—but count me in, Chief."

"I've got nothing planned, Schless. I'm going to pass this information on to the appropriate authorities—keeping your name out, of course." As he said this, his eyes diverted to the floor.

He stayed silent for several seconds and added, "But I would be grateful if I could borrow your car."

Ten minutes later, Ethan pulled the Baja Yellow Jeep Wrangler Rubicon out of Schlessinger's garage and headed toward Interstate 90. After checking his pockets and making sure he had his phone and battery separated for the moment, he glanced over at Kobe as he accelerated up the onramp, and said, "Here's the plan, boy. Pay attention. You might not like it, but—"

CHAPTER 57

For once the gears of the federal government turned faster than Finley imagined possible. His urgent call to President Griffin prompted rapid action from NSA operatives. They reported back within minutes that Galloway's phone had suddenly lit up and they had triangulated his position. It appeared Galloway, at least for the moment, was not moving. Following the president's orders and disregarding any formalities of executing the necessary warrants, they activated the malware previously installed by the Defense Department. Right now, they were in the process of accessing the phone and attempting to download all recent data. They informed Finley that as far as could be determined, no one from the DoD had gone through the motions to commandeer Galloway's phone.

Finley's flight was still about thirty minutes from SeaTac. After a quick discussion with the Gulfstream's pilot, he made the decision to land there as planned. A small airport closer to Galloway's current position appeared out of the question since it had a single grass runway, and the recent rains made the condition of the rutted soft strip too dangerous.

Finley called Olivia Davenport, who had not yet left Seattle to catch up with Governor Blackwell at his next campaign stop. She informed him that from her present location, driving was a better bet than waiting for someone to get a helicopter prepped. Besides, she wanted to do this low-key and avoid spooking Galloway into fleeing before they could confront him. Finley passed on the GPS coordinates as she and two fellow agents climbed into an agency vehicle. The SUV sped out of the hotel's parking garage.

A helicopter would be waiting for Finley and Catori when they landed in Seattle. He estimated that he'd be behind Olivia by no more than twenty minutes. She disconnected the call before he could persuade her to sit tight until he got on scene.

Olivia briefed the two agents who accompanied her to apprehend Ethan Galloway as a person of interest in the attempted assassination of Governor Nicholas Blackwell. She sat in the driver's seat barking orders. By the time she'd outmaneuvered the clogged traffic on I 90 and screamed past the southern edges of Lake Sammamish, Olivia guessed by the look on her colleagues' faces that they had issues with her driving skills and would welcome a firefight with their quarry as a means to settle their nerves.

Smiling, Olivia slid the SUV from the leftmost freeway lane onto the exit ramp and headed north on Snoqualmie Parkway. "Now we're getting into my element. I did my best drivers ed training in the Pocono Mountains near Philly."

She followed the onboard GPS system, taking them farther from the interstate and closer to Snoqualmie Falls. At the last second, she skidded left onto a narrow road in response to the GPS voice instructions. As she slowed the SUV to navigate the winding lane rising up and out of the valley, the agent sitting in the back seat spoke up while staring at the small electronic device in his hand. "I've now got a direct lock on Galloway's phone. We don't need to wait for updates from central control. I'll know the second he starts to move again. And with this little gadget, I can tell you if he bends over to scratch his ass."

The agent riding shotgun turned and smirked. "Only if his ass is as fat as yours."

"Okay boys, let's save it for the bad guys." She glanced in the rearview mirror. "That's why Mommy separated you for this little joy ride."

She located the entrance drive leading to their destination and stopped the SUV alongside a small guardhouse in front of an ornate pair of wrought-iron gates framed into a tapered granite façade. There was a bronze placard embedded in the overhead arch to the gate. When she noticed the embossed logo, a slight shimmy radiated from her gut, suggesting the start of things about to go wrong.

Olivia pushed those thoughts aside and lowered the window as a uniformed guard strutted over and leaned into the SUV.

"Good day, ma'am." The stout man tipped his cap, revealing a receding hairline. "Welcome to Paradise

Resort, where all your desires are pawsible. How may I help you today?"

She did a brief double-take, figuring she didn't hear him right, but shrugged it off and got down to business. Pulling out her fed creds, she said, "Sir, this is official business. Please open the gate."

He glanced inside the SUV and then stood back. "I'll have to call the front desk and get approval to—"

"Sir," Olivia added, using a more official tone, "I've given you all the approval necessary, so please open the gate. And do *not* pick up the phone. In fact, once the gate opens, I'd like you to join us." She turned to the agent in the back seat. "Slide it over, Charlie. We wouldn't want this gentleman to make any mistakes and call ahead to announce our arrival."

With a new passenger in the back seat, Olivia drove through the open gate and headed up the sloped tree-lined drive. After several gradual curves, the road opened onto a landscaped plateau with a sprawling single-story structure set in the center. A series of glossy, black-meshed fencing panels crisscrossed parts of the building's perimeter, but none of them blocked the SUV's access to a paved parking area and the cobblestone walkway that led to a rounded glass entry portico fashioned into the northeast corner of the facility. The walls of the structure were constructed of large white granite blocks. From the building's central hub, long rectangular sections sprouted outward and connected to the fence panels, making Olivia envision that a spider-like flying saucer had landed on this spot and wove a metallic web.

She pulled up to the entrance doors and they all got out. She motioned for Phil, the agent who'd been sitting up front, to take up a position near the SUV and make certain Galloway could not slip by. From the configuration of the fenced barriers surrounding the side and back partitions, it appeared that anyone who exited the building would, by necessity, wind up near the front entrance.

The high-end furnishings and décor in the striking lobby caught Olivia's attention when they walked inside. As they stepped up to a curved ebony reception console, the guard they'd seized from the front gate attempted to push ahead of Olivia and speak to the person standing behind the desk.

Olivia grabbed his arm and pointed him to one of the cushioned chairs lining the side of the lobby overlooking a huge aquarium tank built into a stone-walled grotto. As she once again reached for her creds, a door behind the reception area opened, and a man dressed in a black tuxedo appeared.

"What is all the ruckus about, Miss Leopold?" He stepped up to the desk, and after tweaking his bowtie, placed both hands on the polished copper counter. "We must be cognizant of our guests. It is almost dinnertime, and we would not want anything to interfere with their appetites."

Olivia shoved her creds in the man's face and thought: *Cognizant? What the hell?* She looked over her shoulder and asked the other agent, "You still got a clear fix, Charlie?"

He gave her a thumbs-up.

She turned back to the man behind the desk and scrutinized his officious appearance and contemplated tossing him into the tank of water. A quick glance assured her he'd be the lone penguin in the colorful aquatic milieu of exotic creatures.

"And you are?" she questioned as he studied her credentials with a look suggesting Olivia had waved a rotten fish at him.

He lifted his head and pursed his lips. "I am Dr. Harrington Tricklebank, director and administrator." He raised his head higher, nostrils flaring. "What is the meaning of you people showing up without an appointment?"

Olivia returned his stare, her eyes penetrating deep into the doctor's bloviating character. If he faltered, she didn't notice; but neither did she. "For now, *doctor*, I'll ask the questions. Am I clear?"

The man gave a slight nod while a thumb and forefinger tugged on the sleeve of his jacket, allowing him to check his watch.

Charlie, the agent holding the GPS locator, reached out and placed a hand on Olivia's shoulder. She'd been close to pulling out her handgun and putting a bullet between Tricklebank's eyes. She took a deep breath and spoke, "What other exits are located in this facility?"

"Do you mean for the *guests* or our *staff*?" Olivia pushed in closer and Tricklebank flinched. "All exits beyond this lobby are secured. Any attempt to open the doors or the exterior gates is impossible and will trigger an alarm. I can assure you, none of our guests can get in or out of this facility unless accompanied by a staff member under my authorization." He pointed to the glass-paneled front doors Olivia had just walked through. "Using those doors." He pressed his arms to his chest, pushing the red bowtie into the folds of his neck.

A host of questions shot through Olivia's head as she listened to his words. She decided they'd wasted enough time. She looked back to Charlie. "Where is he?"

"Hasn't moved. Southwest corner of this building."

To Tricklebank, she said, "Doctor? Take us there. Now."

"But—"

Pulling him around the desk by his bowtie, she added. "Let's go."

Tricklebank walked up to a door on the right side of the reception desk and punched in a code on the keypad. A sharp click sounded, and he pushed open the door. When they stepped through, classical music filled the air, blanketing out most of the background noises coming from what sounded like a powerful ventilation system.

Charlie shoved the GPS device in Tricklebank's face. "This is where we're going," he said.

Tricklebank's shoulders heaved as he exhaled. "Why don't you just tell me who you are looking for?"

Charlie looked at Olivia. Olivia shrugged and said, "Ethan Galloway, but I'm sure he wouldn't be using his real name. Charlie, show him the photo."

Before Charlie could reach in his pocket, Tricklebank said, "That won't be necessary. Why didn't you tell me this when you first barged into the lobby?" Shaking his head, he said, "I thought it peculiar. This Mr. Galloway. He told me not to be concerned but mentioned the strong possibility of someone stopping by to question his whereabouts."

Tricklebank turned and headed off around a corner.

CHAPTER 58

Olivia Davenport listened to Dr. Tricklebank's footsteps as he walked away. She turned to her colleague and frowned before they both took off after the director of the facility.

They passed a number of closed doors on the right side of the intersecting corridor. Each with different titles stamped onto oval brass signs attached at eye level next to the doorjambs. Tricklebank stopped at the last door and held out a hand. A look of surprise swept across his face as both Olivia and Charlie drew their weapons.

"Please stand aside doctor—" Olivia started to say.

She glanced at the brass sign next to the door. It read: *Caesar's Roman Suite.*

It all came together, and a sudden cold ripple spread over her: like the air had been sucked from her lungs. She lowered her weapon and pointed to the locking module.

"Unlock the door." The tone acquiescent of what she'd already construed.

Tricklebank hesitated before slipping the key card into the electronic lock. She waved both men back and cracked open the door. Peering through the narrow gap, she saw two razor-sharp eyes focused on her.

Next, she sensed, more than heard, a low rumbling, its intensity escalating. A deafening barrage erupted from inside the room and a dark shape launched itself at her. She pushed hard, closing off the assault as the powerful body crashed against the door.

Leaning her back against the wall, Olivia closed her eyes and let out a series of obscenities. As she took several deep breaths, she felt a faint vibration shaking the facility, accompanied by the familiar *thump-thump-thump* of an approaching helicopter swelling above the harshness of the ventilating fans and the congruent notes of Ludwig van Beethoven's *Moonlight Sonata*.

Dr. Tricklebank, clucked his tongue and shook his head. "My… my… my. Mr. Galloway did mention that Mr. Kobe liked his privacy."

Olivia's eyes opened. "I don't suppose Ethan Galloway is also one of your guests?"

Tricklebank frowned. "We are a luxury retreat for canines. I can assure you we do not cater to *humans*."

Olivia was still struggling with a pithy response when she heard a distant door slam open and footsteps clacking against the floor. She looked up in time to see three figures turn down the corridor.

"I'm sorry, Dr. Tricklebank. This man demanded I bring him back here. I had no choice. He showed his credentials—just like these two agents did." The receptionist's eyes darted at the exposed weapons held by Olivia and Charlie, and her hand flew to her chest. "Oh! He has a gun too. But I think his is bigger." As an afterthought, she pointed to the person standing next to Finley and shrugged. "And this young lady is with him."

As Olivia recounted the situation to Finley, Catori slipped from Finley's side. Tricklebank still held the key card in his right hand. She gently tugged it free and used it to release the locking mechanism on the door. Her cheerful words faded as she disappeared inside Caesar's Roman Suite.

When Catori reemerged with Kobe on a leash, Olivia and Finley were still engaged in an agitated discussion. Holding the door open, Catori looked at Finley. "There's a large duffel bag on Kobe's bed you might want to check out. And there's a cell phone sitting next to it. I'll take Kobe outside for a little fresh air."

"But, Miss," Dr. Tricklebank called, "it's time for Mr. Kobe's dinner."

"Could you please put it in a doggie bag? I think Mr. Kobe might be going on a trip."

Finley waved for Tricklebank and his receptionist to give them some space. He pulled the door to Kobe's room open wider and walked across the threshold, staring at the plush carpeting and the oversized square fluffy bed in the corner. On the far wall was a large flat-screen TV. Kobe appeared to have been watching an old *Lassie* rerun. Charlie followed Finley into the room and looked over his shoulder at Olivia.

"You guys go ahead and examine his bag," she said. "I'll join you in a minute. I've got a few calls to make." After the door closed, Olivia followed Tricklebank back to the lobby. She pulled out her phone and headed outside.

When Olivia ended her third call, she had a few words with Phil, who was still leaning against the SUV. He nodded twice. She looked around the landscaped grounds and saw Catori and Kobe walking in a fenced-in rectangular space with multi-colored artificial turf, shaded benches, and several fire hydrants. She walked over but chose to stay outside the potty area when Kobe gave her a long stare. Catori exited, leaving Kobe inside to explore one of the fire hydrants. Olivia spoke in hushed tones. Catori's face clouded over, and her lips tightened. She grabbed hold of Olivia and hugged her.

She whispered in Olivia's ear, "You don't have to do this."

Olivia stood back. "Yeah, I do." She turned and sprinted down the road and onto the open expanse of lawn.

Finley had returned to the lobby carrying the camouflaged canvass duffel bag from Caesar's Roman Suite, when he heard the helicopter's blades spinning as the engine reached maximum RPM and began to lift.

As he burst out the facility's front entrance, Catori grabbed his arm.

CHAPTER 59

An hour after a pissed-off Mike Finley watched his helicopter lift-off, he received a text message from Olivia Davenport with a belated explanation of her plan. The two agents who accompanied Olivia to apprehend Ethan Galloway had dropped Finley and Catori off at SeaTac. They drove away from the airport without a word. Finley suspected Catori knew more than she professed, but she refused to comment on what Olivia had told her back at the luxury canine boarding facility near Snoqualmie.

Sitting in the tiny office space in the rear corner of a general aviation building at SeaTac, Finley wrestled with the potential consequences of Olivia's plan.

Catori tried to lighten the moment. "Maybe it's the governor you should worry about."

Finley's eyes cut into Catori, but his expression softened. "Why didn't she tell me about this? I could've helped. At least have some input."

He paced the cramped space and leaned his forehead against the windowpane. He then stared back at the phone, deciding whether or not to smash it against the wall. Or throw it on the floor and stomp the crap out of it.

"Because you two would still be arguing about it back at the dog kennel."

Finley didn't answer. He nodded.

Catori pointed to a table—at the stack of papers that had been delivered by the NSA. "Your guys picked through the data from Ethan's phone in record time."

"It's almost as if Galloway thumbed his nose at us by leaving the damn phone with the dog. Didn't learn much from the call records. The only recent outgoing calls were to his son's cell phone."

"You mentioned Corey and Patas left a message on his voicemail. What do you make of it?"

Finley scratched his head, nodding. "Hard to say. Patas seemed spooked about being identified by the governor's security team. If they did recognize her, they should've notified Olivia or one of the other agents."

"Let's say Blackwell's people did recognize her. If that's true, it's a safe bet that with their manpower and motivation, she didn't get away this time. But what reason would they have to take matters into their own hands?"

Finley shrugged. "It's clear from Galloway's internet searches that he's trying to get a grasp on the governor's real estate holdings. It's likely he's concerned the governor grabbed his son and the girl—and stashed them away someplace."

"Wouldn't that be risky with all the media hype surrounding the election? Not to mention the feds providing the governor additional protection. Eyes are on him all the time."

"*If*—for some reason—they did kidnap those kids, they wouldn't take them to any place linked publicly to the governor or his wife's family."

Catori's face darkened. "If they don't want Patas or Corey talking to the authorities, why would they keep them alive?"

Before answering, Finley let out a deep breath. "I'll get somebody to comb through databases and see if we can dig deeper into the governor's finances and holdings." He bit his lip. "Of course, they could easily stash them at a place with zero ties to Blackwell or his wife."

Catori closed her eyes. "For what it's worth, I'm sensing the kids are still alive." Her body shivered. "But... I'm not sure for how long."

After a tight smile, Finley said, "I'll text Olivia and make her aware of the possibility that someone on the governor's payroll might've grabbed those two kids. Right now, this could be Galloway's biggest motivation. One way or the other, if he gets close to the governor, I don't think the governor will get a second chance."

"I don't need any special powers to agree with your conclusion."

"And as soon as I get those details out of the way, I'm going to interrupt the president again. I don't care how close it is to the election; he's getting a piece of my mind. He could've filled me in on Olivia's plan." He paused and added, "At least they took some precautions."

"What do you mean?"

"According to Olivia's text, before she reported for duty at the governor's mansion last week, they implanted a locating sensor under her skin. Problem is… the transmitter will go dead in less than two more days."

CHAPTER 60

Ethan Galloway's paranoia level had ratcheted down several notches since leaving his cell phone with Kobe at the canine boarding facility near Snoqualmie. He bore a twinge of regret about abandoning Kobe, but with what he had planned there were no other good choices.

The Jeep Wrangler he'd borrowed from his old SEAL buddy in Seattle came with a number of useful items stashed in a non-factory installed hidden storage compartment under the rear cargo floor. Before turning over the keys, Schlessinger handed him an extra ammo container and several duffels filled with additional equipment that might come in handy.

After dropping off Kobe, Ethan headed east, putting as much distance as possible from Seattle on the first leg of his journey through the central and eastern portions of Washington. Although he didn't think anyone could trace Schlessinger's vehicle to him, he felt nervous driving across the stark basalt-rich terrain of the Columbia Plateau in the not-so-easy-to-hide Baja Yellow Rubicon.

"Nervous is okay," he mumbled. "But not as good as paranoid."

He made several side trips and bypassed parts of the interstate on his eastbound journey. Now and then he caught a few hours sleep but tried not to sit still for any length of time. One of his detours took him into Spokane, where he purchased additional items. Not wanting to leave any traceable actions, he spread out his acquisitions in several stores. He declined to use any credit cards, instead paying in cash. This drained most of his funds, leaving barely enough for a few groceries. With what he was planning, that might be all he would need.

Just west of Butte, Montana, he picked up Interstate 15 and headed south, back into Idaho. He followed the GPS instructions and eventually crossed into Wyoming. When he entered Jackson, the hub of tourist activity in the Jackson Hole valley, he turned north and drove the ten plus miles to Blacktail Butte. He parked at the far corner of the small parking lot.

Getting out of the Jeep, Ethan stretched his arms and tilted his head upward. The sun provided a contrasting warmth to the brisk fall temperatures. His gaze went to the ragged peaks of the Tetons to the west and then settled on the massive tangle of rocks and trees in the foreground. After stuffing key items in his backpack and grabbing a heavy sweatshirt, Ethan trudged off on the foot trail leading him toward the base of Blacktail Butte. He looked to the sky one more time and watched a series of vast white clouds parading across the vivid blue canvass. Right now the fall temperatures felt pleasant. Although skirting near sixty, he would've preferred it a bit cooler for his arduous trek. Once the sun set behind the Tetons, the temperatures would plummet into the low twenties. He planned on being back in his Jeep by then, not wanting to share the night wrestling with a pack of wolves or an ornery grizzly bear. He was ready to deal with predators, but not the four-legged variety.

Following the GPS coordinates entered into his handheld unit, one of the extra pieces of equipment provided by Schlessinger, Ethan left the obvious hiking trails and worked his way through dense stances of native pines, firs, and spruces. As his boots stepped over a bed of fallen leaves, he observed the bare limbs of the aspens contrasting with the rich foliage of the more abundant evergreen varieties. Winding up at a craggy outcropping approximately nine hundred feet above the Jackson Hole valley floor, Ethan slipped off his backpack and reached inside for the binoculars. Whenever involved in missions in unfamiliar territory, he liked to take in the big picture before worrying about the finer details. He spread his extra sweatshirt on a flat expanse of rock facing in a southwesterly direction and eased himself down. Propped by his elbows, he gazed through the binoculars. He first scanned the site of the Jackson Hole Airport, observing its overall layout but paying particular attention to the general aviation section.

If the governor's secret service detail had set up a base of operations at the airport, he'd spot the subtle presence of any federal activities in the immediate area. The lack of any telltale agency personnel gave him confidence that his intel had been accurate. The governor had opted to rely on his private security team for this final campaign getaway. Keeping this location a secret trumped the support of guarding his life.

Once satisfied with the airport scene and getting a better grip on the surrounding terrain, he glanced again at the GPS monitor and guided the binoculars on a specific trajectory beyond the airport. He studied the main residential structure and how it fit in to the adjacent topography. He traced the roads and trails abutting the property; and the barriers, both natural and man-made, that isolated and sheltered the dwelling.

Ethan opened up a folder containing maps he and Schlessinger printed out from their earlier database searches. He scribbled numerous notes on the pages while verifying the data using the binoculars. After returning everything to the backpack, he stood up. Looking skyward, he then checked his watch, smiled, and spoke to the heavens.

"Thank God for Google, but I'll take boots on the ground over virtual 3D imagery any day."

As the sun began to cradle between the highest peaks of Grand Teton, Ethan sensed the thin mountain air losing its hold on the fading warmth of the departing rays. He turned, heaving the backpack over his shoulder, and retraced his steps to the Jeep. By the time his hand pressed the key fob and unlocked the door, dusk had taken over and the temperature had already plummeted below freezing. Once inside the Jeep, he welcomed the cover of darkness and began to focus on the details of his next moves. The idea germinating since he left Seattle coalesced into a hardened plot. His latest observations gave him hope of gaining access to his target, but not what would happen once he got inside.

CHAPTER 61

Ethan toyed with the notion of executing his plan now but couldn't be certain if Corey and Patas were even in the house. Besides, until Governor Blackwell arrived, a major part of this saga could not be culminated.

After returning to the Jeep following his reconnaissance mission on Blacktail Butte, Ethan drove the short distance to the Jackson Hole Airport. He considered stashing the Baja Yellow SUV in one of the designated long-term parking rows and grabbing a rental vehicle but didn't want to broadcast his location with another credit card transaction.

He walked through the terminal for a more close-up inspection, looking for evidence of heightened security measures but found nothing out of the ordinary. Pausing for a moment in front of Jedediah's, the airport's sole restaurant, he noticed they were preparing to close.

Good thing, he thought, watching the bartender polishing glasses in front of a tempting display of bottles lining the mirrored wall. He headed off down the ticket lobby, dropped coins into a vending machine, and grabbed a Pepsi.

When he got back to the Jeep, instead of exiting the airport he drove through the general aviation section. He noted a Brazilian-made Embraer Legacy 650 sitting alone at the far end of the apron. Running a finger down one of the printouts Schlessinger gave him, he matched the airplane's registration number to an obscure holding company traced to Daniel H. Chauncey, Anita Blackwell's father. He contemplated if this finding changed anything about his current plan but didn't think it provided any concrete information. And he knew for a fact that the governor remained on the campaign trail, still scheduled to fly into Sacramento to vote before heading to Jackson Hole.

After finishing the loop around the general aviation area, Ethan drove to the airport exit. He turned right on Hwy 26 and plotted his next GPS course for a look at another asset owned by a different holding company, but otherwise traced back to Daniel H. Chauncey.

He first made a single pass using the lone public access road to the estate where he believed the governor planned to wait out the election results. His nerves were on fire—the demons screaming to get out—but he needed to tamp down his anger and wait for the right moment to act.

Chapter 62

It was the last night before the presidential election. The neighborhood surrounding the Calvin L. Rampton Salt Palace Convention Center in Salt Lake City braced for the arrival of Governor Nicholas Blackwell, the democrat candidate. In light of the recent publicized attempts on Blackwell's life, security for this last-minute campaign event had been beefed up to the point of gridlock in the entire central city area bordered to the west by I 15 and to the south by I 80.

The governor's short ride from his suite at the Hilton Salt Lake City Center went without a hitch. Before the limo pulled to a stop in front of the convention center, the security hardened into an impenetrable barrier from the thickening crowd of onlookers.

Secret service agents, known for their stoic poise, intense demeanor, and unflappable persona, formed this evening's first line of defense in guarding the candidate.

Almost before the limo's wheels stopped turning, an alert agent reached out to pull open the rear door. It swung at him so fast he barely got his hand out of the way without having several fingers broken.

He recovered, until his gaze fell to the female exiting the vehicle.

"Mother of God!" The words popped out like a Steyr TMP in full auto mode. Too late, he realized his brief diatribe had been broadcast to the entire unit via his lapel mike.

Trained to observe and analyze everything within his field of vision—in a split-second moment he'd catalogued the polished high-heeled pumps and an eyeful of smooth, tight flesh as a leg whipped free of the slitted, mid-calf-length sheer white fabric. His head shot upward as the figure emerged.

She stood tall, reflecting a generous display of cleavage from the gown's plunging neckline. Using both hands, the woman teased back the thin spaghetti straps struggling to contain her breasts and avoid a potential wardrobe malfunction.

"Agent Davenport?" he stuttered and then had the wherewithal to add, "I'll be damned if I can tell where you're carrying your gun."

Olivia stared at the agent, waved a compact purse, placed a wide smile across her face, and said, "Agent Cleveland, if you keep staring, you won't be able to hide your back-up weapon. Unless it's the short-barreled model." Her eyes darted toward his crotch.

Olivia Davenport's smile faded, and she spun back to the limo. "Okay, Governor Blackwell, we're ready to get you inside."

The stunned agent caught a glimpse of the gown's low-cut back and Olivia's snuggly framed backside. He swallowed hard while trying to hide any raspiness from his voice while issuing orders into his mike.

With a phalanx of security, the governor was ushered inside the convention center and escorted down a service corridor to a small room near the rear entrance to the Ballroom. Olivia peeked through the door leading to the capacity-packed room of supporters seated at the tables and awaiting the appearance of their candidate.

Closing the door and making a show of flipping the locking mechanism, Olivia twirled toward the governor with a grace honed from hours on the training mats practicing martial arts moves. "This is your night, governor." She paused and took a step forward, coaxing her eyes into dreamy pools of green liquid. She'd rehearsed this guise earlier today while getting dressed. "It's a pity *Mrs.* Blackwell can't share it with you. I do hope she'll be feeling better soon. Where did you say she was staying until election day?"

Captured by her gaze, the governor looked bemused, but recovered quickly. "Anita's resting at one of our getaways. I'll join her tomorrow after I make a public show of voting. She's already mailed in her ballot."

Olivia slinked closer to Blackwell, her breast grazing his suit jacket. She was tall, but the governor's height gave him an almost six-inch advantage, allowing a savory glimpse into the inviting cleavage sprouting from the satiny material. She slowly placed a finger in her mouth, licking the tip and dabbing it at a corner of the governor's lip.

"You wouldn't want to face your loyal supporters with a smudge on that perfect mouth." Her finger lingered on his cheek for an additional moment. She backed away and strutted to the loveseat as Blackwell's tongue slivered out to engage her finger while his right hand was moving toward the scant fabric covering her lower back and buttocks.

God, she thought. *Guys are so predictable. I could've got him going without wearing this slutty dress.*

She wiped the grin off her face as she turned around, dropped onto the loveseat, and crossed her legs. Sitting back, she threaded her fingers behind her neck, stretching apart the dress's neckline and showcasing her goods.

Thank God Mike's not here to see this. I wonder who he'd shoot first.

She almost forgot about Blackwell, but when she looked, he had removed his jacket, throwing it over the arm of the loveseat. He placed one hand on her knee while swinging himself around to join her, when a quick triple knock reverberated from the door.

Someone tried turning the knob, and when it failed to respond said, "Governor? Is everything okay? We're ready for you."

Olivia whispered in Blackwell's ear. "This is my final shift on protection duty. I'm free in the morning to perform whatever private duties you desire."

Olivia jumped to her feet and winked at Blackwell, who'd collapsed onto the loveseat. "He's coming."

CHAPTER 63

On the morning of the election, Governor Blackwell made his final public appearance outside a polling place in Sacramento, giving the media and the crowd of onlookers his trademark smile and a grand wave. As the SUV streaked out of the capitol city and toward a waiting private jet, the governor turned to the passenger sitting next to him in the rear seat.

When the governor's hand slithered up her thigh, Olivia Davenport thanked God she'd switched to a pair of jeans and no longer wore the slinky gown from the previous evening. She had to give him something, so she covered his groping fingers and dug fingernails softly into the back of his hand. Shutting her eyes, Olivia leaned in closer to nibble his earlobe and whisper in his ear. She guessed it didn't matter what she said because at any moment the asshole might rip off her high-necked sweater and mount her right here in the back seat as they buzzed toward the airport. If that happened, she'd have to pull out her P228 and put a bullet in his manhood.

But then she remembered that before boarding the early morning flight from Salt Lake City to Sacramento, one of the governor's security men had pulled her aside. He informed her that since her protection duty assignment with candidate Blackwell ended this morning, she needed to follow the governor's personal security policy that guests are not permitted to carry firearms—or—cell phones when traveling with the governor.

"What's so funny, Olivia?" The governor spit out the words while navigating a sweaty hand beneath her heavy wool sweater. The driver discreetly kept his eyes on the road and braked for the airport exit.

Your ass would sure make a great target, she thought. *Too bad the asshole took my gun.*

"Nothing, Nicky. I'm a little nervous. It's scary doing it with the soon-to-be president-elect of the United States. And maybe a bit kinky with the next first lady maybe joining in too."

She might've been more anxious with the current situation if the agency hadn't talked her into getting the locator device implanted. It had a limited range, but she counted on Finley being close enough to cover *her* ass.

Last night, after the campaign banquet and rally, Blackwell had tried to seal the deal with Olivia, begging her to return with him to his hotel suite. She'd done a good job getting his juices flowing before the banquet. It was all she could do to keep the son of a bitch at bay this long.

Olivia almost thought he would cry when she told him she didn't get off duty until six o'clock this morning and could not compromise his security. Once her temporary assignment ended, she'd be free to take advantage of his hospitality. She remembered him moaning out loud. She had to check the front of his pants to make sure he hadn't finished without her.

What a pathetic loser. Who the hell could consider voting for this bastard?

* * * * * *

The level of activity at Jackson Hole Airport had escalated from when Ethan Galloway earlier scoped out the territory. The governor's second luxury jet touched down on the tarmac and taxied to a position next to the Legacy 650. A waiting Cadillac Escalade whisked off the disembarking Governor Blackwell and Olivia Davenport.

The governor had opted out of his secret service coverage. He also chose to keep the media and everyone else in the dark as to his current destination. The official press release from the governor's office stated that Governor Blackwell and his wife would attend the gala celebration at the Moscone Center in San Francisco following today's election returns.

Without her cell phone, Olivia Davenport had no opportunity to update Finley. She felt naked without her firearm and counted on Finley to have observed her boarding the governor's jet in Sacramento and verified the flight plan to Jackson Hole.

The governor's estate was less than a five-minute drive from the Jackson Hole Airport. As they approached the property and the driver punched in the code to open the gate, Olivia noted the eight-foot-high stone and stucco walls enclosing the ten acres of private land. The Escalade rode along a cobblestone drive that ended in a circular turnabout with a multi-tiered bronze fountain as a centerpiece. The house was a huge, rambling contemporary-styled ranch with a combination of cedar and stacked-slate siding and an excess of floor-to-ceiling windows. Most of the ten-acre grounds were wooded, leaving about an acre of manicured lawn surrounding three sides of the house. Several stone paths meandered into the copse of trees. Olivia couldn't be sure but thought she had seen the outlines of several smaller structures tucked into the forested portions of the property.

Although not an unexpected revelation, when Olivia stepped inside the main house, Anita Blackwell looked miffed by her husband's latest choice of house guests. She half-smiled, half-sneered at Olivia. "This is a surprise, Agent Davenport." She pointed to the far end of the high-ceilinged foyer. "The governor's chief of staff is in the great room. He can fix you a drink. We'll join you in a minute."

Olivia smiled and nodded as she watched Anita grab her husband's arm and lead him down the opposite corridor. Victor Petricello, who had accompanied Anita into the foyer to greet her husband, started to follow Olivia, but the governor's wife signaled for him to join them in the governor's office.

Olivia entered the great room, her eyes gazing at the white-washed, cedar-planked cathedral ceiling and a stone fireplace on the inside wall. The outside wall consisted of huge windows facing the Snake River and the multiple peaks of the Tetons off the west side of the dwelling. Beyond the French patio doors, between the rear of the house and the river, an enormous man-made pond abutted a narrow flagstone patio. The roaring sounds of the Snake River rapids penetrated the glass.

"Spectacular scene. Normally at this time of year, the whitewater phenomenon you're seeing has been reduced to a mere trickle. But with the unusually rainy fall season, this section of the river is still quite dangerous. Only the most expert rafters, or perhaps the most stupid, would attempt riding those rapids."

Olivia turned away from the views at the sound of Thomas Steadman's voice from behind a copper-topped bar counter in the rear corner of the room.

"What's your poison, Agent Davenport?"

"Seltzer with a twist of lime on the rocks."

Steadman shrugged. "Well, it is a tad early to celebrate the victory of our new president, but so far the exit polls are showing a definite positive trend."

Olivia followed his eyes to the flat screen monitor on the wall behind the bar as her thoughts turned to the more pressing problem she faced.

Chapter 64

Several hours after the governor and his guest, Olivia Davenport, drove off to his nearby estate, a Gulfstream G550 landed at Jackson Hole Airport and disappeared inside an old cargo hanger. A small group of federal agents exited the aircraft and took up shop inside the hanger's cramped office. With the repeater device placed on the nearest road to the governor's estate, they picked up the faint and fading signal from Olivia's implanted locator.

Catori Torrence, who'd accompanied Mike Finley and his small team, sat in a corner trying to stay out of the way. She stroked the back of Kobe's neck while keeping a close eye on Finley. All the bad vibes she'd encountered since meeting Ethan Galloway at Mayacamas Shepherds pointed to the nearby location on the shores of the Snake River. And with Catori, bad vibes didn't do justice to the depth of her empathy.

"You need to relax, Mike," Catori said. "You should know better than anyone. Olivia can take care of herself."

Finley stared back at Catori, whose eyes still veiled the wizened remnants of an inner vision. One that had manifested itself only minutes ago during the flight from Seattle.

At the heart of her vision was Coyott, the ghost of the ancient god of light. This time the mythical trickster had been startled awake from a protracted slumber after spending a millennium carving paths through vast mountainous barriers. This feat could either destroy the intervening plains that stretched toward the Pacific Ocean and wipe out countless tribes along the way or provide an endless supply of food by connecting the Columbia Gorge with this inland preserve.

On a butte high above the churning river borne of its work, Coyott gazed down at the handicraft of a family of beavers attempting to block the flow of the escaping waters and grasp the unsuspecting creatures as they swam to a new destiny. Coyott pondered this dilemma, stretching its frame and digging its claws over the surface of the rocky ledge.

A sudden shift in the Gulfstream's airspeed and attitude jousted Catori from her brief vision, sending Coyott back into the deep crevices of her mind.

The landing gear locked into position and Catori glanced out the jet's window as the sleek craft banked and aligned with the runway at Jackson Hole Airport. She extended her arms and smiled to herself. Whenever Coyott's image entered one of her visions, she couldn't help but conjure up memories of Lomasi, her grandmother—matriarch of the family—and once guardian of the Kootenecti's tribal lore. A job now entrusted to Catori.

On the jet's final approach, she marveled at the contours and outlines of Blacktail Butte to the east and the fury of the rushing waters of the Snake River to the west.

* * * * * *

Finley stopped staring at Catori and paced around the office. His response to her words wiped out the lingering images of Coyott, but not the possible link to today's mission.

"You know what today is, don't you?" He turned and looked at Catori.

Catori raised her brows. Kobe tensed and sat up on his haunches. She thought that Kobe, with his shining, jet black fur, could never be mistaken for Coyott—the creature was as pure a white as the fresh-fallen snow—but Lomasi had once mistaken Kobe's dam, Amber, for the ghost of the ancient god of light.

If Finley discerned any change in the dog's manner, he didn't show it. "This is election day. And the last thing President Griffin needs is a scandal starting off his second term. Especially one that Olivia is up to her ears in investigating."

Catori tilted her head. "And which investigation is that?" She stood up after giving Kobe a quick hand signal and watching him drop back down. "The investigation into Agent Kostelecky's suspicious death? The governor's promiscuous undertakings? His wife's family businesses? The supposed assassination attempts? Or the role Ethan Galloway plays in this?"

Finley was about to answer when Catori added, "Or the disappearance of those two kids." She paused, and in a lower voice added, "This will all end today, Mike."

Finley rubbed his hands against his face and tightened his lips. He gave Catori a slow nod.

She knew he was not about to question her presumptions.

Finley busied himself by rehashing the data received on Ethan Galloway while occasionally glancing at his phone and cursing. They'd heard nothing from Olivia since she and the governor left Salt Lake City early this morning.

And Catori knew there was a good reason for that. Watching from a distance, she and Finley had witnessed a brief exchange between Olivia and one of the governor's security men before Olivia boarded the waiting luxury jet. She'd watched Olivia hand over her gun and cell phone. The items had then been passed on to another man who stuffed them into a leather pouch and headed back to the terminal. At least they knew she had flown here on the governor's jet and was now inside the governor's nearby estate. But only hours remained before the locator signal would die out.

Catori watched as Finley stewed and grew more fidgety by the minute. The tiny office in the non-descript hanger on the periphery of the Jackson Hole Airport was suffocating her. Noting the minutes turning into hours as the hands on the analogue wall clock swept in endless circles, she decided on a plan and headed to the door.

Catori was long gone before Finley realized she and Kobe had disappeared.

CHAPTER 65

Ethan Galloway missed the arrival of Finley's Gulfstream at the Jackson Hole Airport. At that particular moment, he was hunkered down in his Jeep at a nearby visitor center for Grand Teton National Park, catching up on some needed sleep.

Today's sun made only a fleeting appearance before a brisk surge of clouds tumbled in and obliterated the pleasant fall weather. Heralding in the approaching winter, waves of chilling rain stung the Jeep's exterior. As the day wore on, an intermittent drizzle persisted, and the temperatures barely flirted with the forty-degree mark. Inside the Jeep, Ethan rested, undeterred by the harsh elements. He'd slept through a whole lot worse.

What eventually disturbed his respite came from within him. And when it hit—it hit hard. He gasped and lurched forward; only the steering wheel prevented his head from smashing against the windshield. Long accustomed to combat situations, he was fully alert and aware of his environment in a matter of seconds.

Outside the Jeep, the world remained the same, while the turmoil inside Ethan's head pounded. Not unusual, but nevertheless disquieting. He took several deep breaths and reached for his water bottle, taking a long pull. Even as the cold winds whipped outside the vehicle, trickles of sweat cascaded down the back of his neck.

He mumbled to himself, "Just when you think the nightmares are gone—" He bit back the last words, his eyes scanning the parking lot. The last thing he needed was for someone walking by to see a deranged man huddled in a Jeep and talking to himself.

The occurrence of this latest episode made him realize how different he had felt over the last few days, with less thoughts ricocheting between reality and the alternative world as he had come to expect.

Like the doctors told me: get used to it, Galloway.

Then another notion hit him.

If this is normal, maybe I've already gone over the edge.

But something about this incident *was* unique. Like watching a breaking news story on TV; the details surreal and conflicting. He almost got it—but then a muzzle flash forced him to look away. Reverberating echoes of a phantom gunshot had startled him awake. In the instant between vision and reality, faces danced across his head. He strained to recognize them. Familiar and important faces—who were they? And why did they dwell in his memories?

Ethan took another swig of water and checked his watch. Almost time to get ready. He reached for the last emergency ration bar he'd found in the survival pack

Schlessinger gave him. The rest of his meager food supply was gone. Wanting to clear his head and loosen his muscles, he glanced around the parking lot and decided to check out the inside of the visitor center.

Tourists were still lingering at the exhibits when Ethan walked inside the building. He read the sign on a small table near the door and glanced again at his watch. The *Craig Thomas Discovery and Visitor Center* would close in thirty minutes; and not reopen until next spring. He wandered past the exhibits, but his mind concentrated on reviewing the details from his reconnaissance work.

Ten wooded acres surrounded the governor's single story, approximately twelve thousand square foot contemporary-styled mansion. High walls and fencing bordered three sides of the property. The rear portion of the grounds dropped down to the whitewater rapids of the Snake River. These barriers provided ample deterrents for local amateur thieves or vandals from gaining access but were not designed to ward off a direct assault on the occupants of the home. The Blackwells never entertained such a possibility. Since the property had no direct ties to either the Blackwell or the Chauncey family, that scenario had not entered into the equation.

And today, the governor had shrugged off the offered protective services provided to presidential candidates. Keeping this property a secret overrode any additional security arrangements. Only a small contingency of Blackwell's private security team had been deployed for this short stay. The governor planned to remain at the estate until news of his victory. If the polls were accurate, he would then join his loyal supporters at the Moscone Center in San Francisco and proclaim himself to be the next president of the United States.

Last night Ethan observed the approximate number of security personnel present outside the main house and anticipated only a few additional guards after the governor's scheduled arrival earlier today. From the detailed security reports Schlessinger had appropriated, he was confident that no motion detectors had been installed on the grounds of the estate, nor did they employ any trained canines to patrol the property.

Ethan returned to the Jeep and pulled out of the parking lot before the gates closed. He drove toward the nearby bridge that spanned the Snake River. Before reaching it, he turned left onto a gravel access road paralleling the river. He eased the vehicle into a small clearing within a wooded expanse about ten yards from the riverbank.

Even with the windows shut, the roar of the surging rapids filled the interior of the Jeep and stoked Ethan's desire to finish the job he'd started on the Delta King in Old Town Sacramento. But this time he planned on getting a whole lot closer to the governor.

Chapter 66

Darkness spread as the cloud-shrouded sun dipped behind the Tetons. The already cold temperatures dropped further. Ethan ran the scheme through his head one final time as he finished getting his equipment ready.

With a grim smile, he muttered to himself, "I've spent more time in the water these last few days than all my tours in the Middle East."

He spread out the inflatable raft and powered up the electric pump. Swinging aside the Jeep's rear cargo door, Ethan grabbed one of his recent purchases, a Navy surplus drysuit, and began the arduous task of donning the bulky fusion-styled outfit. Once set, he strapped on a watertight backpack and attached the coiled nylon rope and grappling hook to his utility harness. He dragged the inflated raft down the sloped gravel bank underneath the bridge and slipped it into a shallow eddy pool near the shoreline—climbing in and paddling the rubber boat until it got caught up in the rapids.

The raft picked up speed, and the frigid, foaming waters sprayed over his head. Once the lights on the bridge faded, he switched on the night-vision goggles. The whitewater turmoil was dangerous in daylight and close to suicidal at night. The distance from where he entered the river to the governor's property was short, and Ethan knew he'd get only one shot at this before the rapids swept him too far downstream.

At several points he almost lost it. The raft spun and bounced about while he struggled to guide it close to the eastern banks and avoid the more treacherous currents. The raft pummeled down a sheer wall of water. He fought to avoid capsizing when a spidery web of knurled branches clutching the water's edge burst into view. He spotted the western border of the governor's estate rising up behind it. A sudden flux in the undercurrent had the raft spinning and bobbing back to the center channel.

Digging in with the paddle, he succeeded in momentarily switching directions and slid back toward his target. The raft went airborne at the exact moment he swung the grappling hook at one of the branches projecting over the river. The craft jerked out from underneath him as the steel hooks snagged onto its mark and the rope snapped taut. Ethan's body hung suspended for less than a second before crashing back down into the churning onslaught. His world grayed as the night-vision goggles ripped free from his head. The drysuit's tough outer layer caught on a protruding branch but pulled free before ripping into the inner neoprene layer.

Ethan clutched the rope and struggled to pull himself toward the bank. At last his feet touched bottom, and he began to win the battle against the torrents of water trying to suck him back into the murky depths and crush his body against the rocky bed.

Close to exhaustion, Ethan dragged his aching body up a muddy slice of embankment and onto dry land. He dropped to his knees and spit and coughed out mouthfuls of the icy water. He gave himself about ten seconds and then got busy shedding the cumbersome drysuit before tossing it back in the river.

From his knowledge of the grounds, he knew a large man-made pond extended across the entire rear side of the house and overlooked the Snake River. Although he'd given thought to utilizing it as cover to get a closer glimpse at the inside, he decided the water games were finished for the evening. He preferred any close-in fighting to be done without the restrictions of the drysuit.

After double-checking his equipment, he shimmied up the incline and dug himself in behind a row of hedges. The insistent roar of the rain-swollen rapids at his back prevented him from picking up any sounds from the nearby perimeter of the house. This worked in his favor since his presence would also go unnoticed by posted guards checking the grounds. Besides, no one would expect any intruders to approach from the river. The loss of his night-vision goggles didn't concern him because eave-mounted spotlights allowed him to maneuver, while still staying hidden in the shadows.

Ethan spotted a lone man standing at the north end of the patio. He wore a heavy hooded jacket and held a lit cigarette in one hand. The other hand rested inside a pocket. A handgun was holstered on his belt. The man's gaze wandered along the fence spanning the north side of the property, but his attention level appeared low. Ethan could see several people inside the house, standing near an enormous fireplace set into a stone wall at the far side of the room. The bright interior lighting washed through the floor-to-ceiling windows facing the patio, obliterating the possibility of anyone observing his movements. Ethan checked the grounds once more and homed in on the one visible guard.

Moving forward, he eyed an arched wooden footbridge that crossed over a narrow section of the man-made pond. He crept across the bridge, toward the patio, keeping his body below the solid side railings. When he reached the end of the bridge he peered over the railing. The guard, still facing away from the pond and the river, was stamping out his cigarette and stretching both arms upwards, stifling a yawn. Without taking his eyes from the man, Ethan's hand slipped to his utility belt and closed around one of the attached devices. He released the trigger lock but left it in place. He covered the final ten yards to his target without drawing the man's attention and attacked from behind.

Ethan wrapped his right arm across the guard's throat tight enough to prevent him from screaming out. He pushed him to the ground while wrenching the man's arm backwards and spiking his knee into the prone man's back. Slipping the device from his utility belt and jamming the barrel into the meaty flesh of the guy's neck, Ethan pulled the trigger. A low popping noise emanated from the syringe jet, injecting the fast-acting tranquilizer. After several seconds, the man stopped struggling and his body fell limp. Ethan dragged the man into the bushes on the side of the house. He reached for a different syringe jet and injected a second, longer-acting sedative into the prostrate body and proceeded to wrap duct tape across his mouth and fasten zip ties to his hands and feet.

Ethan needed to repeat this sequence two more times. He found the second guard sitting in a chaise lounge on the front porch. Him being sound asleep made Ethan's task easier. Disabling the third sentry proved a bit more challenging. The man had just finished inspecting the front gate to the property. When he turned, he stared straight at Ethan. His hand reached inside his jacket, trying to extract his weapon. Before completing the act, Ethan launched himself at the startled man and wrestled him to the ground. This time he deployed a left hook to silence his adversary before continuing with the same routine used on the other two men to make sure they'd present no threats to his plans.

Ethan had just finished hiding the last body behind a raised garden bed near the front gate when he heard it.

"Sonofabitch," he muttered.

This kind of mistake could get him killed.

CHAPTER 67

Ethan dropped to the ground behind a rocky formation and reattached the device to his utility belt. He cursed himself for getting cocky and missing this during his earlier surveillance—relying on outdated information. No syringe jet was going to neutralize this particular danger. He pulled out his M11 and listened. He heard it again. Closer and more ominous. A human voice, measured, but emphatic broke in—and then silence.

Ethan held his position, not moving a muscle. He scrambled to analyze his choices. His thoughts were pierced by a repeat of the menacing noise, followed by a pleading voice, and then more silence. His eyes darted about in an attempt to localize the threat. Now he wished his night-vision goggles hadn't disappeared in the river. But something wasn't right. He detected a familiar ring.

One more time he heard it.

Ethan realized the barking—whimpering—pleading—were coming from the far side of the gate—not on the grounds of the estate.

He peered around the rocks in time to see the sleek black body leap against the gate and bark again.

"Please," the familiar voice whispered.

Ethan looked over his shoulder at the house but saw no signs of activity. He stood up, holstered his weapon, walked over to the gate, and stared at Kobe and Catori.

"I paid the kennel for two nights in advance. What? You didn't like the food?"

Kobe pawed at the closed gate.

Ethan turned his eyes to Catori.

She shrugged. "All of a sudden something's got him worked up. He usually responds to my commands." Her mouth formed a tight smile. "Thank God *you* answered the door and not somebody from the governor's security team."

Ethan murmured, "Don't concern yourself about them."

Kobe pawed again and barked, his anxiety still escalating. Ethan followed the dog's eyes. Kobe, looking away from the house, seemed fixated on the wooded area on the south side of the property.

"Give me a second," Ethan said to Catori. He hurried over to a metal electrical box mounted on a steel pipe coming out of the ground. Next to it stood the remote activating module for the gate. Grabbing a set of tools from a sealed pouch, Ethan removed the front panel on the box. He held a tiny LED flashlight between his teeth and got to work. Thirty seconds later, the front gate swung open, allowing Catori and Kobe to join him.

Catori still struggled with Kobe, so Ethan grabbed the lead and stared him down. The dog's demeanor didn't change, and he persisted in pulling toward the path leading into the woods.

"Could be you're not the only one who thinks the governor took the kids," Catori whispered.

"Right, but he certainly isn't interested in the main house." He thought about the maps and diagrams he'd studied. "There's a guest house about a hundred yards down this path."

Catori nodded and swallowed. "Ethan? I didn't come by myself." She reached into her pocket and pulled out a cell phone. "I think we should call in the troops. They're at the airport."

Before she could call Finley, Ethan snatched the phone from her hand and dropped it on the ground. He smashed the heel of his left boot against the screen, spreading shards of glass onto the cobblestone walk.

They stared at each other for a long time.

"That was *your* phone, Ethan. We found it in Kobe's room at the doggie resort. The techs gave it back after they finished with their data mining. Kobe liked having it close to him…."

"Paranoia is not only dangerous, but at times can be costly."

He turned to Kobe. "Let's go, boy." Kobe didn't need any prodding.

The background sounds from the raging river faded as they entered the thick copse of trees. Ethan tried to keep Kobe silent as they approached the guest house. The stone cottage with a steep slate roof appeared unguarded from the outside. Ethan again pulled out his M11. He walked around the building and saw no signs of life inside. He stepped onto the front porch and tried the door handle. Locked. Standing back, he raised a foot and kicked. After the second attempt, the door popped open.

Ethan rushed inside to check things out when Kobe charged at a closed door off the kitchen and barked at a feverish pace. Muffled shouts came from the other side. Ethan slid back a heavy latch and opened the door. Standing in front of him were Corey and Patas.

After a brief reunion and a longer period of arguments and pleads, they returned to the front gate of the governor's estate. Ethan stared at the still squabbling voices of Catori, Corey, and Patas, along with a whining black German Shepherd.

"Catori," Ethan said. "Get everybody back to the airport. Including Kobe. Please."

She shot him a look but didn't move.

"I've got a little unfinished business inside the governor's house. It won't take long, and I'll be done before you get back."

"Wait! There's a federal agent inside. She's working undercover. We don't know her situation. If the governor suspects anything—"

Ethan looked at Catori. "She?" He shook his head; his thoughts turning to what the governor did to Patas. And what the governor did to Kinsley. And what the governor did to countless other women. Not only the governor. But the governor's wife too.

He turned away and said, "Then... I guess you better hurry."

"Dad!" Corey pleaded.

Ethan heard the words but ignored the stabbing pain in his heart and ran toward the house.

CHAPTER 68

Mike Finley had just finished his tirade against the other agents for neglecting to inform him of Catori's disappearance. He directed most of the anger at himself for failing to deduce her objective.

The door to the office burst open and Catori, the two kids, and Kobe bounded inside. Everyone screaming and barking at once. Finley raised his arms and tried to calm them down.

Catori grabbed Finley and pulled him outside the office. Her strength surprised him. She spit out the information—which wasn't much. But there was no question about what Ethan Galloway had in mind.

Finley conversed quietly with the other two agents. Against Catori's protests, he locked her, along with the kids and the dog, in the hanger's office.

* * * * *

Ethan closed the distance to Blackwell's house in less than a minute and skirted the outside of the building to get a closer look into the large room facing the river. He counted five people either sitting or standing near the bar cabinet in the corner of the room. He recognized Governor Blackwell, Anita Blackwell, and the governor's chief of staff, Thomas Steadman. The other man standing away from the others looked familiar. Ethan had him pegged as part of the security team. He had one arm held across his chest; the hand hidden beneath his jacket. With him being this close to the governor, he assumed it was Victor Petricello: the governor's security chief. Ethan did some rough calculations in his head and concluded there could be at least one or two additional security personnel still unaccounted for.

An attractive woman sat stiffly on the sofa with Governor Blackwell at her side. She had to be the federal agent Catori mentioned. And she looked ready to blow her cover. The fingers of the governor's left hand were stroking her dark brown hair. His other hand slivered up and under her heavy wool sweater. Ethan turned toward the governor's wife. He tried to decipher the expressions flashing from her hooded eyes. Through the thick glass of the floor-to-ceiling windows, he sensed radiating surges of lust, rage, and scorn coming from her. He didn't know if they were directed at the governor, the agent, or both.

The security guy had his eyes riveted on the agent, while Steadman, who looked uncomfortable, walked to the bar and poured himself a drink.

Ethan broke away from the unfolding drama inside the house and vanished into the shadows. He reverted back to his original plan of gaining entry to the sprawling ranch by breaking through a side service door. This move took him directly to the basement. With the floorplan of the main level ingrained in his head, he recalled the main staircase in the center of the mechanical room he now stood in, led up to a doorway off the pantry alcove in the kitchen. He moved the beam of his flashlight around the room and considered his options. He grabbed several sturdy plastic storage bins and stacked them against the rear wall, underneath the open treads of the wood stairs.

Without making a sound, he climbed to the top of the staircase and unscrewed the bare light bulb from the wall fixture. He returned to the basement and did the same for the remaining two lights in the room. Picking up a short length of galvanized steel pipe from the floor, he took a deep breath and banged it against the sheet metal sides of the furnace; then hurried under the stairs. He squatted on top of the storage boxes and waited, hoping his previous calculations did not prove him wrong.

From upstairs, he heard muffled shouts followed by clatters of fast-moving footsteps. The source appeared to come from the same room he'd observed from outside. Then another set of footfalls joined in, these originating from the front of the house. They converged in the pantry. The door swung open. He listened as someone flicked the light switch repeatedly. After a series of curses, someone cast a flashlight beam into the basement. The stairs squeaked as the first man crept down. Ethan saw a gun drawn in one hand while the other scanned the mechanical room with the flashlight. The guy had proceeded about halfway down when a second person started to follow.

Ethan thought, *Can they be this stupid?*

He reached through the open stair and grasped the ankle on the second man's leg. Thrown off balance, the entire weight of his body slammed against the first man, sending them both tumbling the rest of the way down the stairs. Ethan cringed from the sickening thud as the first man's head smashed against the floor. His gun and flashlight slid across the cold concrete. The flashlight broke on impact and the room darkened, illuminated only by the dim shaft of light coming through the basement door.

The second man flailed his arms trying to separate himself from his unmoving partner. A hard blow to the side of his head from the butt of Ethan's M11 caused him to slump beside the first body. Ethan retreated behind the furnace and listened. No additional footsteps could be heard. He waited several more seconds and then peered out from behind the furnace. He flicked on his flashlight and checked out the two fallen security guards. To play it safe, he pulled out the syringe gun and blasted a dose of the long-acting sedative into each man. More than a little surprised that no one else had responded, he decided to make his way to the first floor—when a gunshot rang out.

CHAPTER 69

Finley's men made quick work of getting to the outer perimeter of the governor's property where they paused by the open gate. Finley exited the SUV and took several steps toward the house, scanning the grounds. With not knowing Olivia's situation, and Ethan Galloway poised for an assault on the governor, Finley felt torn, but he needed to act. As he sprinted back to the SUV, from above the distant roar of the Snake River rapids, he discerned a familiar report.

Muffled, and almost blotted out by the rushing waters, it could still not be mistaken for anything but what it was—a gunshot. Coming from inside the house.

Finley shouted and leapt into the SUV. It tore through the open gate before his door closed and rocketed toward the sprawling ranch.

* * * * * *

Ethan took the basement steps two at a time and charged across the small pantry, down the central hallway, kicking the double doors to the great room open. Crouching and turning his body, the M11 held out in extended arms. He glanced at the back of the sofa directly in front of him. The governor was no longer sitting next to the woman. On the polished granite floor behind the bar cabinet, a river of blood snaked its way under the bar unit and around a leg of one of the bar stools. When he peered over the sofa, he saw the source. Pooling blood spreading from underneath the inert body of the governor's chief of staff. The governor was crouching behind the bar attempting to pour vodka into a glass while it shook in his trembling hand.

From where he stood, Ethan could see the back of the agent's head and her arms held out to the side at the level of her shoulders. He failed to detect a single tremor in her fingers. Her whole body remained motionless but didn't appear tense. He heard her speak in a soft and calming tone. When Ethan shifted his gaze beyond the agent, he saw Anita Blackwell with a Smith and Wesson .45 caliber pistol aimed slightly above the agent's head; meaning it was pointed right at Ethan's chest. He had instinctively swung his M11 around and aimed it at the governor's wife.

For several seconds no one moved and the woman on the sofa stopped talking. Anita Blackwell smiled at Ethan. "Welcome to my home. Mr. Galloway, I presume?" She nodded to Olivia. "Don't think you two have met. Ethan, this is Olivia Davenport. *Agent* Davenport. Why don't you join her on the sofa."

Without moving her eyes from Ethan or Olivia, Anita said to her husband, "If you can fill the glass without pissing in your pants, I'd also like a drink. Vodka on the rocks—skip the lemon slice."

To Ethan, she said, "Agent Davenport has been looking for you." Her voice hardened. "But I also think she's involved in more than one investigation. Isn't that right, Nicky?" She turned to the governor and shook her head. "You really are a moron, dear. Like Daddy always used to say. He thought he could control your baser instincts. Like he tried to do to me... all those years of therapy gone to waste. Then he introduced me to you, darling. Perhaps he needed both of us to fulfill his greatest dream."

The governor still hadn't accomplished getting any liquid into the glasses.

"And here we are tonight. Waiting to count the votes of the American people. We'll know any minute now. And Daddy's anticipating the big moment with the rest of your supporters in San Francisco. It's almost time to get on the plane and join him. Can't wait to hear your acceptance speech, sweetie."

The gun wavered in her hand. She reached out with her other hand and switched to a two-handed grip, shifting her legs into a more stable position. "Forget the drink, Nicky. I'm kinda busy now. Cleaning up your mess once again." The gun lowered a bit, but a single shot could've still hit Ethan and Olivia.

"You should've stuck with the young ones. They were more to my liking too. I knew this bitch sitting on the couch spelled trouble the first time she strutted her ass into your office."

Anita's eyes welled up and a lone tear worked its way down her cheek. "You wanted a real woman, Nick? I've always been right here. All the rest we played with were just throwaway toys."

Ethan heard it first—behind him in the hallway, followed by a slight movement at the patio door. Anita Blackwell's head turned at the sounds. This provided the opportunity for Olivia to launch herself at the governor's wife.

At the same time, Ethan catapulted over the sofa. The two of them trying to subdue Anita and get the gun from her hands.

From behind the bar, the governor let out a gut-wrenching scream and ran toward his wife.

Finley charged through the interior doors to the great room as the two other agents crashed through the patio doors. Everyone's guns were drawn.

In the background, from the flat screen TV on the wall behind the bar, a newscaster's voice announced that the presidential race could now be called.

All hell was breaking loose in the great room at the governor's estate, while the last votes were tallied and the nation elected its next president.

EPILOGUE

CHAPTER 70

Tonight ended one of the most bitter and hard-fought presidential campaigns in the history of the United States of America. Over the last several years the nation had become further divided as radical ideologies struggled for legitimacy in the face of a system on the verge of collapse.

Results from polling precincts in all fifty states dripped in and teams of analysts poured over the data, but a projected winner could not be called until late into the night. While one candidate collected a clear majority of electoral college votes, the results of the popular vote served to strengthen the nation's differences rather than to unite its citizens and start the long healing process.

One by one the major networks and cable news channels declared a winner. What did not immediately happen in the wake of the decisive electoral count was the losing candidate's customary appearance to deliver a concession speech.

Nor did the winning candidate immediately come forward to declare victory.

* * * * * *

While the nation waited for news from the candidates and confirmation of the election results, a small airport in Jackson, Wyoming, had gone into lockdown. A non-disclosed number of aircraft—federal agencies of origin not declared—converged on the sleepy tourist town cradled within Grand Teton National Park.

All departing flights had been cancelled until further notice and arriving flights were diverted to other airports. Federal authorities escorted all passengers and non-essential personnel off airport grounds. Shortly after the communications blackout began, local and state officials were advised not to interfere in what was being referred to as a national security matter.

Thirty minutes after the last federal jet touched down on the tarmac at Jackson Hole Airport, a lone Gulfstream G550 taxied to runway nineteen and departed, bound for the East Coast. Sitting with Olivia Davenport in the rear of the fast-moving jet, Mike Finley occasionally glanced up at the three additional passengers huddled near the front of the cabin, while continuing an unending series of phone calls. Halfway in between, a black German Shepherd crouched in the aisle and kept a keen eye on the two agents.

After ending one particularly heated conversation, Finley tossed the secure satellite phone onto the tray table and stood, stretching his arms against the cabin's bulkhead. "Goddamn, Olivia. I'm glad all these decisions are way above my pay grade."

She patted his arm. "First of all, Mike, you're retired and have no specific salary—or no salary at all."

"Yeah, and who do I have to thank for getting me involved in your little investigation?"

"You can thank me and President Griffin later, but in regard to the decisions being discussed in D.C.—don't you think that once we exited the governor's estate, a key verdict had already been pronounced?"

Finley pointed to the overhead TV monitor near the front of the cabin. "Looks like the news blackout is over and we're about to hear his acceptance speech. They estimate he'll step up to the podium in about ten minutes."

Taking a seat, he looked at Olivia. "Please. Tell me again—from the top. Before I got to the estate." In a lower voice, he added, "Walk me through it once more. It's likely the last time anyone will ever hear this version."

Olivia took a sip of bottled water, closed her eyes, and relived those last hellish minutes inside the great room at the governor's estate.

* * * * * *

The tone in Governor Blackwell's voice, when he invited Olivia to sit next to him on the sofa, gave no room for argument. Her compliance made more urgent by the threatening look on Victor Petricello's face and the position of his hand underneath his jacket. Olivia set her untouched seltzer on the side table and plopped down on the sofa, hugging the cushioned arm and pulling away from Blackwell.

Naked without her weapon, she cursed herself again for not carrying any back-up. Although the thorough frisking she'd endured at the hands of the governor's slimy security guy at the airport would've no doubt uncovered any additional weapons. The confiscation of her cell phone was no big deal. She once again thanked God for the agency's insistence on implanting the tracking device. Counting on Finley being close by, her only concern was whether or not he remained disciplined enough to not lead a full-on assault of the governor's estate. While uncomfortable with the current situation, and with what she understood about the governor's past actions, nothing serious would occur at this site as long as the governor or his wife remained present. If they suspected anything about her motives, the security team would take her someplace far away from this location before eliminating the threat. She had hoped to have uncovered enough information, so when Finley rode in they'd have something more concrete to nail the governor's ass to the wall. The same scenario would take place if the governor had the two kids stashed on the estate. Unless they'd already been killed. She prayed this was not the case.

Olivia reacted with a slight start at the touch of Blackwell's fingers sliding through her hair like the tentacles of some prehistoric reptile. She recovered quickly and by the time his other hand began groping under her sweater, she switched her focus to Anita Blackwell. When his hand tunneled beneath her bra and cupped her breast, she attempted to tune out his disgusting presence. Right now, she was more concerned about his wife's demeanor than his bumbling advances.

Thomas Steadman refilled Anita's empty martini glass the moment she slapped it down on the copper countertop. Anita's eyes transitioned from deep pools of intense hatred to a more frightening glow of something far more primitive. Her face contorted through a kaleidoscope of emotions, and Olivia questioned who was the recipient of her contempt. Given the volume of alcohol consumed by the woman, Olivia began to sow the first seeds of doubt regarding her earlier conclusion of nothing untoward occurring at this present location.

Her thoughts were interrupted by a loud clanking noise coming from somewhere else in the house. The governor appeared unaware of the sound and got to work in earnest, now using both hands to fish underneath Olivia's sweater and undo the clasps of her bra.

Petricello drew the pistol from his shoulder holster, holding it at his side. "I'm going to have a look, governor. Sounded like it came from the basement. Probably the old furnace acting up again."

"Need some help, Victor?" Olivia said.

Blackwell licked her ear and whispered, "Victor's a big boy and can take care of it by himself."

Olivia had reached her limit as the governor yanked the bra off her chest and started to lift the sweater over her head. She drew her left arm across her chest, poised to elbow Blackwell in the ribs when Petricello leveled his weapon at her. "Don't even think about it, Davenport."

Petricello hesitated a moment and nodded at Steadman before he headed off to the basement. "You're armed, Tom. Make sure this bitch behaves herself and cooperates with the governor."

Steadman reached inside his jacket and pulled out a Smith and Wesson .45 caliber semiautomatic pistol. He placed it on the bar counter, resting his hand on top. Petricello looked at Olivia. "Don't think he won't use it." As Petricello sprinted out the door, Olivia heard him call to the other security man inside the house. Their footsteps faded down the hall.

Olivia considered her options. She'd never make it from the sofa to the bar to grab the gun before Steadman could get off a shot. From the beads of sweat forming on his brow and the way his hand shook, any sudden movements might cause him to pick up the gun and start shooting.

When Olivia's eyes settled on Anita, she saw something that made her blood turn to ice.

In the next instant, Anita Blackwell swung her half empty glass at Steadman, the contents splashing in his eyes.

She grabbed the gun from the counter, but Steadman's hand was still wrapped around the handle with his finger looped inside the trigger guard.

It happened so fast, Olivia had no time to react as a deafening blast filled the room and Steadman lurched back into the wall. His hand went to his chest, and he slid to the floor, leaving smears of blood plastered down the rustic wood paneling. The governor bolted up and stood staring at his wife.

Olivia had taken two steps forward before Anita had the pistol aimed at her chest.

"Sit down!" Anita screamed.

Both Olivia and Governor Blackwell sat down on the sofa.

Anita looked at her husband. "Not you—you fucking moron. You place one more hand on this bitch, the next video you watch will be of your dick hanging from the fireplace mantel like a shriveled-up Christmas stocking."

In spite of her predicament, Olivia had to close her eyes and bite her tongue to wipe that image from her head.

Stunned, Governor Blackwell got up from the sofa. His legs shook and he grabbed onto the armrest for support. He headed toward the bar, still clutching Olivia's bra in his right hand. As he placed one foot in front of the other and stepped over the body of his chief of staff, the silky undergarment dragged through the pooling blood.

Olivia took several deep breaths and, in a casual effort, spread out her arms. She attempted to talk the crazed woman down but didn't think any of her words were getting through to Anita's alcohol-sodden brain.

* * * * * *

Finley hadn't moved a muscle since Olivia started her story. His knuckles remained white, hands clutched onto the Gulfstream's leather armrest.

"That's when Ethan Galloway burst into the room," Olivia continued. "Anita Blackwell proceeded to introduce me to him and gave a touching account of her husband's political career—along with his other endeavors. And right in the middle of all that, the federal government— meaning you—saw fit to intervene."

She touched the bandage on her right temple.

"So, sorry, Mike, but I'm a little blurry on what happened next. You're gonna have to refresh my memory."

Mike Finley let out a deep breath.

The rest of the picture still percolated in his head. He and only a few others would take this story to their graves.

* * * * * *

The first thing Finley saw when he entered the great room was the blank stare in Anita Blackwell's eyes. For a moment, they were aimed right at him. He watched Olivia leap out of her seat. An instant later, Ethan Galloway followed suit by jumping over the sofa. Both charging toward Anita Blackwell.

As Olivia grabbed for Anita's gun, she slipped on the wet floor and the broken glass. Before she could recover, the governor's wife slammed the butt end of the gun into her temple. Olivia crumpled to the floor, dazed and temporarily out of action.

Ethan sidestepped the stricken agent. Anita had the weapon aimed at Olivia's head when he grabbed for the gun with both hands. His own gun dropping to the floor.

At that moment, Governor Blackwell staggered into the picture, screaming and calling out to his wife. Blocked by Ethan's body, none of the agents witnessed the details of what happened next.

The gun fired as Ethan wrestled Anita to the floor.

There was a blood-curdling scream followed by another loud report from the .45 caliber pistol.

Finley dashed around the sofa as Ethan slowly stood up and backed away. Finley's eyes first went to Governor Blackwell and the large rent in his chest—gaping at the blood spreading across his shirt and the foamy exudate from his lips. He turned to Anita Blackwell, who lay motionless in front of the fireplace. The gun still clutched in one hand with her arm resting across her stomach. Her head listed to one side. The small hole in her forehead. And the larger exit wound covered in blood, bits of tissue, and fragments of granite.

Ethan looked down at his M11 resting under one of the bar stools. He stared at the blood covering his leather gloves and turned to Finley, raising both arms high. "I understand you've been looking for me."

* * * * * *

Olivia glanced out the Gulfstream's window. Below, a blanket of almost invisible clouds. Above, an infinity of stars, staring down on one tiny planet in an eternal universe, making her feel small, insignificant in the scheme of things. Ignoring all that, she turned back to Finley: narrowing her eyes and tilting her head. "So… you never saw what happened?"

Finley followed Olivia's previous gaze to the heavens. He shrugged. "As far as I'm concerned…." He pointed again toward the TV monitor. "The president is about to inform the nation about this unfortunate tragedy. And his version will be good enough for me."

"A wise man once said the truth has no versions."

"Guess he didn't work for the federal government." Finley smiled and reached for the TV remote, punching up the volume and sitting back as President Tyler Griffin stepped up to the podium in the main ballroom of the New Jersey Convention and Exposition Center. He addressed the crowd of supporters—and the entire nation.

CHAPTER 71

The ballroom turned still. The crowd had expected a triumphant winner to walk up to the podium, not the solemn figure of President Tyler Griffin, face outlined by dark shadows.

"I apologize for keeping you all waiting," the president said.

For most of the evening, exit polls had painted the picture of a race too close to call. And then the electoral college scale tilted toward Griffin. In swing states, a series of narrow victories were all decided in Griffin's favor. But even when Griffin surpassed the magic number of 270, strongholds of democrat support helped Governor Nicholas Blackwell maintain a clear edge in the popular vote.

In the days, weeks, and months to come, the consequences of the election results and the arguments over mandates and legitimacy would be front and center for debate by a divided nation and fueled by the stunning loss of the opposition party. Pundits would give little thought to the fact that the democrat candidate was dead. The reelection of President Tyler Griffin would serve as a reminder to the status quo of both political parties in Washington that the movement that had started during President John Connor's administration, the Restraint in Government Alliance, was not lying down or going away.

But tonight, none of that concerned the nation.

The rumors originated at the Moscone Center in San Francisco, the site where Nicholas Blackwell planned to give tonight's acceptance speech. After the election had been called in Tyler Griffin's favor, the stunned and subdued crowd waited to hear from the governor.

Although federal officials tried to maintain an absolute blackout over events in Jackson, Wyoming, leaks regarding a major news story began trickling into newsrooms across the nation. For the last hour, a frenzied media on the brink of a meltdown had bombarded the administration for confirmation on the evolving saga. President Tyler Griffin now stood at the podium, poised to release the floodwaters to the nation.

"First, I would like to commend the media for its constraint in not going public with the tragic news I am about to deliver." The president's deep-set, virtually black eyes stared straight into the cameras as if he could see the face of every American sitting at home and listening to him speak.

"The FBI's field office in Denver has informed me that the bodies of Governor Nicholas Blackwell and his wife, Anita, have been found in a house near the town of Jackson, Wyoming. The body of Thomas Steadman, the governor's chief of staff, was also discovered. The FBI's investigators, working in cooperation with local and state authorities, have released a preliminary statement. Based on the evidence at the scene and testimony by the head of the governor's security team, Anita Blackwell appropriated a weapon from Thomas Steadman and fatally wounded the governor. In the struggle, Steadman also died. Anita Blackwell then turned the gun on herself. This account will be verified once the forensics investigation is completed, and the results of the autopsies are analyzed."

The president paused and scanned the hushed audience.

"We've already encountered a series of leaks about Anita Blackwell's deteriorating mental health during the latter half of the campaign, and the speculations regarding increased bouts of anxiety and depression."

Griffin motioned to the first lady, and she joined him at the podium. "Tonight, Alison and I wish to extend our sympathies. Our hearts, and the hearts of the nation, go out to the families of the governor and his wife."

Griffin spent the next several minutes praising Nicholas Blackwell's work as the governor of California and congratulated him on a hard-fought campaign. He thanked his supporters and the American voters for helping him achieve the decisive electoral college victory and pledged to continue his job in the White House, working to mend the differences that divided the nation.

"Let us pray for the families involved in this horrific tragedy. And may God bless the American people." President Griffin bowed his head before turning away from the podium. With the first lady at his side, and joined by his four children, he lowered his head and strode off the stage.

* * * * * *

When Finley looked away from the TV monitor, the eyes of his fellow passengers focused on him. Olivia nudged him and pointed to the others. He walked up the narrow aisle of the Gulfstream, carefully sidestepping Kobe. Olivia remained two steps behind him as he stopped across from the galley table where Ethan, Corey, and Patas sat with expectant gazes.

"If you guys have any questions regarding the president's acceptance speech," Finley said before pausing and pointing a finger at Olivia, "I'm sure Agent Davenport can provide the appropriate answers."

He placed a hand on Olivia's shoulder, squeezed around her, and returned to his seat in the rear of the cabin. He tilted back the seat and folded his arms across his chest. Before Olivia could protest, he was sound asleep.

Olivia turned her attention to the three passengers. "There are still a lot of unanswered questions regarding the events over the last couple days. That's one reason you're going to be guests in Washington for a while. The president appreciates your cooperation."

Corey and Patas looked at Ethan.

As Ethan's thought processes continued to clear, allowing him to see past events in a far different light, he had begun to grasp the potential outcome of his recent actions. But more telling was the fact that he still saw no good reason to trust the government.

He raised his brows in response to Olivia's remarks but remained silent.

CHAPTER 72

A week after his election night speech outlining the tragic deaths of Governor Blackwell and his wife, President Tyler Griffin again addressed the nation. This time he sat in the Oval Office. He aimed tonight's message at the purported Islamic jihadist group responsible for both the attempted assassination of Governor Blackwell in Sacramento and the second botched terrorist plot in Seattle. Griffin reassured the nation that the investigation into determining the specific Islamic organization involved was still ongoing, but the United States of America would not tolerate any foreign entities undermining the American election process.

When the camera crews had packed up and left, Mike Finley entered the Oval Office by the side entrance. The two men stared at each other, and without a word they sat down in front of the fireplace: the coffee table separating them.

"So, you think that blaming a phantom terrorist group will put an end to all this?"

The president glanced up at the portrait of George Washington on the wall above the fireplace before answering. "With all the issues facing this nation, Mike, I hope to God it does. It's time to heal. The last thing the nation needs—is to find out the extent of corruption and depravity in a person almost elected to the highest level of our government. Maybe the personal deviances and the financial shenanigans of Blackwell and his wife could be dismissed by some ideologically extreme voters, but hopefully not the rapes, the murders, and the staged terrorist plots."

Finley nodded.

He chose not to remind the president that the attempted assassination of Nicholas Blackwell in Sacramento had been real and carried out by a sixteen-year-old Muslim girl, although ostensibly driven by the governor's own deplorable actions. In the end, however, the governor did use that event to garner sympathy and bolster the legitimacy of blaming a radical Islamic terrorist group for the planned bombing on the hijacked Seattle-bound ferry. And then he tried to take credit for providing intel that helped authorities discover the plot and prevent the explosives-laden ferry from achieving its goal at the Seattle Aquarium.

Olivia Davenport's continuing investigations into the governor's involvement in the death of Agent Kostelecky had uncovered potential motives. In addition to Kostelecky's original focus on activities of political corruption associated with the governor and his wife's family, Kostelecky had discovered ties between Blackwell's staff and people who wound up linked to the

Seattle terrorist plot. And like Kostelecky's fate, those individuals had either disappeared or had shown up dead. A long-standing tradition that seemed to shadow the Blackwells and the Chaunceys.

Other than the claims coming from the governor's office, no involvement of any radical Islamic organizations could be found. It was all a hoax perpetrated by the Blackwells and Daniel Chauncey.

Finley felt the president's eyes staring at him. He kept his thoughts to himself and smiled at Griffin.

Griffin let out a long sigh. "So... how's retirement life treating you?"

"Can't say it's all been on easy street." He stretched and sighed. "Glad to be of help, but I'm looking forward to heading back to Florida and catching up on my fishing."

The president reached inside his coat pocket and pulled out an envelope. He leaned forward and dropped it on the coffee table.

Finley looked at the envelope and then back at the president. He narrowed his eyes but didn't speak.

"Came across this in my desk drawer this morning, Mike. Seems I must've forgotten to sign off on your retirement papers."

Finley wiped his hands over his face and muttered, "Olivia."

"Speaking of which," the president said, checking his watch, "I think it's time we invite our guests to join us." He pressed a button and spoke into the small device sitting on the coffee table. Moments later, a door opened and Olivia Davenport entered the Oval Office, followed by Ethan and Corey Galloway, and Patas Ta'anari.

The president rose and nodded to his guests, taking the time to greet each one and exchange a few words. When he faced Ethan Galloway, the president saluted and then extended his hand. "Thank you for your service, *Master Chief Galloway*."

Finley saw a slight change in Galloway's expression at the president's words. He'd just been promoted. Maybe Griffin didn't believe Galloway should've retired either. It appeared the federal government used a lot of tactics similar to the Mafia.

The president directed everyone to take seats near the fireplace.

"I apologize for any inconveniences you fine folks may have been subjected to," the president said in a voice absent of any real regret, "but we needed time to get to the bottom of this mess."

Griffin turned to Patas and smiled, causing her to blanch and sink deeper into the sofa. "As you know, Ms. Ta'anari, on the evening of the attempted assassination of Governor Blackwell, a number of reliable witnesses positively identified you as the suspect fleeing the scene. And, of course, the forensic analyses from the vest and the pieces of blood-stained clothing recovered from the river verified the eyewitness reports."

Patas stopped breathing, looked straight ahead, and avoided all the stares.

"What you might not yet have heard—in fact, the story is scheduled to run on this evening's major news channels—is that the body of Patas Ta'anari has been pulled from the Sacramento River. Earlier this morning, divers found it snagged by underwater debris about a half mile downstream from the explosion."

Patas's mouth opened wide.

"Moving on… it seems your father has denied any knowledge of your activities leading up to the incident at the theater. He stated that your brother acquired the necessary materials and the skills to help you assemble the suicide vest. He has disavowed you as his daughter, demanded you be stoned, and has insisted fatwahs be placed on you. We consider this tantamount to admitting his awareness as to the governor's despicable actions. And I've also learned that your brother has not been seen since the night in question. We have reason to suspect he's fled the country, but so far there are no traces of where he might be."

The president leaned forward, and his voice softened. "Patas, based on all the evidence, including your own depositions and what you recovered from the governor's mansion in Sacramento, plus the startling additional evidence discovered at the Blackwell estates in Malibu and Jackson, we find no reason to charge you with any crime."

Before Patas could speak, Ethan Galloway jumped in. "Additional evidence, Mr. President?"

The president turned to Finley and urged him to explain.

Finley recounted the melted plastic found in the fireplace the night they'd investigated Kobe's strange appearance outside the governor's mansion. More recently, investigators uncovered the stash of DVDs in the armoire in the master bedroom suite. While this particular collection had items missing, duplicate copies were found at the governor's Malibu estate and also the property in Jackson. He described these new findings and recapped the incriminating evidence against Blackwell found on the soiled linen napkin recovered from the mansion by Ethan and Patas.

The president went on to detail the plans to set up a new identity for Patas. He informed her that they were in the process of locating a family where she could stay on a temporary basis until a more permanent solution could be arranged. Under no circumstances could her family be told that she was still alive.

As the president outlined this, Finley observed a quick exchange between Ethan and Corey. When Ethan smiled at his son, Corey's face turned bright red.

The president paused and faced Corey. "Son, I understand your actions on the ferry helped facilitate the Coast Guard's men to get the vessel under control. I'm still trying to comprehend how you and Patas slipped off the ferry without being identified by any of the authorities."

Checking his watch, the president stood. "Corey. Patas. It's been a pleasure meeting both of you today. But now I'd like a private word with Master Chief Galloway."

After Olivia escorted Corey and Patas out of the Oval Office, she returned and handed the president a file folder.

Griffin glanced at the contents and placed the open folder on the coffee table. He looked up at Ethan and smiled. "Would you mind if I called you Ethan?"

"Please do, Mr. President." He cast a quick glance at the papers in front of the president.

Griffin nodded. "First things first, Ethan. Officially, neither the fingerprints nor the SR25 sniper rifle found on the Delta King have been linked to a Master Chief Petty Officer by the name of Ethan Galloway. So, you get to keep your name, Ethan. And along with it goes your new rank. Don't worry though. Your discharge remains valid, although it's changed from general to honorable. You are still a retired Navy SEAL."

The president glanced at Finley and winked. He tapped a finger on the open folder. "From what I recall reading, the particular sniper rifle in question had an unusual custom-made stock. I'm guessing whoever it belonged to might like it back. But since we have no idea who left it on the riverboat, the best we can do is make sure it goes to another SEAL. If you wish to take possession of the rifle, Mike will get it to you after we're finished."

Finley watched as Ethan self-consciously tugged on the sleeve of his jacket. Catori had finally confessed to first seeing the tattoo when Ethan had visited Mayacamas Shepherds and had verified it was identical to the one engraved on the sniper rifle found on the Delta King.

Griffin closed the folder and slid it across the table to Ethan. "There is one thing I'm going to insist on. You're going to be our guest at the Bethesda Naval Hospital."

Ethan jumped to his feet. "Sir? I've already spent countless hours over these last several days getting grilled by a bunch of VA doctors—"

"Ethan, please let me finish. I've authorized an investigation into a now defunct joint military/CIA program that relates to certain specific duties you encountered as a SEAL sniper. The program had no official sanctions and should've been buried years ago, before any operations took place. Somehow a rogue group of agents revived the program on a limited basis. And you are now the sole surviving SEAL to have been exploited for this particular use."

Griffin paused and motioned for Ethan to sit down. At first, Ethan looked like he would bolt out of the room but then relaxed and dropped back onto the sofa.

"Just to be upfront with you, Ethan, those *doctors* you spoke to this week were actually agents assigned to the investigation. From their reports, it appears pieces of your memories are returning. And they implied you may remember a lot more than you let on."

"Sir, if I may be upfront with you, I don't have a whole lot of trust in the military, the VA, or the federal government."

"After seeing your undoctored military record, I tend to agree with you. But now it's time to make sure we do everything possible to straighten out whatever the hell those sonsofbitches did to you. And while they examine you at Bethesda, I want you to read your unabridged military record. This folder contains the whole goddamn truth of how you were hypnotized and given a continuous regimen of drugs to maintain the memory blocks."

The president shook his head. "You can read about the illegal missions these operatives had you unwittingly participate in. An impressive list—including one or two assassinated heads of state. Of course, you'll need to read it in the presence of one of our agents, and it will then be destroyed."

After a moment, President Griffin stood and motioned for Ethan to do the same.

He once again saluted and shook the former Navy SEAL's hand. "I thank you for your service, Master Chief Galloway, and deeply regret what this government did to you."

The president watched his visitors leave the Oval Office. For a long time, he sat staring at nothing in particular. He then picked up the phone. "Please, send her in."

CHAPTER 73

Following a sharp knock on the door, Griffin called out, "Come in."

He finished sifting through a number of documents on his desk and stood up. Walking across the Oval Office, Tyler Griffin stopped dead center on the presidential seal sculpted into the carpeting and greeted his new guest with a long embrace and a chaste kiss on her cheek.

The president took a step back and smiled.

"It's been way too long, Edie."

Edie Pauling narrowed her eyes. "We were at your campaign victory party last week."

"No, I'm saying it's time you get back to work. The kids are all grown up so it's just you and that crazy firefighter now."

"All grown up? Rosa's in preschool and T.C.'s sleeping in his stroller right outside in the reception area with Steve, who, by the way, is still on the federal payroll. Besides, I'm already working—"

"I mean back in politics. Not fooling around writing about government conspiracies. Those days are over."

"Some people might disagree. Seems as if we're smack in the middle of one hell of a conspiracy right now."

The president smiled and winked at Edie. "As you may know, Ms. Pauling, many politicians in this town consider the US Constitution to be a right-wing conspiracy."

* * * * * *

Outside the West Wing portico, Ethan and Corey spoke in hushed voices. Ethan had brought up the possibility of Patas living with them until more permanent arrangements could be made. Corey looked stunned and didn't know what to say.

Patas, with two agents by her side, walked through the door. They started leading her to a black SUV, but she asked them to wait while she talked to the Galloways.

"Looks like they're not finished with me," Patas said, shrugging.

"Patas," Ethan said, "I've been thinking… maybe you could stay with us… at least until things get sorted out."

Corey's eyes opened wide as his face flushed. He glanced at his father, took a quick look at Patas, and then stared at the ground.

Patas stuttered a few incoherent words. The agents motioned for her to get moving or they'd be late.

She bit her lip. "Gotta go, guys. I'll talk to you as soon as I can." She hugged Ethan and grabbed Corey's shoulders, kissing him on the forehead. She turned and fled toward the waiting SUV.

Ethan and Corey watched them speed off and disappear through the West Gate.

The look on Patas's face almost broke Corey's heart. He couldn't fight the feeling of never seeing her again.

THE END

Author's Notes

Justice Matters is the sixth book in
The Amber Restrained Series.

In this tale, Steve, Edie, and Amber take back seats to a new cast of individuals who get caught in a web of government corruption and personal tragedy. The storyline and supporting characters, however, are continuous with the previous volumes in the series. Steve and Edie return in the next segment of *The Amber Restrained Series,* along with the aging, but still determined, Amber. Please keep an eye out for *Amber Waves of Grain,* the follow-up to the current saga.

<<ronvergona.net>>

Books by Ron Vergona

Opposition Reflex
Terrible Swift Sword
The Guarding State
Targeted Validation
Amber Alert
Justice Matters